The Eighth Guest

and Other Muzaffar Jang Mysteries

Madhulika Liddle is best known as the author of the Muzaffar Jang mystery series (*The Englishman's Cameo, Engraved in Stone* and *Crimson City*). Madhulika lives in New Delhi and also writes fiction in other genres, including humour. In 2003, her short stories won the top prize at the Commonwealth Broadcasting Association's short story competition. Her other passions range from history to classic cinema, travel and food: writings on all of these can be found at www.madhulikaliddle.com.

Praise for *The Eighth Guest and Other Muzaffar Jang Mysteries*

'The writing is crisp and taut, just the way a good mystery tale should be told. At the same time, the essence of the book is not lost... *The Eighth Guest and Other Muzaffar Jang Mysteries* still stands as a testimony that Indian writers can write a good mystery. Madhulika Liddle is a writer to watch out for.'

– *IBN Live*

'It is vividly descriptive with attention to detail and it is simply delightful to read the way the words just flow with no attempt to flummox the reader... Where others would be lost for being too commonplace, Liddle has been ingenious in creating a detective who is set in a time which places him far ahead in any competition.'

– *Asian Age*

Praise for *The Englishman's Cameo*

'The mystery is intriguing, but it is Liddle's historically accurate portrait of Shahjahanabad, complete with the moonlit Yamuna, the paandaans, the palanquins, the noblemen's parties and bustling market places, that make the novel come alive. The plot will intrigue you and the narrative will enthrall you.'

– *Hindustan Times*

'*The Englishman's Cameo* is a genuinely promising debut. Its originality and freshness [are] its strongest point[s], and – after the dramatic resolution – one shuts the book hoping that Madhulika Liddle will continue with her literary project and act as a path-breaker for other history-mystery writers in order to build this fabulous genre's South Asian avatar.'

– Zac O'Yeah, *Deccan Herald*

'The writing style is vivid and descriptive... With the young and hot-blooded Muzaffar Jang following the trail to help his friend from being executed we have an Agatha Christie style plot in hand.'

– *The Hindu*

Praise for *Engraved in Stone*

'The language is contemporary and fresh; the way of thought and movement is too. The narrative style is casual, the stuff of which young urban linguistic India is made.'

– *The Hindu*

'*Engraved in Stone* is a historical whodunit, racy and engrossing. Liddle painstakingly adds details from the period to make the story as authentic as possible.'

– *Time Out*

'...[I]t's the whodunit and adventure sequences that make up for the niggling irritations of the unlikelihood of someone like Muzaffar Jang actually existing, and that make *Engraved in Stone* such a pleasurable read.'

– *Sunday Guardian*

The Eighth Guest

and Other Muzaffar Jang Mysteries

MADHULIKA LIDDLE

hachette INDIA

First published in 2011 by Hachette India
(Registered name: Hachette Book Publishing India Pvt. Ltd)
An Hachette UK company
www.hachetteindia.com

This edition published in 2015

SRD

'The Hand of an Artist' was originally published under the title 'Murk of Art' in *21 Under 40* (Zubaan Books, 2007).

ISBN 978-93-5195-030-1

Hachette Book Publishing India Pvt. Ltd
4th & 5th Floors, Corporate Centre
Plot No. 94, Sector 44, Gurgaon 122003, India

Typeset in Minion 10.5/12.5
by Inosoft Systems, Noida

Printed and bound in India by Manipal Technologies Limited, Manipal

FSC www.fsc.org MIX Paper | Supporting responsible forestry FSC™ C043100

To Swapna and Gourab,
with gratitude

Contents

The Missing Corpse

Muzaffar Jang, a handsome man of twenty-five, stretched out his tall, broad frame on the mattress and winced as his hand brushed against the bolster. His brother-in-law, Farid Khan, the kotwal of Dilli, bestowed a sympathetic look on the younger man. Khan Sahib's wife, Zeenat Begum, looked daggers at her husband, as if he were to blame for her beloved brother's pains and aches.

Muzaffar noticed the look and grinned. 'I am the one who plunged into those adventures, Aapa,' he said. 'If I'd left Faisal to his own fate and not gone looking for the real murderer, I wouldn't have got hurt. And I couldn't *not* look out for Faisal, could I?'

Less than a week had passed since Muzaffar's adventure revolving around a pair of mysterious Englishmen and the courtesan – alas, cruelly murdered – who had loved one of them and had been in the know of certain highly reprehensible activities against the Imperial Exchequer. Matters had been cleaned up satisfactorily. Muzaffar's friend Faisal, a jeweller's assistant, had been exonerated of the crime of murdering a wealthy amir. Muzaffar's other dear friend Akram – who had begun by being Muzaffar's enemy – had been consoled on the sad blow to his love life, and Muzaffar was nursing a shoulder and a hand that had been injured in the course of his escapades.

Zeenat Begum sniffed, unconvinced. She had brought him up after their mother died in childbirth; Muzaffar knew that her concern for him was both that of a loving sister and of a mother. He watched, his face carefully expressionless, as she examined his hand.

'I will go to the kitchens and prepare a salve for this,' she pronounced, finally. 'Keep it still, here – on the bolster. Don't let it hit anything. Do you have a clean handkerchief? Yes? Give it to me, I'll drape it over your hand so that it remains protected.' She muttered something about the heat and dust of summertime Dilli as she fussed.

She had been gone a few minutes when the curtain at the door was pulled aside and Khan Sahib's young servant Rashid stepped deferentially into the dalaan, ushering in a slim figure that looked vaguely familiar to Muzaffar. Recognition came a moment later; Ibrahim Hussain was a well-known face in court, known more for the elegance of his attire than for his ability to ride the waves of court politics. Now, looking at the untidily tied turban and the crumpled choga, Muzaffar could only surmise that Ibrahim Hussain had left home in a hurry.

And so it proved. Hussain Sahib, initially reluctant to discuss matters of delicacy in the presence of a stranger, was eventually persuaded to at least divulge the essence of what perturbed him. He directed a worried glance at Muzaffar before saying to Khan

Sahib, 'I fear a murder has been committed in my house, and that too by one of my close relatives.'

Muzaffar straightened, wincing as the action jolted his still-healing shoulder. Kotwal Sahib exchanged a quick, wordless look with Muzaffar, noting the sudden interest in the younger man's eyes. He gave a brief smile. 'This intrigues you, doesn't it, Muzaffar?' he said. Then, addressing Ibrahim Hussain, he added, 'Muzaffar unearthed that scandal surrounding the death of Mirza Murad Begh.'

Interest flickered momentarily in Hussain Sahib's eyes. 'The embezzlement of the taxes? *Ah.*'

'Ten days ago, I would not have imagined that my brother-in-law could have shown such a talent for investigation. Today, I must admit to a respect for his adeptness. It would do you no harm, I think, to speak out in front of Muzaffar. I can vouch for his discretion, and he may well be able to provide valuable insights that would help *me.*'

Ibrahim Hussain's haveli had a restrained, sophisticated beauty to it. The dalaan to which Muzaffar and Khan Sahib were escorted by a steward, a small retinue of lamp-men and their host himself, was an elegant plastered chamber, its walls polished to an alabaster-like sheen. The carpets were Persian; the porcelain, flower vases and lamps in the niches of the walls understated and fine; even the sherbet chilled and sweetened to just the right degree.

'I sent my servants off to search the grounds for the body,' said Ibrahim Hussain, 'while I came rushing to meet you.'

Kotwal Sahib nodded. 'And you said you feared the murder had been committed by one of your own relatives. Whom do you suspect?'

For a few moments, the man looked discomfited, caught between the necessity of asking for help and reluctance to wash dirty linen in public. Finally, he replied, 'My younger brother, Zafar. We had a quarrel earlier today, and then this happened… I went to the qutb khana to get a book, and found it in a shambles. There was –'

Muzaffar cut in, 'I would suggest we go to the qutb khana and see it for ourselves.'

So Hussain Sahib, with the steward and the lamp-men again forming part of the procession, led them through the khanah bagh, the central garden of the haveli, now cloaked in darkness, and to the qutb khana, the library that lay beyond. Off to the left loomed the single-domed bulk of the household mosque. To the right was the mahal sara, the quarters of the ladies of Hussain Sahib's household. The qutb khana was housed in a single, mid-sized hall, with a narrow veranda in front. The little retinue made its way up the four steps to the wide cusped arch that formed the main entrance to the library. Two servants had been stationed outside the hall. In response to Hussain Sahib's query, one of them reported that nobody had approached the qutb khana since the discovery of the incident.

'Are men always on guard here?' Muzaffar asked Ibrahim Hussain.

'No. There's no need. There are guards at the gate; they're sufficient to keep out intruders.'

The three omrah stood on the veranda, waiting for the lamp-men to illuminate the qutb khana. 'I dare not keep the lamps burning while the qutb khana is unoccupied,' Ibrahim Hussain explained. 'What if a fire broke out?' He shuddered, eyes closing briefly at the mere thought of the potential catastrophe. 'I would sooner have my fortune decimated than lose my books.'

'You are fond of reading?' Muzaffar asked.

Kotwal Sahib smiled, well aware of Muzaffar's own passion for books. 'I doubt there is another amir at court so well respected as a man of the pen.'

'Hardly a man of the pen, Khan Sahib,' Ibrahim Hussain said, with a modest inclination of his head. 'I am only as poorly or as well read as any of my colleagues. But ever since I arrived in Dilli and discovered the many opportunities here for obtaining fine books, I have become an unabashed fanatic. I suppose I can lay claim to a love of books that not many others share. Not just for the classics, but for *any* book. I am,' – he turned to Muzaffar, eyes aglow with a passion that Muzaffar guessed even surpassed his own – 'a lover of paper and ink and paints and gold leaf. I can exult over the beauty of calligraphy and the excellence of a miniature painting, even if what is written is not considered to be literature of the finest order.'

The lamp-men had finished lighting up the qutb khana. They emerged in single file, the steward bringing up the rear. Ibrahim Hussain, with a wave of his hand, indicated that Kotwal Sahib and Muzaffar should precede him into the qutb khana.

It was a plain, unpretentious room. The walls were white plaster, a mere hint of a painted arabesque running along the bottom the only form of decoration. The niches in the walls were similar to those of the dalaan, but instead of Chinese porcelain and flowers, they held newly lit lamps. At one end of the qutb khana were a few takhats, low wooden platforms covered with white-sheeted mattresses, each with its complement of bolsters. On one takhat sat a small wooden desk with an inkwell beside it. The walls on three sides of the room were lined with shelves, along with a few heavy wooden chests on the floor below. On the shelves were books, each manuscript wrapped in a piece of silk. The chests, too, Muzaffar realized, would contain books – the more valuable ones, perhaps, which Ibrahim Hussain would not want to put out on a shelf. There would be the usual volumes, of Sa'adi – *Golestan* and *Bostan*, definitely – of Omar Khaiyyam; also classics like *Yusuf u Zulaykha* and the *Dastaan-e-Amir Hamza*; and, if Hussain had been diligent in searching out rare manuscripts, perhaps a copy of the *Tuzuk-e-Jahangiri*, the memoirs of the late Emperor. There may well be oddities here, he guessed, maybe even a copy of the *Nimatnama*, that hedonist's treasure-trove of recipes.

Muzaffar walked forward towards the wall, looking

at the shelves of books. Ibrahim Hussain's qutb khana was not, as he would have had them believe, a manifestation of a frivolous – if expensive – love for the paintings in books; this was a bibliophile's qutb khana. Each shelf was labelled, the classification going as far as to follow the system used at the Imperial Qutb Khana: every topic and every subject neatly slotted into one of thirteen categories. There were commentaries on the Qur'an and books on law and theology; there was poetry, music, astrology and medicine; philosophy and philology, astronomy, geometry and Sufism. It was an impressive library.

'Look at that,' Ibrahim Hussain said. He was now in the far right corner of the room, pointing to the floor. The polished plaster was splattered with bright red blood that had still not dried.

Muzaffar grimaced. 'A lot of blood.'

'And no corpse,' Ibrahim Hussain added. He indicated a chest that stood about five feet from where they were. 'Come and look at this.'

The three men moved across to the chest, a heavy wooden affair inlaid with geometric patterns in silver. Here were more stains: drops and splatters of blood, some as large as a man's palm, some barely enough to have spilt from a cut finger. Ibrahim Hussain pulled up the hasp of the chest and hauled the lid back. The fragrance of camphor, placed inside to guard against moths, wafted out. Inside the chest, stacked in haphazard piles, was part of Ibrahim Hussain's collection of books.

Each book had been wrapped in an individual piece of silk, to keep it safe from grubby fingers and mould. But the silk had been no deterrent to a knife wielded by a madman intent on destruction. Kotwal Sahib winced and Muzaffar frowned as they gazed down at the brutally ripped silk, the pulled threads and the hacked, vandalized binding showing through. Someone had attacked the books, flinging them about in the chest, pulling them askew, tearing into them with a ferocity Muzaffar found incomprehensible.

'There are bloodstains on some of these coverings,' Muzaffar said. 'Why would anybody try to murder someone *inside* a chest?'

Kotwal Sahib shrugged. 'Perhaps you better tell us how and when you discovered this, Hussain Sahib,' he said.

'There isn't much beyond what you see,' the amir said. 'I have recently acquired an especially fine copy of the *Akbarnama*. It was delivered this morning. About an hour ago, I came to the qutb khana to retrieve the book. I wanted to study it at my leisure. When I arrived, this is what I found.'

'Nothing more? Just the blood and the slashed books?'

'Yes – and some books have been stolen.'

Muzaffar raised an eyebrow. 'Oh? Which ones? Can you tell?'

Ibrahim Hussain looked mildly embarrassed. 'The *Makzan-e-Afghan*,' he said, after a moment's thought. 'And a work on astronomy, not very good, I'm afraid. But as to the others – I can't name them all. I can tell they're missing, though; there should be more books in this chest.' He gave a watery, resigned smile. 'Perhaps I should be grateful that they weren't especially valuable books. Certainly not irreplaceable.'

Muzaffar and Kotwal Sahib exchanged a puzzled glance. 'Let me get this straight,' Khan Sahib finally said. 'The more valuable books in your collection are safe? Untouched?'

Ibrahim Hussain nodded. Muzaffar, standing next to the vandalized chest, looked down into it reflectively. He had assumed that Ibrahim Hussain stored his more valuable books in the chests; that, it seemed now, had been a mistaken notion. He bent and flipped through some of the books. This was a mixed lot; there were old, shabby books here, a few, now moth-eaten, ones inscribed with a name not Ibrahim Hussain's own. 'Those are mainly duplicates,' Hussain said. 'An uncle bequeathed to me the contents of his qutb khana. I didn't have the heart to throw them away.'

Muzaffar lowered the lid of the chest. Kotwal Sahib asked Ibrahim Hussain, 'You said you suspected your younger brother of having done this. A quarrel, you said? About what?'

'He is much younger than I am. He was a baby when our father died. I brought Zafar up, and I have controlled his finances all this while. Now that he is seventeen, Zafar feels he should be allowed free rein. He does not want me to say a word about where and how he spends his money. But he is still a child, Khan Sahib, impetuous and extravagant. If I don't guide him, he will certainly drive himself into debt – or bring disgrace to the entire family.'

'And you think Zafar may have done this? To spite you?'

'It shows all the signs of a tantrum, doesn't it?'

'Who was murdered?' Muzaffar said, breaking the awkward silence that followed.

Ibrahim Hussain blinked. Muzaffar had a fleeting suspicion that the man had forgotten all about the yet undiscovered dead body. 'My servants are searching the grounds,' Ibrahim Hussain replied. 'They will report once they have finished – or found the corpse, of course.'

Muzaffar glanced towards the trail of blood from the chest across the floor. His gaze wandered further. There were more traces of blood: small, barely visible stains that went all the way to the doorway. Muzaffar moved forward, following the trail. He stopped at the door and looked back at Kotwal Sahib and Ibrahim Hussain. 'I think I will join your servants in their quest, Hussain Sahib,' he said, and stepped out.

Muzaffar had supposed that anyone dragging a corpse through the grounds would have left signs of passage. Flattened grass, broken twigs, perhaps a stain on the low bushes bordering the garden.

He found nothing, not even in the blaze of the lamps held by two lamp-men.

Behind him, three sets of footsteps – the lumbering, steady thudding of Khan Sahib's feet, the lighter and more graceful steps of Ibrahim Hussain and the quick gait of another man – descended the steps leading from the qutb khana into the garden. With the two noblemen was now one of the men who had been guarding the qutb khana.

'This man may be of some help, Jang Sahib,' Ibrahim Hussain said by way of explanation. 'He knows which way the servants went.'

The servant, a wiry man with bright eyes shining out of an intelligent face, dipped his head in salutation to Muzaffar, and pointed ahead, to the left. 'That way, huzoor,' he said. 'Some have spread out across the grounds, searching elsewhere, but the ones with the dog went that way.'

'They got a pariah dog from somewhere,' Ibrahim Hussain added. 'A short while ago, since I returned from your haveli, Khan Sahib.'

Ahead of them, half-screened by the trees inside the outer wall, hovered a shifting group of men – a group that moved like a snake, coiling silently forward, fanning out, then coming together and huddling close. Men left the group, then came back; others joined, their silhouettes sharp against the flames of the torches. The sounds of excited chattering and the persistent yapping of the dog drifted on the breeze.

The dog had found something. One man, who had tied a rope around the animal's neck, was pulling the creature back from digging up whatever it was.

The ground had been disturbed here – partly, perhaps, by the dog. Muzaffar got the impression that whoever had scrabbled at the soft moist earth had made a very half-hearted, amateurish attempt to hide their tracks. Loose earth lay scattered about a small mound. A fresh branch, heavy with foliage, had been placed over the mound, a few leaves tugged off it and scattered about.

'That isn't large enough to bury a corpse,' Khan Sahib observed.

Muzaffar beckoned to the nearest lamp-man to hold his lamp closer to the ground. He bent, peering at the leaves and the branch, then looked up at Ibrahim Hussain and Khan Sahib. 'There's dried blood on the leaves. Let's see what lies underneath.'

With the help of a short, sturdy branch and two servants, Muzaffar was able to unearth what had been interred so clumsily. 'Books,' he said, shaking off the earth from one tome as he pulled it out. Another, and yet another, emerged. By the end of it, seven books – or what remained of seven books – lay in a bloodied, muddy, ragged pile beside the hole. Muzaffar, opening the cover of the topmost book, read the inscription on it. 'It's your *Makzan-e-Afghan*, Hussain Sahib,' he said. 'I think we've found your missing books. And these are in a much worse condition than the ones in the chest.'

He ordered the servants to stand aside while he pushed a hand down into the hole and searched again, his fingers systematically sweeping the damp interior, from side to side and up and down. Around him, faces aglow in the flickering light of the lamps, stood the kotwal, the master of the house and the servants.

Muzaffar suddenly stiffened, his eyebrows snapping together.

'What's the matter?'

'I've found something.' His fingers worked, pushing away the soil, pulling at the elusive alien hardness buried in the earth along with the books.

Finally, triumphantly, he drew forth a knife. It was an ordinary, unornamented knife, its rounded hilt devoid of all decoration. Muzaffar held it by the very tip of the hilt. 'Here we are,' he said. 'A bad attempt at concealment. I'm pretty certain there's nothing else to be found here.' He turned to look up at Ibrahim Hussain. 'Perhaps the dog could be taken around the rest of the grounds, to see if it can find anything else.'

But the dog found nothing. It ran, nose to the ground and barking in a frenzied way, up to the water channel that bisected the garden; and there the trail went cold. The dog whined, disappointed; and Ibrahim Hussain invited Khan Sahib and Muzaffar to accompany him back to the dalaan. 'It's more comfortable,' he said. 'And it's time we had dinner.'

It was on the way back to the dalaan that the muffled sounds drifting from the mahal sara – sounds that Muzaffar had initially assumed were the usual ones of a household – began to resolve into a definite, distressed disturbance. Somewhere inside the mahal sara, a woman was weeping, her sobs interspersed with words, muted and distorted by the walls of the low building. A quivering, half-hysterical voice, carrying on a harangue: 'Who knows how long I shall live? Perhaps I will be gone soon – it is unforgiveable –'

Kotwal Sahib was pretending he had not heard. Muzaffar, mentally classifying this as an instance of a neglected wife indulging in a fit of the sullens, walked on quietly. Ibrahim Hussain, his face set and his shoulders rigid, began talking in a hoarse, hurried tone about his brother Zafar. 'If Zafar is the culprit, I *cannot* have the family's name dragged through mud. It can be hushed up, can it not?'

Khan Sahib looked grim. 'That depends. You may choose to overlook the destruction of your books. But what about the kin of the victim? What is to keep them from demanding justice?'

'But surely a fine – that is often the penalty, isn't it? If we were to pay a considerable amount as a fine to the family, that might be sufficient –'

'It depends,' Khan Sahib repeated. 'Let us not talk of that yet. Once we have ascertained the identity of the victim, we may make conjectures about possible solutions to this problem. Not before that.'

So Ibrahim Hussain, with a final despairing glance at the kotwal, led the way into the dalaan. Servants were preparing to serve dinner here, a youth laying out bowls of cool yoghurt alongside pickled limes and ginger, while another brought in a vast platter of rice cooked with chickpeas. Other servants followed, loaded down with kababs, with lamb cooked in yoghurt, with haleem – crushed wheat cooked with ground meat and spices – and with naans, rotis and an array of chutneys and murabbas.

'I can't understand it,' Ibrahim Hussain said as they ate. 'Where did the corpse disappear? And why are there no drag marks anywhere? Anybody who took a corpse all that distance must have carried it to leave nothing but a few drops of blood along the way. Has there been a giant demon at work here, a rakshas as the Hindus call it?' He grinned feebly. After a moment, his expression reverting to its original gravity, he added, 'What worries me even more is: *who* was killed?'

'Is everybody in your household accounted for?'

Ibrahim Hussain shrugged. 'The family, yes. As for the servants, I have ordered the steward to conduct a muster. We'll know soon enough.'

But the steward could find nobody missing. All the servants – the guards, the water-bearers, the lamp-men, the cooks, the palanquin-bearers, the eunuchs and maids in the mahal sara, the dozens of other people who kept Ibrahim Hussain's large household – were present. 'A maid wishes to convey a message from Begum Sahiba, huzoor,' the steward added.

A minute later, the maid, a diminutive woman with her face well hidden, was giving Hussain Sahib the message from his mother. Begum Sahiba begged that her son pay her a visit. It had been a long time since she had had the pleasure of his company; she missed him.

'Tell my mother that I shall present myself at the mahal sara as soon as I am free,' Ibrahim Hussain said in a tight, uncomfortable voice. 'Tomorrow, perhaps.'

The woman murmured a barely audible acknowledgment, and turned to go. 'Why have you come with this message?' Hussain Sahib said, bringing the maid to a halt. 'Where is Fatima?'

'She is unwell, huzoor,' the maid said. 'So Begum Sahiba sent me instead.'

When the maid had gone, Ibrahim Hussain turned to his guests. 'I beg your pardon,' he said stiffly. 'With increasing age, my mother has becoming increasingly demanding. Since I am her oldest living offspring, she tends to be possessive.' He glared back defiantly at Khan Sahib and Muzaffar, as if daring them to say that a son's first duty was towards an aging mother. But Muzaffar and Khan Sahib held their tongues, and Ibrahim Hussain, after an awkward harrumph, added, 'And now this Fatima is ill. She's the only one my mother listens to, somewhat. I hope she mends soon; I can't have her lying in bed for days altogether, leaving my mother to whine and pine and drive herself into a frenzy.'

With a shrug, he abandoned the topic. 'There seems to be nobody missing from the household,' he said. 'Family and servitors are all accounted for. That means an outsider was murdered, I suppose.'

'It seems like it,' Khan Sahib said. 'You have guards at the gate, though – what do they know of who came in during the day?'

'My steward asked them, but they were hardly of any help. People come and go all day long. Grain and vegetables and cloth and whatnot are delivered; messengers and petitioners and guests come and go. It is impossible to keep track of all who visit.'

Muzaffar picked up a slice of musk melon. 'Not many of those people would be able to make their way to the qutb khana. It's too deep inside the grounds for the average messenger or wagoner to penetrate without being noticed.' He took a bite out of the slice, wiped his mouth with the back of his hand and continued: 'And then there's the entire setup, which seems very strange indeed. The fact that *your* books were ripped up suggests an attempt to get at you. But that an outsider was murdered – that seems as if the grudge was not against you, but against someone else.' He bit into the melon again, chewed with a distant look in his eyes, and then asked, 'Do you know if your brother harbours an enmity for someone outside this household?'

'Possibly. I do not know.'

'I would like to speak to him. But, to return to the original premise, what we have to find out is if there is anybody who may possibly wish to harm you and an outsider. The outsider more than you.'

'The killing of the outsider could have been an accident,' Khan Sahib remarked. 'But think, Hussain Sahib – is there anyone who may wish to harm or at least inconvenience you, *and* perhaps harm another – an outsider?'

Ibrahim Hussain frowned, his eyes focused on the tray of melon on the white sheet in front of him. He reached across, forehead puckered in concentration, and lifted a slice. Then, drawing a jade-hilted dagger from his cummerbund, he began slicing the melon into thin, precise slivers. When he glanced up at Khan Sahib, his eyes were narrowed. 'There is only one such man I can think of,' he said. 'Abdul Qadir. He was my librarian till I dismissed him two days ago.'

Khan Sahib exchanged a glance with Muzaffar. It was Muzaffar who spoke. 'Why was he dismissed? And what reason would he have for murdering one not of your household?'

'Do you know Mohammad Shahnawaz? He too is a lover of books. We often find ourselves competing to procure the same books, but we are friends nevertheless. Two days ago, Mohammad Shahnawaz brought me a book that he had been offered – for a large sum, I may add – by a man named Ahmed Qadir. Mohammad Shahnawaz has visited my qutb khana often enough to be familiar with my books. He persuaded Ahmed Qadir to allow him to keep the book for a day to examine it.'

'Which book was it?' Muzaffar asked, intrigued.

'The *Tutinama*. It is a beautiful piece of work, with over 200 illustrations.'

'That must be splendid.' The *Tutinama* – 'Tales of a Parrot' – written in the 14th century by the Sufi saint and physician Nakhshabi, centred around a woman called Khojasta, whose husband goes on a journey of fifty-two days. Through those fifty-two nights, to keep Khojasta chaste and faithful to her husband, her parrot relates to her a moralistic story each night. The stories were entertaining enough; embellished with the miniature paintings that traditionally accompanied the text, the book could be priceless.

'Anyway, though the cover did not have any inscriptions regarding its ownership, Mohammad Shahnawaz thought the book looked familiar. He brought it to me, and sure enough, I recognized it as mine. My copy was missing, and this one had marks I knew as having been in my *Tutinama*. It is a favourite of mine; I have read it and admired its paintings often enough to be able to distinguish it from amidst ten other copies.'

'I suppose this Ahmed Qadir turned out to be a relative of your librarian, Abdul Qadir?'

'His brother. Ahmed was a fence, Abdul was the one who stole the books and removed some traces of their ownership. I will probably never know how many books they stole from me.'

'Didn't you miss any of these books?'

The man looked sheepish. 'I have a large collection. And I would think he probably searched out books that he knew I rarely, if ever, looked at. He must have been terribly daring to steal the *Tutinama*. I was certain to have missed it sooner or later.'

'You think he would want to have his revenge on you and Mohammad Shahnawaz, then?'

'It seems plausible.'

'Yes, but we had better put it to the test.' Muzaffar beckoned to the servant who held the sailabchi, and washed his hands in the stream of water the man poured over his hands and into the lattice-covered bowl underneath. 'Let us pay Mohammad Shahnawaz a visit.' He wiped his hands on the napkin the servant held out. 'And then, if you should know where Abdul Qadir may be found, him too. But first, I should like to meet – alone – your younger brother.'

Zafar suffered from bad skin and had an air of being withdrawn, as if he would rather not have anything to do with the world. He stared fixedly at his feet while Muzaffar introduced himself and explained the reason for his visit. It was only when Muzaffar said, 'Would you know anything of what happened?', that Zafar's head tilted up. He had vivid greenish-brown eyes, large and disconcertingly bright. His gaze met Muzaffar's, then turned back to his feet.

'How should I know what happened?' he said in a gruff voice that hovered on the edge of belligerence.

Muzaffar waited.

Finally, after fidgeting restlessly for about a minute, Zafar said, 'My brother's books got stolen, and there was blood everywhere, wasn't there?' He laughed, a bitter laugh devoid of all happiness. 'Serves him right! I hope the thief took away his most precious books.'

'You did not happen to see anything, did you?'

The youth shook his head vigorously. 'Not me. I have better things to do than to prowl around the qutb khana. I'd run the risk of being caught and given a lecture by my brother. No, thank you.'

'So where were you this evening?'

'Here, in my room. And I went to the mahal sara for a while to visit my mother.'

'Ah. That must have pleased her. She has been missing her sons, I believe.'

Those bright eyes looked up again, and this time continued to look into Muzaffar's eyes unblinkingly. Zafar said nothing. It was Muzaffar who finally looked down, at the younger man's hands. They were clenched into fists at his elbows as he faced Muzaffar, his arms folded across his chest. Zafar's hands, Muzaffar noticed, were long-fingered and beautiful; elegant hands that would have been perfect if they had been completely clean – but they were not. The fingernails held traces of the dark soil that Muzaffar had had to scrub so hard to get off his own hands before he sat down to dinner.

He gestured towards Zafar's hands. 'Where did you get so much mud on your fingers?'

Zafar looked down at his hands, his eyes widening suddenly. 'The servants told me some books had been found. I went to see for myself. I must have got some dirt on my hands then.'

'Blood, too,' Muzaffar said mildly, indicating the cuff of Zafar's sleeve. A smear, reddish-brown and dried now, marked the edge of the thin muslin. 'I remember there was blood on those leaves. Anyhow, I shall not trouble you anymore. Should you recall anything that may be of significance, you will inform Hussain Sahib, won't you?'

Mohammad Shahnawaz was not at home. 'He has been gone since the afternoon,' his steward explained. 'I do not know where he may be, but I shall inform you once he returns, if that is what you wish, huzoor.'

'Also inform Hussain Sahib if your master should *not* return by morning,' Muzaffar said, and left the steward looking puzzled.

Abdul Qadir was at home, sullen and tetchy. Muzaffar and Khan Sahib, guessing that the presence of Ibrahim Hussain may well spark off a row between the man and his former employer, had insisted that Ibrahim Hussain return to his haveli.

To Muzaffar's question about whether he had visited Hussain Sahib's haveli that evening, Abdul Qadir's response was accompanied by a petulant sniff.

'No. I didn't go.'

'You have an alibi, of course,' Muzaffar murmured. 'Someone who will vouch for you?'

'My brother. Will you accept his word?'

'I'm not inclined to. How did you spend your day?'

Abdul Qadir thought for a few moments. 'I was at home till lunch. Then my brother arrived, and we went out. He had promised to introduce me to an amir who lives near Lahori Darwaza.'

'Who?'

Abdul Qadir named a man whom both Muzaffar and Khan Sahib recognized by name. 'And till when were you with him?'

'Till an hour back. He has ambitions of expanding his qutb khana and making it as grand as that of the Shahzada Dara Shukoh's. He offered me the post of librarian, and since I intend to accept, I spent a good deal of time discussing the matter with him.'

'That is easily verified,' said Khan Sahib, as he and Muzaffar made their way out of the narrow lane in which Abdul Qadir had his home. 'We both know the man; he may not move in the first circles, but I would never doubt his word. If he says Abdul Qadir was ensconced with him through the evening, I will believe it.'

'Like Khan Sahib, I too didn't think Abdul Qadir would have lied about going to visit the amir,' Muzaffar said the next day. It was close to noon. Muzaffar and Khan Sahib had been ushered into the dalaan at Ibrahim Hussain's haveli by the steward, who had confirmed that despite renewed searching – all through the morning, and with the help of a dog to sniff out the trail – they had not been able to find the corpse. Or anything else, for that matter.

Ibrahim Hussain had entered the dalaan shortly after, anxious and irritable enough to even forget that etiquette demanded he offer his guests refreshment. It was the steward who suggested politely to his master that perhaps sherbet should be sent for.

So sherbet had been served, and Khan Sahib had reassured Ibrahim Hussain that they had not, as he feared, forgotten all about the calamity that had struck the household. Khan Sahib had then gestured to Muzaffar to speak up.

'The amir – no doubt you know him too – is a man of his word. And to lie about visiting him would be a tricky affair; it would mean involving many people in the lie: the amir himself, his servants, his guards – *everybody* who would know whether or not Abdul Qadir spent those hours with the amir yesterday.

It would be risky to attempt a lie on such a scale. Someone or the other could slip up.

'I guessed, therefore, that Abdul Qadir really *had* gone to meet the man and had spent a long time there. That he had an alibi. In any case, it would be stupid for him to attack you or Mohammad Shahnawaz. He got out of this scrape very lightly: most people would have dragged a thief like him to the kotwali and insisted on a heavy fine or a flogging. Abdul Qadir escaped with a mere dismissal; and two days later, he's already got another job. He has little reason to be vindictive.'

Khan Sahib said, 'Also, a message came from Mohammad Shahnawaz's haveli early this morning, that Shahnawaz had arrived home a little past midnight.'

'Which means, Hussain Sahib, that Mohammad Shahnawaz is not our missing corpse. In fact, unless there really was a rakshas striding around in your backyard last night, I'd say there wasn't *any* corpse.'

Ibrahim Hussain sat up with a jerk that sent a small goblet of sherbet tumbling to the floor, its contents pooling onto the floor. He ignored it and stared at Muzaffar. 'No corpse? How – what do you mean? We all saw the blood, we followed the trail. There *has* to be a corpse; it's just that we haven't found it yet.'

'Your men have looked all over. And the dog, last night? It followed the trail up to the water channel.' Muzaffar paused. 'May I make a request, Hussain Sahib? Can you send for your brother Zafar?'

Ibrahim Hussain looked stricken; he turned to the kotwal and said in an agonized whisper, 'Khan Sahib, please; I beg of you…' His voice trailed off. Khan Sahib's face remained unreadable. 'Send for him, Hussain Sahib.'

So Zafar – a clean, neat, scared-looking Zafar – stepped into the room. The bravado of the previous evening was gone, dissolved like a river mist with the rising of the sun. This was a frightened child, even if a wisp of a beard had begun to sprout on his chin. He glanced at his brother, at Khan Sahib, and finally at Muzaffar, who gestured to him to sit down.

'Tell us,' Muzaffar said, 'about your relationship with those in your family.'

Zafar blinked. 'My family? I don't understand. Whom do you mean?'

'With Hussain Sahib here, for instance.'

Zafar looked at his brother, his eyes large with anxiety. The two brothers were very similar in some ways, Muzaffar realized; that anxiety was mirrored in Ibrahim Hussain's eyes. The older man was worried, and that too not just at the thought that his family would be dishonoured, but at the thought that his younger brother might be hurt.

Zafar spoke. 'We have our differences.'

'On what? Women? Wine? How you spend your time?'

The young man grinned, slightly embarrassed. 'No, no. None of those.' The grin vanished as suddenly as it had appeared. 'Only – only about money. My brother feels I am too young to take charge of my inheritance. I don't think so. I am old enough to know right from wrong. I refuse to be treated like a child any longer.'

'And how about your mother? Do you have differences with her too?'

This time Zafar did not look either at his older brother or at the two guests. He was sitting cross-legged, his hands fidgeting in his lap; now he stared fixedly down at his hands, gazing at them as if they were the endlessly moving hands of another person. His jaw was rigid and his face expressionless as he murmured, 'I would give anything to be able to say I had any relationship with my mother.'

Muzaffar waited for the remark to be explained; when Zafar remained silent, Muzaffar glanced towards Ibrahim Hussain. The older man sighed. 'It is not a matter I would have wished revealed, but it is necessary, I suppose.' He pinched the bridge of his nose between the tips of his thumb and forefinger. 'I and my five sisters were born within the first seven years of our mother's marriage. She has always been devoted to *me*, possibly because I was the firstborn. Much later, my father married again, had more wives and other children. I think my mother had always imagined she would be Abba's only wife, his ever true love. His marrying again embittered her, made her feel betrayed. And then, long after I had grown up, my father –' he faltered, reddened noticeably, and finally continued in a choked voice,'– he forced himself on her. Zafar was born. Then Abba died a month after Zafar's birth. Ammi said Zafar was inauspicious, that he'd killed his own sire.'

Zafar's knuckles were pale, his fists clenched so tight that the bones stood out, hard knobs of white under taut skin.

'Somewhere, Ammi must still have harboured a great passion for Abba, I think, for her to have blamed his death on Zafar… but the point is that she has never considered my brother her own. Zafar has never been important to her. Whether he is in the house or not, whether he visits her or not – she does not care.'

'But you,' Muzaffar said to Zafar, 'you, Zafar Hussain, even if your mother does not love you – you love her, don't you? You would even get yourself into trouble to save your mother, wouldn't you?'

Zafar looked up, his eyes watchful. It was his brother who spoke, in a low, nervous voice. 'What do you mean, Jang Sahib?'

Muzaffar switched his gaze to Ibrahim Hussain. 'Yesterday evening, when we were returning from the qutb khana, we heard the cries of a woman lamenting the absence of some man. Later, when we were at dinner, a maid came from your mother, begging you to visit her. Have you been neglecting your mother, Hussain Sahib – or at least making her feel neglected?' He did not expect a response to the question; he saw a flicker of what could be construed as guilt in Ibrahim Hussain's eyes, and then he continued. 'And Begum Sahiba has been getting increasingly desperate. Tell me, what is it that has taken precedence in your life? Your own wives and children? The court? Or your books?'

The two brothers were now staring at Muzaffar, almost identical expressions on their faces. Kotwal Sahib, leaning back against a bolster, smiled: a fond father watching a well-loved child effortlessly recite a piece of difficult poetry in front of guests.

'Your books, your qutb khana – isn't that so? That's a new distraction, one you admitted to having acquired ever since you arrived in Dilli. Before that, I suppose Begum Sahiba only had to vie with your wives and children for your attention. Now, with these books filling up your days, she finds herself constantly having to even beg for a visit from you. Is that how it is?'

Ibrahim Hussain bit his lip.

Muzaffar paused to collect his thoughts. 'Last evening, Begum Sahiba grew frantic – or was it just furious? At any rate, she decided the books were the cause of her enforced estrangement from the son she adored. So she grabbed a knife and burst into the qutb khana, with the intention of ruining some of those books.

'Perhaps even in that frenzy, she didn't want to *truly* harm your interests by damaging the more valuable books you possessed – which had intrigued me. There were all these books, fine and rare and very precious books, just a few feet away and there for the taking. But whoever had stolen or damaged the books, had chosen the least valuable ones. A thief, such as you had imagined Abdul Qadir, would have picked those that would fetch the best price. A man who held a grudge – Abdul Qadir, or Zafar – would also have damaged the books dearest to you. But Begum Sahiba just wanted to vent her spleen; she loves you too much to actually hurt you greatly.'

'Ammi? Ammi ripped the books? But – but why did she take some of them away and bury them?'

'She didn't do that.' Muzaffar turned to Zafar. 'You did, didn't you?'

'*Zafar?*' Ibrahim Hussain blurted. 'But what about the blood? Who was murdered?!'

'I told you, Hussain Sahib,' Muzaffar replied softly. 'Nobody was murdered. Remember, no corpse was found. But Fatima, the maid so devoted to your mother, and about whom you asked that other maid yesterday – Fatima is ill, is she not? So ill, she cannot carry a message from the mahal sara to this dalaan?

'But Fatima isn't ill. Just seriously injured. I think she discovered what your mother intended to do, and so she came after Begum Sahiba and tried to stop her. With the result that she got slashed with the knife. Accidentally, I am sure.' He glanced at Zafar, who was now sitting up straight and looking a little more composed. 'When did you arrive on the scene?'

The youth licked dry lips. 'Just about then. I had entered the khanah bagh, when I heard Ammi's cries. Fatima was pleading with her to stop, and then I heard Fatima cry out, too. I ran to the qutb khana – I could tell that was where they were – and then I went in.' He swallowed. 'It was terrible. Fatima's shoulder and arm were dripping blood; there was so much of it around that both of them – Ammi and Fatima – were pretty much covered with it. So was the floor, and all the books Ammi had pulled out of the chest and hacked at.'

'So you took charge.'

'I had to. Ammi had gone to pieces. She was sobbing and begging Fatima to forgive her. And Fatima was close to fainting. So I sent them back to the mahal sara, and told them to leave it to me.'

'And you tried to tidy up. You took the books and the knife, and went out and buried them. Why did you do that? You could have left them in the qutb khana and nobody would have been any the wiser. It wasn't as if you were able to remove all traces of the incident from the qutb khana... or had you intended to return, after you had disposed off the books and the knife, to clean up further? You left behind only those books that weren't so terribly mutilated. You'd hoped that if you rewrapped them carefully and stacked them in the chest, nobody may ever know? Because your brother rarely even looked at those books.'

Muzaffar paused. 'Well? What made you leave the task undone?'

'My brother arrived at the qutb khana while I was heading back after burying the books.'

'After you'd stepped in the water channel and walked in it to wash off the trail, just in case someone thought of using a dog?'

This time Zafar looked up at Muzaffar with something akin to awe in his eyes. 'How did you guess that –' he shook his head. 'No, of course. That's obvious, isn't it? The trail ended at the water channel. But how did you guess it was me?'

'Because you had blood on your cuff,' Muzaffar said with a grin, relieved that the end of this business was in sight. 'Blood that had dried on your cuff. And you suggested you must have got it on you when you went to look at the unearthed books for yourself. But when *I* found them, the books had dried blood on them, not fresh. They wouldn't have left bloodstains on your clothing.'

Piercing the sudden quiet of the dalaan, from the mahal sara came the sound of music, the light strumming of a tambura as someone launched into a lilting, joyful song of love and hope.

The Sullied Baoli

'This reminds me of my village,' said Salim to Muzaffar as they topped the rise of the hillock.

Muzaffar's friend was very different from the young nobleman: a scrawny, weather-beaten old boatman who had no compunctions about airing his views. Theirs was an odd friendship, a bond that had brought together opposites and made them regard each other almost as equals. With him, Muzaffar had gone boating and watched elephant fights. Salim had helped in Muzaffar's quest that summer to find the man who had slain the nobleman Murad Begh. And Salim was the one who had saved Muzaffar from drowning after the young man had been struck by a would-be assassin's arrow.

Now Salim looked around him. He gazed fondly at the buffalo tied to a post, the toddlers scuffling in the dust and the woman making griddle-shaped dung cakes for fuel, rows of them drying in the morning sun.

'Hot, isn't it?' He grinned at Muzaffar, his face covered with a film of sweat and dust. 'Not looking our usual pretty selves. Come, let's find a well and have a wash. We mustn't turn up at Qutb Sahib's dargah looking like bandits.'

Muzaffar nodded. The shrine of the Chishti saint Khwaja Syed Mohammad Qutbuddin Bakhtiyar Kaki, now dead over 400 Hijri years, was much venerated. To arrive at it covered in the dirt of their jaunt from Shahjahanabad would be sacrilegious. At best, they would attract scowls and sniffs of disapproval from the other pilgrims thronging the dargah to offer flowers and tiny scraps of paper or cloth, scrawled over with the pleas of a soul in need. At worst, the white-clad men at the entrance would usher them out politely, hinting that cleanliness was next to godliness.

'I'll ask that woman if there's a well nearby,' Muzaffar said.

A sudden scream of distress rent the air. The woman's head snapped up. The children stopped mid-squabble. Even the buffalo, its nose buried in hay, lifted its head. Muzaffar glanced about, trying to place the direction of the scream from memory. Nothing remained of it, not even an echo – but the woman had risen, wiping her hands on a rag as she hurried down the dirt track into the heart of the village. Muzaffar and Salim followed.

A few metres on, and the sound of loud crying made itself heard. More people were appearing now, many of them obviously having been caught in the middle of some chore or the other. One man held a half-lit hookah. Another, a thin white-haired man, was leading a large goat. A woman, her bulging odhni covering what was apparently an infant at her breast, appeared to have sacrificed decorum to curiosity.

The crowd jostled and shoved, everybody putting forward theories about what had happened. 'Where are we headed?' Muzaffar asked his neighbour, the man leading the goat.

'The baoli,' the man replied, tugging ineffectually at the goat. It had stopped to nibble at a wayside clump of grass and refused to budge. Muzaffar reached across and wound a hand round the rope, yanking the goat away. The man smiled toothlessly at Muzaffar in gratitude. 'That shriek came from the baoli,' he explained.

As step wells went, the baoli wasn't especially impressive. The steps – arranged in three sets of ten each – were rough-hewn. They led down to a small square tank of water, tucked away under an overhang to protect it from dirt and evaporation. In the style typical of baolis, cells to house travellers had been built on three sides along the top of the baoli. The well and steps, the bare essentials of a baoli, were of sturdy grey quartzite. The cells were brick, quickly made and cheap. Signs of a short-lived burst of philanthropy on the part of some nobleman, thought Muzaffar. A fine and generous start that had petered out after the rudiments were ready.

A group of women streamed down the steps of the baoli. On the middle set of steps, huddled against the wall was a bundle of yellow and green. It was a girl, her ghagra billowing about her ankles, an odhni covering her head, face, torso – everything down to her waist. She was sobbing hysterically.

'What's the matter? Is she hurt?' Salim asked in a whisper.

'Maybe. There's no blood that I can see… Oh,

dear.' The girl, hauled to her feet by her neighbours, was now babbling, pointing a shaking finger towards the water in the baoli.

'*What?*'

'I can't tell. I think there's something in the water.' Muzaffar glanced about, attempting to recognize some figure of authority, a chowkidar or a village elder, amidst the people milling about. These, however, were not those who mattered in the village. This was the riffraff which had been busy in menial tasks, sweeping floors and washing clothes, making dung cakes and milking buffalos, when the scream had pulled them here. The wealthier, more powerful inhabitants of the village would come later, at their own convenience. Or not at all. It would not do for a venerable patriarch to be found gawping at what may only be a dead crow floating in the water of a step well.

But then, a dead crow would not have driven anyone to such panic.

'Come on,' Muzaffar told Salim. 'I want to see what this is all about.' He led the way down.

The women had coaxed their sobbing friend up the steps to the top of the baoli. Behind her, on the steps where she had sat huddled, lay the shards of a broken water pot, dry and empty. The girl was babbling something about a dead man floating in the baoli. Muzaffar, her nearly-incoherent words still buzzing in his ears, glanced back towards the water. Deep in the shadows under the overhang, he saw a flicker of something white, drifting gently on the water. He descended the remaining few steps and knelt briefly, peering into the gloom. Rigid limbs clad in waterlogged clothes floated on the surface of the water. Muzaffar stood up again, looking up at the crowd spread across the steps.

The men were staring anxiously down at the water, curious but unwilling to go any closer to what may well be a gruesome sight. A few were beginning to drift back to tasks left incomplete.

The owner of the goat had placed a hand briefly on the shoulder of the weeping girl as she had passed. He had said something to her, and she had responded with a vigorous shake of her head. The conversation had been brought to an abrupt end by the other women, who had hustled her out. The man was now standing silent, twisting the end of the rope absently while the goat, for want of anything better to chew on, sucked at the end of its master's dhoti.

'Everybody's leaving,' Muzaffar said as he climbed back up. 'Won't anyone pull out the corpse? Identify it?'

'That is the job of the chowkidar,' the man with the goat mumbled, his voice low and indistinct – a combination of missing teeth and embarrassment. 'A lad has been sent to fetch him.'

Even as he spoke, Muzaffar saw a thickset man come striding purposefully in through the square-sided stone pillars of the gate. He was in his early thirties, clad in a white dhoti and kurta, with a massive turban on his head. Close on his heels came a young man, his muscular chest shining with oil. The few men still remaining within the precincts of the baoli called out subdued greetings, which the newcomer acknowledged with a brisk nod. 'What's been happening here? Ganesh told me Radha found a dead body.'

At close quarters, the chowkidar looked the stereotypical officer of the law, his eyes wary, even suspicious when he noticed Muzaffar and Salim. The man had a strange face: fleshy and large, with all the features pulled towards the centre, the mouth too near a disproportionately small nose, the eyes too close together, the eyebrows meeting below a wide forehead, the jowls too heavy. A self-assured man, well aware of his own power.

Some uncomfortable murmuring ensued, until the man with the goat spoke up. A few explanations were tacked on by the others, and the chowkidar descended the steps, trailed by the youth who had accompanied him. Muzaffar and Salim followed.

At the level of the water, the chowkidar lowered himself onto his haunches, peering into the gloom below the sheltering overhang. He huffed as he got to his feet, then stood up and said to the young man beside him: 'Ganesh, get something to fish him out with. A bamboo or a branch.'

Ganesh scurried off. The chowkidar, hands clasped behind a broad back, turned to the outsiders and asked, 'And you, huzoor? What might you be doing here?'

'We were passing by,' Muzaffar replied. 'On our way to Qutb Sahib's dargah. We heard the girl scream and came to see what the matter was.'

Behind them, Ganesh had reappeared, scampering down the steps with a long, thin branch clutched in one hand. At the top of the baoli, just three men – either more curious than the others, or with less to do – now remained. Among them was the man with the goat.

'Do you mind lending a hand?' the chowkidar asked. His tone was flat, as if he saw no reason for Muzaffar and Salim to refuse help. 'That lot wouldn't help if we were fishing out their grandfathers. *Bastards.*' His nose wrinkled in disgust.

The chowkidar took the branch, and poked and prodded in an attempt to get a hold on the sodden clothing of the dead man. 'Why don't I dive in?' Salim suggested. 'I'm not squeamish. If he's caught on something, I can help.'

'There's no need,' the chowkidar said. 'It just needs some patience, that's all.'

A little manoeuvring, and the end of the branch caught onto a fold in the dead man's clothing. The chowkidar pulled, and the body drifted closer, finally bumping against the stone edge of the tank. It was face down, still without a name. The chowkidar hooked thick, strong fingers in the collar of the dead man's waterlogged kurta; Salim and Muzaffar grabbed other bits of clothing and hauled. The corpse emerged, and with a single swift pull, they turned it over onto its back, on the lowest step. Rivulets ran down the steps and into the water.

There was a sudden yelp, and from the top of the steps, the old man, goat in tow, came hurtling down. 'It's Manohar!' he screeched. 'Hai bhagwaan, it's Manohar! Why are you just standing there – fetch help!' He turned to the young man, Ganesh, prodding him in the centre of his deep, glistening chest. 'Go! Get the vaid! The longer you delay, the less chance there is –'

The chowkidar placed a restraining hand on the old man's arm. 'Calm down, Govardhan.' He waited for the man to look up at him, still blinking dazedly, before he continued. 'Ganesh will fetch the vaid' – he waved Ganesh away – 'but there's nothing *anybody* can do for Manohar. At the most, the vaid can say how he died.'

'I think that's clear enough. His throat was slit, and then he was dumped in the water.' Salim, crouching beside the body, looked up at his audience. 'He was probably killed sometime during the night,' he added, turning back to look at the corpse, a gnarled finger indicating the grotesque gaping gash in the dead man's throat, clear from one ear to the other. 'The blood's had enough time to wash away. And the skin's all wrinkled and waterlogged. He's been lying in your baoli for a few hours, at the very least. Maybe even since last evening, after dark.' Salim placed his hands on his knees and rose with a sigh. 'But get your vaid. He will, perhaps, be more precise.'

The identification of the body – of the unfortunate Manohar, his windpipe slashed and his breath forever choked off – had driven Govardhan to the brink of hysteria. He had refused to believe that Manohar was dead; it could not be, he had insisted, it could not. *What would become of Radha?*

'Is Govardhan a relative of Radha's?' Muzaffar asked Ganesh.

The young man scratched his chest pensively, then examined his fingernails and rubbed them against his dhoti-clad thigh. 'Her uncle,' he said. 'Her parents died years ago; Govardhan has looked after her ever since.'

'And Manohar? Was he a relative too?'

Ganesh sniffed at his fingertips and made a face. 'No, Manohar was no relative. But they may well have become relatives: Manohar wanted to marry Radha. She's a beautiful girl. I saw her once near the well –'

'Ah, yes. I recall someone mentioning the well. So the village has a well in addition to the baoli, does it?'

Ganesh laughed, as if at the mindlessness of the question. 'Of course we do! We aren't as backward as some city folk think.' He winked. 'Very few women go to the baoli to fill water; just those whose houses happen to be near it. Everybody else goes to the well. No trudging down the steps to get to the water. No finding corpses in the water.'

The three men – Muzaffar, Salim and Ganesh – were sitting under a banyan tree in the square at the centre of the village. It was a venerable old tree, its girth the thickness of ten men, its silvery bark knobby and its dark leaves spreading in a shady canopy over most of the square. A platform had been built around the base of the trunk, to serve as a meeting ground for the village elders, bed for the homeless and itinerant, and – as now – a place to sit and satisfy one's curiosity. Around them, the village had begun to recover from the sudden shock of discovering that one of its inhabitants had been murdered. A pair of boys was herding a dozen buffalos, probably to some grazing ground outside the village; a man was walking past with a large cane basket full of vegetables on his head; two little girls were exulting over a tiny red bangle.

'Don't bother yourself about this business,' Ganesh said easily. 'The boss will look after it.'

'You mean the chowkidar?'

'Hmm.' The man grinned, showing fine white teeth. 'He won't let anybody who was the cause of distress to his Radha go scot-free.'

'*His* Radha?'

'He's fond of her. Wanted to marry her, too, but that greedy Govardhan thought wealth was more important. Tchah! If I was her guardian, I'd rather have her married to the chowkidar than to a soldier. Here today, dead tomorrow; that's how it is with soldiers. Who cares about all that money? It won't last forever. Here's Govardhan now,' he added. 'He'll tell you.'

Muzaffar looked over his shoulder towards the baoli. He and Salim had hung around there while the chowkidar had sent Ganesh off to fetch the village vaid. Though the chowkidar had glared at them, obviously regarding them as intruders, they had waited to see what the vaid's assessment would be. It had been similar to Salim's. Manohar had been killed probably shortly after sunset the previous evening before being dumped in the water.

A distressed Govardhan had stood by, tugging impatiently at his goat's tether as he watched the proceedings. When the vaid had begun to take his leave of the chowkidar, Govardhan had interrupted, begging to know why anybody would kill Manohar. The vaid had clucked sympathetically but helplessly; the chowkidar had simply said, 'Go home, Govardhan. I know this is a bad blow for you, but nothing can be done about it.'

While the vaid had ascended the steps, the chowkidar had instructed Ganesh to spread the word that the baoli would remain out of bounds until it had been cleaned. 'As if anybody would *want* to use its water,' Salim had muttered to Muzaffar. Then, more loudly, he had said to the chowkidar: 'I can get started with that, if you like. You can't expect people to stay without water. If this Ganesh helps me, we can start draining the baoli.'

The chowkidar had directed a hard, cold gaze at Salim. 'There's no need,' he had said. 'Most people go to the well to fetch water. It's not as if the village will go without water. And I'll get labourers to come tomorrow to get started on it. We can't afford to have amateurs doing a shoddy job.'

And with that remark, the chowkidar had ordered Ganesh to escort Muzaffar and Salim out of the baoli.

A rude dismissal, but the two men had acquiesced without complaint, leaving Govardhan alone with the chowkidar. Outside the baoli, Ganesh had tried to shake them off, but Muzaffar had shown a burst of shameless tenacity. When Ganesh had pleaded that he had to tell people about the chowkidar's decision to cordon off the baoli, Muzaffar had said, 'You will welcome some assistance, then.' They had trailed alongside Ganesh as he went about telling passersby of the chowkidar's order. Then they had taken themselves off to the banyan tree and seated themselves under it.

Here, now, was the man Muzaffar wanted to talk to. He rose, brushing his choga off as he did so, and went to meet Govardhan. From near-panic, the old man had sunk into a fit of the sullens. Tying his goat to one of the long, hanging tresses of the banyan tree, he said, 'There's nothing to ask now. With Manohar gone, there's nothing left.'

'You held him in great esteem?'

Govardhan turned his head away and spat, narrowly missing the goat. 'In esteem? Manohar? No, I didn't. But he'd have made a good match for my niece.' He regarded Muzaffar with interest. 'Why do you ask? Mere curiosity?'

'To some extent,' Muzaffar confessed. 'But, more than that, the desire to see justice done. A man who kills another should not get away with it.' He paused, noted Govardhan's grunt of disbelief, and played what he hoped was his trump card. 'And you, who are so distraught by Manohar's slaying – don't you want to know who was responsible?'

'I don't see how it will help, seeing as he's dead and gone,' Govardhan mumbled. 'But have it your way.' His gaze wandered enviously down Muzaffar's choga right to the tips of his gleaming boots.

'Good. Can we talk for a while? Somewhere private?'

Govardhan's house stood at the other end of the village, a good ten minutes' walk from the baoli. It was the usual village home: wattle and daub, the tiny courtyard swept clean and with a placid buffalo tied in one corner under a neem tree. A charpoy stood outside the door leading from the courtyard into the house; Govardhan invited Muzaffar and Salim to seat themselves on it, while he gathered his dhoti tight around lean, stringy thighs and sat down on his haunches.

'Here!' he yelled to whoever was inside the house. 'We have guests! Get some buttermilk!'

A stout female figure, only dusty toes and muscular forearms visible under an all-covering odhni and ghagra, came to stand at the open door. 'There is no buttermilk,' she said, her voice peevish. 'The household has been in a flurry ever since Radha got back. She's too shaken up to start churning the butter and I have a thousand other chores to do.'

Muzaffar interrupted. 'We do not need refreshment, thank you. You are Radha's aunt?'

The woman dipped her head wordlessly.

'Has she recovered? Is she well enough, perhaps, to answer some questions for us? If Manohar had been her intended bridegroom, I assume she would want to help find his murderer –'

The woman broke in with a low, mocking laugh.

'She didn't *want* to marry Manohar, if that's what you've been led to think.'

'Whom did she want to marry, then? The chowkidar?'

'Who told you that?' Govardhan snapped. 'Did the chowkidar say that? Just because I was inclined to let him marry her once upon a time doesn't mean I can't change my mind.'

'Radha wanted it too,' his wife said angrily. 'She was happy to be promised to the chowkidar. But then Manohar came along, flashing those silver coins at you, and of course *you* couldn't say no –'

Muzaffar, sensing the start of a quarrel, intervened by asking Govardhan's wife, 'What has Radha said, though? When did she spot the corpse?'

'She was going down to fetch water when she saw it.'

'Where on the steps was she?'

The woman shrugged. 'I don't know. You can ask her yourself.' She waited just long enough to note Muzaffar's nod, then vanished into the house, re-emerging a few moments later with Radha in tow. The girl came to a halt beside her aunt, and tugged a slim golden arm free of the older woman's grasp. The Radha who had screamed hysterically at the baoli had gone; this one, even though he could see nothing of her face through the odhni, was much more in control of herself.

'I apologize for bothering you so soon after such a harrowing experience,' Muzaffar said formally. Beside him, Salim smirked, and Govardhan looked taken aback. Muzaffar continued, 'There are a few details, though, that I am curious to know. When did you first see the corpse?'

There was a moment's silence. When the girl spoke, her voice was soft. Not educated, but low, even alluring. 'On my way to the water. When I was going down the steps.'

'I see. But – let me get this straight – when the other villagers reached, you were sitting on the middle set of steps, about halfway down to the water. Was *that* where you had been when you first saw him?'

A nod.

'You hadn't run up from the water in your panic?'

'No.'

'Very well. That's all. Thank you.'

The girl nodded again, acknowledging him. Then, without a word to anybody, she retreated into the house.

'Whatever anyone might say,' Govardhan said, breaking the silence, 'Manohar was a bridegroom in a thousand. Not everybody comes back from a battle with a pot of silver. He would have kept Radha in style.'

Radha's aunt snorted. Muzaffar ignored the unspoken insinuation. 'So Manohar was a soldier, was he?'

Govardhan nodded. 'With a mansabdar near Firozabad. Manohar's parents used to live in this village, very close to the baoli. His father died ten years ago. Then Manohar left to seek his fortune, and his mother stayed on here with Manohar's sister.'

'Are they still here, then?'

'No. The mother found a husband for the girl a few years back. After the girl got married, the mother decided there was no longer any point in staying on here, since she was all alone and there was no knowing when Manohar would return. She went off to stay with her relatives. Somewhere in the hills, I think.'

'When did Manohar come back to the village? Recently?'

'About a fortnight back. He'd done well in the service of the mansabdar. Then he got injured, an arrow went through his leg and he developed a fever, so he came back to recuperate.' Govardhan paused in his reminiscences. 'And when he came to meet me, he saw Radha.'

'Next you will say it was love at first sight,' his wife jeered. 'When all that happened was that he needed a wife to look after him. And to clean up the house and keep it going. *And* to give him children that would keep the family going. If it hadn't been Radha, it would have been some other girl. He just chanced to see her here. A young, healthy girl. What better?' She tilted her head. Muzaffar could imagine those veiled eyes boring into her husband. 'And you were the only one desperate enough to give away a girl for only half a pot of silver.'

'You mentioned a pot of silver earlier too,' Muzaffar said to Govardhan. 'What was that about?'

'I told you. He fared well with that mansabdar he was working for. I don't know where he got that silver – perhaps it was his pay, perhaps it was plunder he managed to sneak past his officers. Who knows? But he had it, all right; he showed it to me.' Govardhan sat back, sighing heavily as he rubbed the heel of his hand against a stubbly chin.

'You asked for half the pot to allow him to marry your niece?'

Govardhan scowled, indignant. 'I didn't ask for it. He offered it, of his own accord. He said the day Radha became his wife, he'd hand over half of that silver to me.'

'If this Manohar had spent his entire life in the village, it would have made things a lot easier, wouldn't it?' Salim said as he sat on the platform under the banyan tree, beside Muzaffar. The village had quietened down, the excitement of the morning gone. A stone thrown into the water of the baoli, thought Muzaffar. A great splash and many ripples disturbing the surface – but, a brief while later, stillness again.

'Well?' the old boatman asked, when his friend did not respond. 'What do you think?'

Muzaffar blinked. 'Do you mean that his stint with the mansabdar may have earned him enemies who would want to do away with him?'

'What else?'

'But why follow him all the way here from Firozabad to kill him? If I wanted to kill a man, I'd do it where it was least likely to cause inconvenience to me. Not a place I had to cross half the land to reach. And certainly not in the man's own village, where he might have friends and relatives who would want to exact revenge if they discovered I was the culprit.'

'But it's possible.'

'Of course it's possible.' Muzaffar reached out and picked up a pebble from the ground. 'What intrigues me is the girl Radha's part in all of this.'

'Radha? You think she had a hand in the murder? You think – *ya Allah!* – she didn't want to marry Manohar, isn't that so? Perhaps she decided the best way to get out of a marriage she didn't want was to get rid of the bridegroom!'

'No. Do you think she would've been able to slit the throat of a soldier all by herself? You've seen Radha. She's slight.'

Salim's eyes widened. After a moment's thought, he whispered, 'But you think she had a hand in it?'

Muzaffar scratched absently at the packed earth of the platform with one end of the pebble. He etched a large rectangle in the mud and carefully began drawing parallel lines, in groups of ten each, down the length of the rectangle. Still silent, he drew a square across the far end of the rectangle, opposite the parallel lines. 'This is the overhang. It's dark under it. Remember how the chowkidar had to peer to see Manohar's corpse? The only way one could have seen that corpse would have been to go down to the level of the water, and stoop. If Radha had descended to the bottom step and knelt to draw water, she would probably have seen the corpse. But from halfway up the steps? No. If she says she saw the corpse from there, she's lying.'

Salim mulled over Muzaffar's words. Finally, he reached across, took the pebble from Muzaffar's hand, and made a mark near the edge of the square nearest the parallel lines. 'You forget, Muzaffar. A corpse floats. Manohar's body could have been near the edge of the steps then.'

'And it drifted to the back in the few moments that it took for Radha to attract half the village with her screams? From the moment she first shrieked, to when all of us trooped into the baoli, not more than a minute could have passed.'

Salim flicked the pebble disgustedly away. 'I hadn't thought of that.'

'She may not have killed him, but I'm pretty sure she knows who did it.'

They sat on in silence for a few minutes, then Salim said, 'I'm confused. If she was involved in it all, why draw attention to the murder? She should have kept her mouth shut. If I'd been in her place, I'd have stayed clear of the baoli.'

'Yes. And why dump the body in the baoli? It wasn't as if Manohar had been drowned; you and the vaid both agreed he'd already been dead when he was put into the water. Why contaminate perfectly good water?'

He stared blankly at the rough diagram of the baoli that he had made on the earth platform. When he looked up, Salim was watching him with an indulgent smile.

'Let's go to the dargah, Salim,' Muzaffar said. 'I think we've spent enough time here.'

'I thought we'd finished with the Manohar story,' Salim grumbled as they trudged back through the village in the afternoon. 'I thought we weren't coming back here.'

'Don't you want to know who killed Manohar?'

'Why should it matter to *me*? I'm not Govardhan, who would have got half a pot of silver if Manohar had stayed alive. I'm not Radha, who didn't want to marry the man. What difference should his death make to me? In any case, as Govardhan said, it's the chowkidar's job. He'll find the killer.'

Muzaffar glanced quizzically at his friend but did not say anything.

'What's the matter?'

Muzaffar shook his head. 'I – no, nothing. Just a vague suspicion. I want to visit Manohar's house. I'm hoping Govardhan will guide us there.'

Govardhan, like many of the older men of the village, was enjoying a postprandial siesta. He was stretched out on the charpoy, belly distended and one bony forearm flung across his forehead, when Muzaffar and Salim arrived. Their host was irritated at being roused, but a few reminders of all that he had lost as a result of Manohar's death eventually won his co-operation.

'But before we leave, I want to speak to your wife,' Muzaffar said.

Govardhan's wife emerged from the house in response to her husband's peremptory summons. She listened to Muzaffar's question, but hesitated before answering. When she finally did speak, it was with caution, even reluctance. 'Yes, we always draw water from the well. It's much closer.'

'Then why did Radha go to the baoli?'

'She – she hadn't meant to go there. It just happened. She had gone to meet a friend who lives on that side of the village. The girl was busy with her chores, I think, and needed water fetched. So Radha offered to get it.'

'Who is this friend? What is her name?'

'Lakshmi. She lives in the house next to the old peepal tree.'

With that, the woman had darted back into the house and Muzaffar had set off, along with Govardhan, for Manohar's house. Salim, now sleepy and tired, had taken himself off to the platform under the banyan tree for a nap.

'I don't think you'll find anything,' Govardhan said as he unlatched the door of a small house similar to his own. Manohar's house was tucked away near the baoli, a tiny overgrown grove of guava trees separating it from the rest of the village. A low mud wall surrounded the house. It was an isolated dwelling, the sort of house where blood could be shed without attracting attention.

Inside the two rooms was the usual sparse paraphernalia of a house long deserted and only recently reoccupied, and that too by a soldier, a man of few needs and used to living in camps. One pot with a spoon. One griddle for making chapattis. A helmet, battered. A lance. A bow and a quiver of arrows. A large heap of clothes lying in one corner of the room, along with a leather tunic, much scarred. But no pot of silver.

Govardhan, surprisingly perceptive, said, 'The chowkidar's already been. He came with Ganesh to have a look. If they had found the pot of silver, they would have taken it with them.'

'Did you see them?'

'Yes. That's how I knew they'd come here.'

'Were they carrying the pot?'

Govardhan shook his head.

'What sort of pot was it, by the way?'

'The usual. A water pot, but used to store silver instead of water.'

Muzaffar let his eye wander around the inside of the room. The marked lack of any furniture made it easy to see, even at a single glance, that there was no place here for a man to have hidden anything as obtrusive as a pot full of silver. There were no niches, no boxes or chests, and the floor – which may conceivably have been dug up to inter an item – looked as if it had not been disturbed in years.

'Manohar showed you the pot? Yes? Do you know where he kept it?'

Govardhan chewed his straggly moustache. 'He made me wait while he fetched it. I stood outside, in the yard. He went around the side of the house and returned a little later with the pot.'

'Show me, if you will, please.'

The yard – if it could be distinguished with that name – surrounded the house on all four sides. The side in front of the house was the widest, with about five feet of sun-baked earth separating the outer wall from the house. On the sides and the back of the house, the distance between the wall and the house varied between two feet and three. Govardhan led Muzaffar around to the front of the house and pointed to the low gateway, just a break in the wall, which led onto the dirt track outside. 'Manohar made me wait here at the entrance. He went off that way, towards the back.'

Followed by a curious Govardhan, Muzaffar walked around to the back. Finding nothing except undisturbed mud walls and ground, he circled the house and returned to the front.

'I don't think Manohar hid the silver here,' Muzaffar said. 'Nobody has dug up the ground recently. And the mud plaster on the wall hasn't been touched for a long time.' He thought for a while, then asked Govardhan, 'How long did you have to wait for Manohar to bring the pot? Do you remember?'

'About five minutes. Probably more.'

Muzaffar chewed his lip. 'I will spend some more time here,' he said eventually. 'I do not need you to stay, but I will have no objection if you would like to wait.'

'I'll wait.'

So Govardhan waited at the entrance while Muzaffar went off once again to the back of the house, climbed over the wall, and made his way into the grove of guava trees. A few minutes, and he was back, a relieved smile on his face. 'There's a hole in the ground – large enough to have accommodated a pot – at one end of the orchard,' he told Govardhan.

'Radha?' The woman named Lakshmi spoke from behind the door. All that Muzaffar could see of her was the edge of a bright red ghagra, and the small restless foot of the baby she balanced on one hip. 'Yes, she came here.'

'What time? Do you remember?'

'I don't know… before she found the corpse.'

'And why had she come? On some errand?'

The baby began wailing. Lakshmi cooed to it, then spoke above the child's whimpers. 'No, no errand. Just like that. To see how I was.'

'Oh. And then?'

'Then nothing. She said she ought to be getting back home, to help her aunt with the chores. So she went.'

Muzaffar frowned to himself. He thanked the woman and headed back towards the platform under the banyan tree, where he found Salim, now awake and cursing the chill of the evening.

Salim sat hunched, wrapped in a thin shawl that he had managed to procure in the village. 'This rain is making the nights too cold,' he grumbled. 'Why are we here, anyway?'

Muzaffar and Salim had positioned themselves in a cell near the top of the baoli's steps. These cells were tiny, almost primitive rooms: a wall at the back, and two pillars in the front holding up the ceiling. That was all. A breeze funnelled through the row of cells. The baoli was dark and still, the water gleaming in the light of a waxing moon. From the village came the sounds of people preparing for sleep: someone vigorously shaking out a sheet, its snapping unmistakable as it swung up and down; a mother singing a lullaby; utensils being scrubbed before being put away for the night.

Muzaffar, sitting with Salim at the back of the cell, where the moonlight could not reach them, replied, 'If I'm not mistaken, we're going to discover where that pot of silver disappeared.'

'How so?'

'Remember how we'd wondered why anybody would have wanted to pollute perfectly good water? I realized later that there *could* be a plausible reason. If everybody in the village knows the water's contaminated, they won't come here.'

Salim, sensing there was more to come, said nothing.

'The idea was to make sure nobody came to the baoli for a few days.'

'Why?'

'You'll see. Now keep quiet and catch a few winks if you want. I'll keep watch. Try not to snore.'

'You don't put me to bed like that! I'm not a decrepit, no matter what you may think –'

'Hush! Keep your voice down!'

'All right. But don't be patronizing.' Salim sulked, huddling into the shawl. 'Where does Radha fit into all of this? And who killed Manohar? Who stole the pot of silver – I suppose it *was* stolen?'

'I'd think Radha's role was to raise the alarm; to let the other villagers know that the baoli's water wasn't fit for use anymore. As to who –' he broke off, suddenly alert. A figure had appeared at the gate of the baoli. The moonlight was only sufficient for Muzaffar, at this distance, to be able to identify the newcomer as a man, dhoti-clad legs protruding below a dark cloak-like upper garment: a large shawl, perhaps.

They watched the man walk, soft-footed and silent, down the steps of the baoli. He kept to the far side, walking almost with his shoulder to the wall beside the steps. At the lowest step, he discarded the shawl and leaving it on the step, slipped into the water.

'What's he doing?' Salim hissed.

'You'll see. Listen carefully, now. If I'm right, he'll emerge soon and come up the steps. When he reaches the top, I'll go for him. Be ready to help, but don't try to tackle him unless it's necessary.'

Before Salim could respond, the man's head broke the surface of the water. He swam awkwardly to the edge, and hoisted up a sack-like object which he deposited on the lowest step. The two men hidden in the cell watched as the man climbed out and rubbed himself hurriedly with the large piece of cloth he had left on the step. That done, he flung the cloth about himself, picked up the sack, and mounted the steps. He had reached the topmost step when Muzaffar stepped out from the shadows of the cell. Behind him, Salim moved forward.

Muzaffar's sudden appearance startled the man; he drew in a sharp breath, but recovered swiftly and ran for the gate. Muzaffar dived after him and the two men fell to the ground in a rolling mass of wet clothing, flying fists – and a dripping, heavy sack full of something hard, which the man swung at Muzaffar's head. Muzaffar ducked and the edge of the sack glanced past his ribs.

But the man was hampered by his wet clothing, and winded by the weight of the sack he had lugged up the steps. The wild swing of the sack sent him off balance, and he teetered just long enough for Muzaffar to get in a decisive blow. Salim came, sandals slapping on the stone floor, running towards Muzaffar, just as the man fell, the breath whooshing out of him, his sack falling.

Muzaffar yanked away the shawl and turned the groaning man's face up. The moonlight washed over the features of the chowkidar.

'It all fits together,' Muzaffar said the next day. The chowkidar, by turn vowing vengeance and pleading his innocence, had been hauled before the bleary-eyed village elders whom Muzaffar had summoned out of their beds. The sack, bulging with incriminating silver coins, had been proof that the chowkidar had stolen Manohar's hoard; that he had also murdered

Manohar was the immediate conclusion. Or so had said the village headman, and no-one had contradicted him. Muzaffar and Salim had made their way back, in the moonlight, to the mansion of a nobleman known to Muzaffar, in whose stables Muzaffar had left his horses, his own chestnut stallion and a smaller grey horse that he had loaned to Salim for the expedition. At the nobleman's insistence, they had spent the night – Muzaffar in a smart guest room, Salim in one of the less smart cells set aside for the servants of guests – at the mansion.

Now, as they rode back to Shahjahanabad in the warm sunlight of a new morning, Muzaffar explained. 'The chowkidar was taken with Radha and wanted to marry her. Radha was amenable to the idea, and so was Govardhan – until Manohar arrived with his newfound wealth. Govardhan agreed to let him marry Radha, and that was when the chowkidar decided to do something about it. He'd enrich himself *and* get his rival out of the way.

'He must have coaxed Radha into helping him execute the plan. I assume he went sometime that night to Manohar's house and bullied him, before slitting his throat, into revealing the whereabouts of the pot of silver. The chowkidar may even have got Manohar to unearth the pot before he killed the man. At any rate, once he'd got the money and killed his man, he had to find a place to hide the money, not leave it buried in the vicinity of Manohar's house, since just about everyone would think of looking *there*.'

'Therefore the baoli?'

'Yes. It was nearby, and the chances of anybody finding it even accidentally were slim. But a pot can be cumbersome to lug around – especially if it's filled with coins – so the logical thing to do was to transfer them to a sack. There either wasn't one in Manohar's house, or the chowkidar didn't have time to look. So he untied Manohar's bundle of clothes, threw out the clothes – thus the heap of clothing that I found in the room – and tied up the money in the sheet. It would have taken him a couple of trips, I suppose, to dump the body and the money in the baoli. And he must have left the empty pot hidden somewhere at the baoli, perhaps at the gate, to be disposed off.

'All Radha had to do was go to the baoli, pretend to discover the body, and get rid of the pot. They didn't realize that Radha would have to account for having gone to the baoli, and she ended up trying to concoct a story for her aunt about Lakshmi needing her to fetch water… which Lakshmi, not being part of the lie, didn't corroborate.'

He took a deep breath. 'So Radha raises the alarm and breaks the pot, which everybody takes to be a normal water pot, not the all-important pot in which Manohar kept his wealth. The chowkidar arrives, takes charge, and later announces that the baoli is out of bounds until it's cleaned. Simple. Now all he needs to do is bide his time and wait for the incident to die down, for people to forget that a pot of silver had gone missing – and for Govardhan to accept his offer for Radha's hand. But you come along, repeatedly threatening to jump into the baoli. He can't afford to have you dive in and find the silver, so as soon as night falls, he comes along to retrieve it.'

Salim squinted up at the sun and turned to grin at Muzaffar. 'See? If it hadn't been for me, the man would never have been caught.'

He clucked encouragingly at his horse, urging it forward, till it had left Muzaffar's horse well behind. Salim turned in his saddle and waved cheekily.

'What would you do without me, Muzaffar?!' he called.

A Pachydermal Puzzle

The Royal Elephant Stables buzzed with activity through most of the day. Animals were brought in, animals were taken out. Animals were exercised. Animals were trained. Animals were decorated with rice powder, their backs covered with brocade and topped with howdahs before they were led off to be mounts for royalty.

And some animals, ill or wounded, were attended to by the salautri, the veterinarian assigned to the stables. The salautri was an elderly man, grey-bearded and brown-eyed, the very picture of wisdom and experience. His hands, gentle and capable, were today wandering slowly, surely, over the distended stomach of an elephant that had wandered into a field of green corn and fed lavishly and unwisely. The animal had been tossing about, biting the tip of its trunk and trumpeting forlornly. It now lay on its side, whimpering while the salautri examined it. Nearby, looking on, was a young man, about half the salautri's age. Unlike the salautri – or any of the other men in the stable, for that matter – the man was obviously an amir: his choga was of expensive cloth and the large square-cut ring on his finger was flawless green jade set in gold.

He was also a strange young man, for no amir, whether important or lowly, would have dreamt of visiting the Royal Elephant Stables. But Muzaffar was a self-confessed oddity, and he had taken advantage of a recent acquaintance with the salautri to visit the stables and see how elephants were treated.

He was standing next to the gatepost when a mahout clad in a muddied loincloth came rushing in and headed straight for the salautri. He bent and whispered something to the animal doctor, and the salautri's hands froze. He looked up, and Muzaffar, from five paces off, noticed the fear in the salautri's eyes.

The salautri beckoned to the ill elephant's mahout even as he rose. As he hurriedly washed his hands and wiped them, he passed on a long and complicated string of instructions to the mahout, who nodded vigorously as he listened. The salautri, with a final pat on the mahout's shoulder, turned to go and noticed Muzaffar. 'Ah, Jang Sahib,' he said, blinking as if he had forgotten Muzaffar's presence. 'I – I have to go to another part of the elephant lines. There is an emergency, the Baadshah's own elephant… if you want, I will get one of these men to escort you out.'

'Do you mind if I come along to see the Baadshah's elephant?'

And so, a minute later, Muzaffar was hurrying through the elephant stables, heading for the far end where the Emperor's very own mount, the elephant known as Kaliqdad, was housed.

'A wound,' explained the salautri. 'Fortunately not in an elephant fight, so it's possible that it's not very severe. It's the fights I hate: the ripping up, the disembowelling, the injuries one cannot even begin to treat. Those are horrible.' He shuddered.

'That fight we went to last week wasn't especially bad.'

'That was a staged fight – army elephants trying to entertain the people. Watch one of the civilian elephants fight, and you'll see what I mean.' He paused, then said, 'There's a land owner called Rai Gangadhar, from Mewar, I think – though he has a spacious haveli in Matiya Mahal. He owns an elephant that's downright vicious; always ripping up other animals in fights. It earns Gangadhar huge sums of money, of course. But Gangadhar's elephant will not fight for a while, I believe. I heard it got hurt in a fight last night. Ah, Kaliqdad, here we are,' he said, breaking off. 'If you want to be of help, Jang Sahib, you could offer up a few prayers. Should anything happen to Kaliqdad, the Baadshah would have my head.'

Despite the coolness of the elephant stables, the salautri was sweating by the time he had finished stitching up the ugly gash in the elephant's thigh. It was a deep wound, four fingers long, just below the mark of the arrow that branded the elephant as a government animal. As he broke off the horsehair at the end of a neat row of stitches, the salautri heaved a sigh of relief. He rinsed his hands at the sailabchi held by a slave, then drew a piece of clean silk from his saddlebags and took it to the small fire that blazed merrily outside the stable. Muzaffar watched as he carefully burnt the silk, reducing it to fine grey ash.

The elephant's keeper was Shahjahan's Chief Mahout, Mahaura Khan, a lean, grizzled old Yusufzai from faraway Kabul, his skin darkened by countless afternoons on the exposed back of the Emperor's personal mount. His face wore a harried, haunted look, and Muzaffar guessed that there was more to it than the knowledge that the Baadshah would be furious if Kaliqdad died.

The salautri had also noticed Mahaura Khan's anguish. After he had pressed the burnt silk on the wound, spread a salve of crushed herbs, and then covered it all with a piece of clean silk, he said, 'Don't fret, ustadji. Kaliqdad is made of sturdy stuff – *you* know that. The wound is bad, but it will mend.'

The worry in the old mahout's eyes did not diminish.

The salautri got to his feet from beside the bulk of the elephant, and added reassuringly, 'Trust me. He will soon be well.'

Mahaura Khan smiled tiredly. 'I do not doubt your skill, huzoor.'

'But something worries you.'

Mahaura Khan sighed. 'I have to perform a task I always find distasteful, huzoor; I have to break the news of a man's death to his widow. The elephant that wounded Kaliqdad also gored his own mahout. Impaled him – the tusk went in through the stomach and came out between the shoulder blades.' He shivered. 'Ram Chand was dead before we knew it.'

The long, uncomfortable silence was broken by the salautri's gentle query. 'How did it happen, ustadji?'

To Muzaffar the remark seemed rhetorical, a mere expression of sympathy; but Mahaura Khan took it literally – as a question to be answered.

'The elephant was at the peak of musth, huzoor,' he replied. 'Violent and aggressive. Ram Chand did what we always do; he tied up the elephant well away from the rest of the animals. Thick ropes around a solid tree trunk, hind legs securely anchored – and no disturbance, man or animal. Just a regular daily visit by Ram Chand, to water and feed the animal, and check the ropes. Today Ram Chand went to attend to the elephant – and next we knew, the animal had killed him and was running amok. Allah alone knows how we got it down to the river to cool off.'

He sighed heavily, then went down on his haunches and extended his hands to the fire, even though the evenings were not particularly cold yet. 'And what bothers me, huzoor, is that I may have sent Ram Chand to his death.'

A stunned silence greeted this astonishing revelation. Finally, Muzaffar asked quietly, 'And why do you say that, ustadji?'

The Chief Mahout stared down at his calloused hands. 'Ram Chand came to me shortly before he died. He said he had been waiting all day to talk to me. But I was tired; I told him to attend to his elephant, that we would talk later. There was no hurry, it could wait.'

He glanced up at Muzaffar, his eyes full of pain. 'If I had not sent him away – if I had listened to him – he may have been alive now.'

'It is the will of Allah,' murmured the salautri. 'And no fault of yours, ustadji.'

Muzaffar chewed meditatively on his moustache. There was something, intangible and insubstantial, but *there* nevertheless, that told him there was more to this tragedy.

'What did Ram Chand want to talk to you about?' he asked. 'Did he say?'

'No, huzoor. Only that it was urgent.'

'And you have no idea what it could be?'

The mahout shook his head. 'None, huzoor. It could have been anything. The Royal Elephant Stables have long been associated with gossip. Some say that the elephant lines know of what is happening in Dilli – or anywhere in the empire, for that matter – before anybody else. Not even Kotwal Sahib's henchmen know half the things that come our way.'

A ghost of a smile flitted across Muzaffar Jang's handsome features, but all he said was, 'And?'

'And Ram Chand, huzoor, was a gossipmonger of the first water, his ears and eyes always open for a whiff of rumour. He attracted gossip.'

Muzaffar's face was expressionless as he murmured, half to himself, 'Gossips are vulnerable men.'

The mahout looked up, his keen, bright eyes suddenly narrowing. He muttered gruffly, 'Do you mean – but no; it cannot be possible –'

'Anything is possible.' Muzaffar's voice was firm, but low enough to be audible to only Mahaura Khan and the salautri. 'A known gossip indicates that he has urgent information to impart. And before he can do it, he is dead.'

'Dead, yes; but killed by his own elephant.'

'True. But can we be sure it was an accident? Could it not be deliberate?'

Mahaura Khan laughed shakily. 'You are reading too much into a mere accident, huzoor. Elephants have been known to kill their own mahouts – and when an elephant goes musth, who is to say what it will do?'

'And what if there were a human hand behind the death of Ram Chand? Could you rest in peace?'

Muzaffar's words were greeted by a tense silence, broken only by the crackle of the flames that danced, golden and red. Mahaura Khan looked deep into the pulsating white heart of the fire and said, 'No, huzoor. No man with a conscience could rest in peace.'

Muzaffar lowered himself onto his haunches, opposite the mahout. Young, alert eyes looked into old, weary ones. 'Very well, then. Let me see what I can unearth. At the very least, your conscience will be clear. Tell me: how long had Ram Chand been a mahout?'

Mahaura Khan frowned. 'Perhaps a little over twenty years. He was a tribal, huzoor – and they begin training their boys to handle elephants when they are barely out of their cradles. Ram Chand was in his thirties. I have known him since he was fifteen.'

'And had he ever been attacked by his own elephant?'

Mahaura Khan shook his head vigorously. 'Never. He was a careful man, an experienced mahout.'

'So it is unlikely that he would have been careless enough to endanger himself when he went to attend to his elephant today? He would have been careful, as always?'

'Certainly. Unless he was terribly agitated about whatever he had to tell me.'

Muzaffar inclined his head in deference. The Yusufzai may be a barely literate elephant handler, but that grizzled old head hid a sharp brain.

'So we come back to what Ram Chand wanted to tell you. What could have been so urgent that he felt it could not wait?' Muzaffar paused, and when Mahaura Khan made no comment, asked, 'How long had it been since he had last met you, ustadji?'

'Not very long – less than a day. Last night, when I went to check on Kaliqdad, Ram Chand was at the stables.'

'And he did not speak of wanting to talk to you?'

'No, huzoor. He was his normal self. Calm, relaxed.'

Muzaffar nodded. 'And today – was anybody else about when he asked to speak to you?'

'The world and his wife, huzoor,' Mahaura Khan replied, with a bitter laugh. 'I was just coming into the lines. There were others with me, coming in, and there were some going out with their animals. There were guards, slaves, mahouts. At least twenty people must have been there.'

Muzaffar grimaced. 'And would all of them have been able to hear your conversation with Ram Chand?'

'Not all. Perhaps some half a dozen were within earshot; but they may not even have been paying attention.'

'Could anyone watching Ram Chand – just watching, mind you, not listening – have been able to guess what he said? Was he agitated, excited – could his manner have alerted someone?'

Mahaura Khan shook his head unhesitatingly. 'Not Ram Chand, huzoor. I told you; he was a canny one. A gossip, but careful about where and to whom his tongue wagged. No; I don't think anyone – unless they were blessed with a sixth sense – could have guessed. *I didn't.*'

The salautri shifted uncomfortably. He had been standing beside the fire, his thin hands stretched towards its warming glow. His gaze wandered to the near-night darkness of the sky above, and he cleared his throat. 'I beg leave, Jang Sahib,' he said awkwardly. 'It is time for me to be heading homewards.'

Muzaffar nodded. 'Yes, and time for all of us, I think. But before I go, ustadji,' – he addressed Mahaura Khan – 'will you take me to where Ram Chand's elephant was tied up?'

The scene of the carnage was a small clearing hemmed in by the brooding canopies of three gnarled old banyan trees. Their rope-like tresses hung to the ground, imparting a markedly sinister appearance to the clearing. Muzaffar felt his skin crawl.

Mahaura Khan held aloft the lantern he was carrying. 'This is it, huzoor. The elephant was tied up here.'

The two men stood alone in the middle of a stretch

of bare earth. All around, till beyond the edge of the clearing, the mud, once packed hard, had been churned up as if by the hands of an enraged giant ploughman. A ploughman who had lashed out at everything in sight: digging deep, slashing madly at the trees, pulling down leaves, strips of bark, twigs, even entire branches.

In the centre of the clearing, an ominous dark stain had seeped across a patch of earth – a patch that still smelt sour and tragic. Muzaffar extended a hand for the lantern, and took it gently from Mahaura Khan. Leaving him standing in the middle of the clearing, Muzaffar began moving in slow circles, stooping as he examined the ground.

Slowly, the concentric circles that Muzaffar trod widened, stretched – went beyond the rim of the clearing. Mahaura Khan watched in silence as the flickering glow of the lantern dimmed, submerged in the menacing shadows of the banyan trees. A few minutes passed, then Muzaffar called over his shoulder.

'Come and look at this, ustadji.' Muzaffar tried not to sound triumphant, but the excitement in his voice was palpable.

He was standing behind one of the larger banyans, and when Mahaura Khan appeared, he lowered the lantern to within three feet of the base. A rope lay on the ground, its thickly plaited fibres frayed and broken.

'This broke when the elephant escaped, huzoor,' Mahaura Khan observed despondently.

'You think so, ustadji?' Muzaffar moved the lantern closer to the tree trunk. A series of shallow, vertical cuts became immediately visible on the bark. '*I* have never seen an elephant that left the marks of a knife on a tree.'

Muzaffar turned to look at the mahout, who was staring at the tree trunk. His eyes were wide and his voice shook as he whispered, 'Which man would do a thing like this, huzoor?' Who would dare come within striking distance of a musth elephant? This could only be the work of an imbecile – someone who had no idea of the danger.'

'Or someone who was utterly desperate,' added Muzaffar drily. 'Come, ustadji, let us return, it is late. But if it suits you, I will come back tomorrow morning. In the meantime, perhaps you could ask around among your men and find someone who could possibly have known what Ram Chand had been up to in the past twenty-four hours.'

'I do not know, huzoor,' Aziz Khan shook his head glumly when Muzaffar questioned him the next morning. 'Ustadji left for the qila in the morning with Kaliqdad. The other mahouts got down to their work, cleaning, watering and feeding their animals. Ram Chand was with them, I suppose – but I cannot be certain. I was summoned to the qila, and returned only late in the evening, when the news of Ram Chand's death was brought to me. So even I do not know –'

'Can you think of anybody who could possibly know?'

Aziz Khan's forehead creased in thought. It was a while before he spoke. 'Ghanshyam,' he said finally. 'Shahzada Sulaiman Shukoh's mahout. Ghanshyam may have some idea, since he came in from the river with Ram Chand. The guard mentioned it to me. Yes, Ghanshyam might know.'

Mahaura Khan shook his head even before Muzaffar could speak. 'It may be difficult to get hold of Ghanshyam,' he said. 'Can you not think of anyone else, Aziz? If Ram Chand went down to the river with Ghanshyam, it is possible some of the other mahouts went as well.'

'Ram Chand did not go down to the river with Ghanshyam, ustadji,' Aziz Khan corrected the Chief Mahout. 'Since Ram Chand's elephant was tied up, there was no question of taking the animal down to the river. Ram Chand went off by himself. But the guard said they came back together, so I assume the two men met at the river.'

Mahaura Khan raised an eyebrow. 'Ghanshyam took his elephant down to the river for a bath? Wounded and all?'

Muzaffar had begun to feel lost; the thread of the conversation was drifting beyond his reach. In other circumstances, he would have held his tongue and let the discussion take its course. But circumstances were far from normal. 'Is Ghanshyam wounded?' he butted in.

The two mahouts turned to look at him simultaneously, but it was Mahaura Khan who replied. 'No, huzoor. Not Ghanshyam; his elephant. His elephant was wounded sometime yesterday morning.' He chewed meditatively on his moustache, then said, 'Aziz, how *did* Ghanshyam's animal get hurt? He never told me.'

'Ghanshyam said it was attacked by a wild boar. Since Shahzada Sulaiman Shukoh is not in town, Ghanshyam took the animal off early for a jaunt in the forest. That was where they ran into the boar. Ghanshyam brought his animal right back to the stables so that he could attend to its wounds.'

Muzaffar frowned. 'Wait. He *didn't* bring the elephant right back here. Didn't he go to the river instead?'

Aziz Khan looked blankly at Muzaffar; it was Mahaura Khan who said, 'Yes, huzoor. He took the elephant to the river first, then came here, along with Ram Chand.'

'Would you do that, ustadji, if you had a wounded elephant on your hands?'

'It would depend, huzoor – on how badly the elephant was wounded. And whether it was thirsty. And whether the river was on my way back to the stables.'

Muzaffar nodded. 'Questions which perhaps Ghanshyam would be in a better position to answer.' He rose to his feet determinedly. 'Perhaps we had better interrupt his care of his elephant. And it may be advisable to call in the salautri for advice. After all, the wound may be more serious than Ghanshyam realizes.'

An hour later, Muzaffar was once again standing by, looking on while the salautri attended to an elephant. Muzaffar was not, however, paying much attention; his mind was hard at work, trying to make sense of all that he had heard and seen.

His interrogations of the guards, mahouts and slaves had not been fruitful. Nobody, it appeared, had noticed anything unusual. All insisted that Ram Chand had been, for once, in no mood to gossip.

There was one whom Muzaffar had not yet questioned. He stood next to his elephant, a tall, muscular man, almost as broad in the shoulder as Muzaffar himself, middle-aged and with a pair of magnificent moustaches that curled upwards towards his cheekbones. He had looked absently at Muzaffar once, but his attention had returned to his elephant. Ghanshyam, Muzaffar guessed, was a devoted mahout.

Somewhere in the background, Muzaffar could hear the buzz of conversation between the salautri, Ghanshyam and Mahaura Khan. They were probably discussing the treatment of the animal; whatever it was, it did not concern Muzaffar. He sighed and leaned back, wondering when Ghanshyam would find the time to talk to him.

'Not as bad as Kaliqdad, at any rate.' The salautri's voice broke in on Muzaffar's thoughts.

Muzaffar looked up to see the salautri wiping his hands vigorously on a large square of white muslin, a relieved smile on his face as he joined Muzaffar. 'And Kaliqdad too is better. Of course, one cannot expect the wound to heal so swiftly, but at least he looked more cheerful.'

The salautri looked down distastefully at the streaks of black his hands had left on the muslin. 'Ugh! Just look at that – and here I thought the man was fond of his elephant. You'd have thought he'd have kept the animal a lot cleaner.'

Muzaffar cocked an interrogative eyebrow. 'Those stains are from Ghanshyam's elephant?'

The salautri scowled. 'Yes. And greasy too. Allah knows what that animal's been wallowing in. And a mean creature too. If the mahout hadn't been there to soothe it, it would probably have gored me. Talk about ingratitude!'

Mahaura Khan, his conversation with Ghanshyam over, came to meet Muzaffar and the salautri. The relief on his face was apparent. 'If Allah wills it, at least we won't have trouble with this one,' he remarked.

The salautri's nose wrinkled as he sniffed suspiciously at his hands. 'Ustadji,' he said in mock annoyance, 'you're losing your touch. Your mahouts are letting your animals roll about in muck, and they can't even control a musth elephant. This particular one has wreaked havoc – one man dead, two animals wounded –'

'Two?' Mahaura Khan interrupted. 'Only Kaliqdad, huzoor.'

'Come on, ustadji. What about this one I've been dirtying my hands over? It was gored too, wasn't it?'

Mahaura Khan shook his head emphatically. 'Not by Ram Chand's animal. Ghanshyam's elephant was in a fight with a wild boar.'

The salautri grinned. 'If Ghanshyam told you that, ustadji, I would want him to show me that wild boar. It must be a very tall boar – I have personally never seen one that could strike five feet high on an elephant's thigh. Or did it jump about like a monkey?'

Muzaffar cut short the salautri's drollery with a swift question. 'Do you mean that wound was inflicted by an elephant, and not a wild boar?'

'I could stake my reputation on it.'

Muzaffar Khan turned to Mahaura Khan. 'What is your opinion, ustadji?' he said. 'Have another look at the elephant, and tell me what you think. And I need to talk to Ghanshyam.'

Ghanshyam, though somewhat reticent, appeared to want to cooperate. He listened attentively to Muzaffar's questions, mulled over them, and replied in a slow, deliberate voice.

'I met Ram Chand down at the river, huzoor,' he affirmed. 'He was there early, and without his elephant. Since the Shahzada Sahib is out of town, I took my animal into the forest well before dawn to allow it to forage.'

'To forage? But why?'

The man smiled. 'My elephant grew up in the wilds, huzoor. I caught him deep in the foothills of the Himalaya six years ago. Even though he's now used to camp life, I can sense that he misses the woods. Any chance I get, I take him out of the city and into the forest.'

Muzaffar nodded.

'Unfortunately, we ran into a wild boar just as the sun was coming up. The creature was snuffling about in the bushes, digging for roots, when we blundered into it. Even though my elephant finally managed to send it flying, it inflicted a serious wound – *you* saw how it was, huzoor.'

'Hmm. But the wound seemed a bit high to have been caused by a wild boar.'

'Ah, that. That was because the boar was up on an earth bank, huzoor. Had it been on the ground, at the same level as my elephant, it would probably not have had the temerity to attack. But up there – it could attack, and it did.'

'So you were on your way back from the forest? What were you doing at the river?'

'My elephant was thirsty, huzoor. And in any case, the river was on my way to the stables.'

'And you met Ram Chand. Did he seem his usual self?'

The man stroked his moustache meditatively. When he spoke, it was in a subdued, cautious tone. 'I would not say that, huzoor. He appeared excited.'

'And did he say anything to you?'

'The usual pleasantries.'

'Nothing else?'

'Nothing else. Unless...' His voice trailed off abruptly. Muzaffar, watching the mahout with interest, took the hint readily enough. 'Unless?'

Ghanshyam cleared his throat a little nervously, and hesitated before replying. 'Unless you pay any heed to what Ram Chand told me that morning.'

'Which was?'

The man was looking downright worried by now. 'I do not know if I should be saying this, huzoor,' he muttered. 'I am only repeating the words of a dead man – and who knows whether he was right or wrong in his suspicions? But if what he said should spread abroad as my opinions, I could get into trouble.'

'You can trust my discretion. If you know something, you may say it without fear.'

Muzaffar's voice was soothing, and the mahout seemed to draw reassurance from it. 'Very well, huzoor,' he said, with a sigh. 'If you say so. Ram Chand implied that he had serious doubts about the honesty of Aziz Khan.'

'Is that so? Why?'

'He suspected all was not right with the rations. The vegetables, grain and molasses for the elephants are brought daily by bullock cart. The rations munshi reports at the gate every morning, to attend to the bookkeeping – but Aziz Khan supervises the receiving and distribution. I think Ram Chand suspected something; he said Aziz Khan and the munshi were possibly making some money on the side.'

'Did he say why he thought so?'

The mahout shook his head. 'No, huzoor. We had reached the stables by then, so he didn't say anything more – other than telling me to hold my tongue, of course.'

Muzaffar nodded, a little absently. 'Interesting. And that was all?'

'Yes, huzoor. That was all.'

Muzaffar straightened, thanked the mahout, and then, just as it appeared that he was leaving, he turned to Ghanshyam and asked, 'May I have a look at your elephant? I am fascinated by elephants. And the royal elephants are a class apart. Do you mind…?'

For the briefest of moments, Ghanshyam looked disconcerted. Muzaffar wondered if he was going to refuse. Ghanshyam may not appreciate an outsider peering at his elephant, but a request from an amir was *not* a mere request. 'Of course, huzoor,' he murmured. 'It is a privilege.'

They made their way into the yard where Ghanshyam's elephant was standing. The dressing on the animal's thigh was still fresh; but the elephant itself appeared to be out of pain. It was bright-eyed and alert, curving its trunk lovingly around the shoulders of a young man who was standing beside it. He turned at the sound of the approaching footsteps, and Muzaffar found himself looking at a younger version of Ghanshyam. The young man appeared to be only about twenty, but his features bore a marked resemblance to those of the mahout. The height, the width of the shoulders – even the curving moustaches – were the same.

But there the similarity ended. Where Ghanshyam was attired in a simple white dhoti and thick cotton kurta, the young man glittered and sparkled. His crimson and yellow turban was massive, and his dhoti was of the best muslin. He wore an intricately worked armband of solid gold; and his shoes were of the finest leather – better, thought Muzaffar wryly, than Muzaffar's own boots. A very smart young man. Definitely not noble; but certainly well-off.

The stranger dipped his head in a salute to Muzaffar and grinned at Ghanshyam. He gave the elephant a final pat on its vast side, then strode off – all without uttering a word.

Muzaffar looked inquiringly at Ghanshyam. 'My brother, huzoor,' explained the mahout briefly. 'He comes visiting occasionally.'

Muzaffar's eyes were on the elephant; his only comment was offhand and almost by the way. 'Your brother seems to have done well for himself.'

'The gods are merciful.'

Muzaffar nodded. 'I suppose so. What is your brother's name?'

'Damodar, huzoor.'

But Muzaffar appeared to have lost interest; instead, he was studying the elephant carefully. Suddenly, without preamble, he reached out as if to stroke the elephant – and Ghanshyam sprang forward, quick as a bolt of lightning. His hand closed over Muzaffar's arm like a vice. '*Huzoor!*' He pulled Muzaffar back, and himself lunged forward towards the elephant, whose trunk had swung out suddenly towards Muzaffar.

Muzaffar backed away hurriedly, fumbling clumsily. Ghanshyam, his hands stroking the animal, his voice murmuring soothingly, calmed the elephant. By the time the animal had quietened down, the young amir had recovered his composure somewhat. He mumbled his thanks, and after an embarrassed glance at the elephant, took his leave.

Out of sight of the mahout, Muzaffar abandoned the flustered demeanour. By the time he had made his way to the gate of the Royal Elephant Stables, his brow was furrowed in thought; and after he had put a few questions to the guards at the gate, he mounted his stallion and rode away.

Muzaffar did not come to the elephant lines over the next couple of days. When he returned, he looked triumphant, and his first words to Mahaura Khan were telling.

'I need to talk to you, ustadji,' he said softly. 'Alone.'

And when they were alone, instead of responding to Mahaura Khan's questions, Muzaffar simply said, 'Wait, not so fast. I will tell you what I know. But you are the man who knows elephants, who knows the Royal Elephant Stables, and who, more importantly, knows the men who work here. So you have to tell me if what I say could be true.'

Mahaura Khan inclined his head in assent.

'Very well. Let us begin with what we know. Ram Chand did not die an accidental death; someone – a desperate someone – deliberately cut the ropes that tethered his elephant. Now, who could have cut the ropes? There are only three groups of people in the elephant lines: the guards, the mahouts and the slaves. The guards remain on duty at the gate, and there is little opportunity for one of them to sneak into the heart of the stables. That leaves us with the slaves and the mahouts.'

He glanced at Mahaura Khan, who simply blinked.

'Let us move on. Ram Chand was killed because someone feared that he was going to impart damning information – possibly a serious complaint – to you. Since Ram Chand had not mentioned the subject to you the night before, it is safe to assume that whatever he had to say arose out of something that occurred the same day.

'So what happened that day? Ram Chand went down to the river early, and there he met Ghanshyam. Ghanshyam's elephant was wounded – supposedly in a scuffle with a wild boar. The two men returned to the stables, and on the way, Ram Chand confided in Ghanshyam. He said he suspected Aziz Khan of conniving with the rations munshi in embezzling the rations –'

Mahaura Khan was incredulous. 'Aziz! Guilty of such deceit? I cannot believe it, huzoor! Surely there is some mistake. Ghanshyam must have heard incorrectly. Or Ram Chand must be mistaken –'

'Had you ever known Ram Chand to be mistaken in his gossip?' Muzaffar intervened quietly.

The Chief Mahout pulled up short, baffled. 'No – but... *Aziz*?'

Muzaffar did not seem to hear the anguish in the older man's voice. 'When you arrived at the elephant lines in the evening, Ram Chand approached you, asking for a word with you. This was witnessed by a number of people. Excluding, significantly enough, the rations munshi, who is on duty at the gate only in the morning. And also excluding Aziz Khan, who was away at the qila.'

'But then that means –'

'That neither Aziz Khan nor the rations munshi could have suspected Ram Chand was going to complain about them? Perhaps. But they could have accomplices – or informants.'

The old mahout shook his head and insisted stubbornly, 'I cannot bring myself to believe it, huzoor. I do not know the rations munshi well, but Aziz I can vouch for. His honesty is beyond all doubt.'

'That can probably be verified by getting the books checked. But if you are so sure, ustadji, then let us, for the moment, assume that Aziz – and the rations munshi – are innocent. Ram Chand, you say, could not have been mistaken. Then we are left with one obvious alternative: that Ghanshyam is lying. After all, we only have his word for what Ram Chand said.'

Muzaffar raised a hand to stall Mahaura Khan, who looked as if he was going to protest. 'Hear me out, ustadji. Tell me: did you examine the wound Ghanshyam's elephant sustained? Yes? And what did you think? Could that wound have been caused by a wild boar?'

Mahaura Khan looked unhappy, as if unwilling to admit – even to himself – what he had seen. 'I saw that wound – or what I could see of the wound; it had been dressed by the time I reached. And no, I do not think it could have been inflicted by a wild boar.'

'Even a particularly ferocious one, standing at a height?'

Mahaura Khan shook his head. 'One cannot say with absolute certainty; but no – I would think it unlikely. A pig rarely tackles an elephant.'

'True; that is what the salautri told me. And now something that may seem unconnected. There is a land owner from Mewar, Rai Gangadhar. He owns a fighting elephant that is said to be a nasty creature.'

'I have heard of him, huzoor,' affirmed Mahaura Khan. 'He has a bad reputation, that one.'

'Exactly. The salautri first told me about him on the very evening that Ram Chand was killed. Salautri sahib mentioned that in a fight the previous night, the elephant had been injured.'

There was no comment from Mahaura Khan.

'Ghanshyam's elephant, like Rai Gangadhar's, is known to be vicious – a born fighter, Ghanshyam himself warned me – and I tested the theory on my own.'

Muzaffar paused.

'Ghanshyam's elephant and the land owner's elephant were wounded within hours of each other. And Ghanshyam is almost certainly lying when he claims that a wild boar did the damage – it seems obvious that another elephant attacked his animal.

'And then there was the black substance that came off on salautri sahib's hands when he attended to Ghanshyam's elephant. I saw it for myself – it wasn't mud or dung, or any of the other dirt that you'd probably find on an elephant; it was oily. I could have sworn it was lampblack.'

Mahaura Khan stared, perplexed. 'Huzoor will pardon the slowness of an old man,' he murmured finally. 'But this tangle is beyond my comprehension. Who killed Ram Chand? Why?'

'Ram Chand went to the river that morning, ustadji, and there he met Ghanshyam, with a wounded elephant. The elephant's thigh was smeared with black, and I suppose Ram Chand came upon Ghanshyam trying to wash off the black. I do not know how Ram Chand guessed the truth – he may have put two and two together, and being the gossip he was, he probably had enough background information to come to the correct conclusion. I doubt if he tried to confront Ghanshyam. At any rate, Ghanshyam suspected that Ram Chand had smelt a rat – and so he got rid of Ram Chand.'

'But *why*? I don't understand, huzoor – what was Ghanshyam guilty of?'

'Of passing off a royal elephant as a commoner's. You see, ustadji, when I met Ghanshyam the other day, I also ran into his brother, Damodar. A debonair young man – definitely much wealthier than I would have expected. And also a man with whom Ghanshyam's elephant – a notoriously bad-tempered animal, as we all know – seemed to be both familiar as well as comfortable. When I questioned Ghanshyam about his brother's obvious prosperity, he was evasive. Evasive enough to rouse my suspicions.

'On my way out that day, I casually asked the guards about Damodar. Nobody seemed to know what he did for a living, but one of the men said Damodar had once mentioned a haveli in Matiya Mahal. That sounded familiar, and I decided to visit Matiya Mahal for myself. At every haveli, I asked for Damodar, and finally ran him to earth – in the haveli of Rai Gangadhar. Who, when asked to produce his elephant, became extremely aggressive and refused to comply.'

'Which means –?'

'That Damodar, along with his master and his brother, were passing off Ghanshyam's elephant as Rai Gangadhar's own animal. They were using it in elephant fights, and making large sums of money out of it. Since Ghanshyam ran the risk of being punished severely, I assume he was compensated adequately, with a sizeable portion of the winnings. His brother apparently earned a good bit; and he appears to have no qualms about flaunting his ill-gotten gains.'

'Lampblack – or something similar – was used to hide the brand on the elephant's thigh. And Damodar himself rode the elephant during the fights; it would have been too risky for Ghanshyam to do so. The chances of someone recognizing him – and reporting the matter – were just too high.'

Mahaura Khan sighed. 'It is a bad business, huzoor. Bad, and utterly needless… but what now? Shall I send for the guards to arrest him? And what of Damodar and Rai Gangadhar?'

'I have informed the kotwali. Both will have been taken into custody by now.'

'I will lead you to Ghanshyam, huzoor.' Mahaura Khan got to his feet. 'And then I will beg leave of you. I should inform Ram Chand's widow that her husband's death has been avenged.'

Author's Note: *Mahaura Khan was the Chief Mahout of Shahjahan for much of the emperor's reign, including the entire time the Taj Mahal was being built. His elephant, Kaliqdad, died shortly after the death of Shahjahan.*

The Eighth Guest

A splendidly attired Akram, on his way to his father's haveli to dine with visiting relatives, had stopped by to show off his new choga to Muzaffar Jang. 'Though why I'm wasting it on country bumpkins like my cousins, I don't know,' he grumbled, stretching a well-kept hand alongside the crimson choga. He squinted at the pigeon's blood ruby glittering in his archer's ring and tut-tutted. 'I had the cloth dyed to match the stone. But they've missed it by a few shades, I think. Eh, Muzaffar?'

When his friend's only response was a distracted nod, Akram raised an eyebrow. 'What ails you?'

'Nothing ails *me*.' Muzaffar sighed. 'I've received a disturbing note from Nawab Mukhtar Ali.'

'Oh. And?' Akram was instantly wary, the ruby and ill-matched choga forgotten for the moment.

'He writes that there has been an *unfortunate incident* at his haveli, and requests my presence.'

Akram slipped off his ring and peered meditatively through the ruby at the lamp flickering beside him. 'So what excuse will you make? I assume you aren't going.'

Muzaffar stirred uncomfortably. 'I don't want to go,' he admitted. 'But the note sounds desperate. If I don't go, it'll weigh on my conscience.'

Akram slid the ring back onto his thumb and stood up. 'I'd better leave or I'll be late. Take my advice and don't go.' He smoothed the front of his choga. 'It's bound to be something unsavoury. You know what his household's like.'

Muzaffar heaved a sigh of resignation. 'Yes, I know. But I can't ignore an appeal for help.'

Half an hour later, ushered into one of the smaller chambers in Mukhtar Ali's haveli, Muzaffar found himself regretting his decision. The dalaan where a party had been in progress earlier that evening was in the middle of the haveli. Off to its left lay the kitchens and the storehouses. On the opposite side of the house, overlooking the garden, was the mid-sized chamber to which Nawab Sahib led Muzaffar.

The room, its air a nauseating melange of rose attar and sweat, was claustrophobic. A Persian carpet in muted shades of red and blue covered the floor, its floral motifs repeated in the inlaid border of cornelian and lapis lazuli along the marble walls. The sheets on the mattresses were crisp and white, the brocaded bolsters a trifle overstuffed. Draped artistically across one bolster, a slender arm trailing on the carpet, was the body of a boy in his late teens.

A pretty boy, thought Muzaffar, groaning inwardly. Nawab Mukhtar Ali's parties were known for the beautiful serving boys he employed: boys who did more than merely pour wine or present platters.

This one must have been the pick of the lot. Flawless lilywhite skin, silky hair, a lightly muscled figure enveloped in light muslin. But the face was frozen into an empurpled mask, the lips pulled into a rictus of horror. The rich brown eyes, disconcertingly brilliant, bulged. A trickle of blood, thin as a brushstroke, ran down to a blotchy neck from a tongue that protruded disgustingly.

Muzaffar turned away, sickened. 'Has a hakim been sent for?' he asked Mukhtar Ali. The nawab, a man in his forties with a beguiling youthfulness which recent events had dimmed somewhat, nodded. 'He's attending to Qizilbash. Gulrez' – he indicated the steward, a portly man in his fifties who hovered in the background – 'will let us know when he's done.'

Muzaffar cast a quick glance across the mattress on which the boy lay spread-eagled. One of the bolsters had rolled off the mattress and sat forgotten on the floor. Beside it lay a cup of rock crystal, a sip of wine still twinkling scarlet in the bowl. Another cup, empty, stood on the mattress near the boy's arm.

'Nawab Sahib,' Muzaffar said, 'could we move out into your garden? I could do with a breath of fresh air.'

'How did this happen?' he asked as they strolled through the moonlit garden. Muzaffar gulped greedily of the cool, clean air, grateful for the faint whiff of night jessamine flowering somewhere nearby. 'And who is Qizilbash?'

'Naseeruddin Hassan Qizilbash. Surely you've heard of him?' The nawab chuckled wryly. 'Jang Sahib, you cannot be an amir in Dilli and *not* know who Qizilbash is.'

'Well, I don't,' Muzaffar snapped.

Nawab Mukhtar Ali lifted a placatory hand. 'Forgive me. I have pulled you into an affair which you no doubt find distasteful. I had little choice. A mere serving boy dead and one of the city's wealthiest men the obvious suspect – I cannot afford a scandal that could antagonize Qizilbash.'

'It would help if you told me who Qizilbash is,' Muzaffar said acidly.

'Yes, yes. He is – well, not exactly a moneylender, at least not by profession, but that's what he does. His father was a land owner and merchant who traded with the Persians and the Uzbeks. Made his fortune out of it, all of which passed on to Naseeruddin. He's rolling in money and has no qualms about lending it to noblemen in need. At slightly above the usual rates of interest charged by other usurers, but nobody minds. He's discreet; never lets on about whom he's helping keep afloat. And he *is* reasonable about being paid back.'

'So he's in great demand. Why so respected then?'

The nawab's eyebrows drew together for a moment. Then, with a self-conscious laugh, he said, 'Not respect, really. I am deep in debt to him. Yes, I know I should be living within my means, but what is life if it isn't lived to the fullest?' His eyes widened in defiance, then brightened in sudden, spontaneous amusement. 'Ah,

Muzaffar, you're brilliant. One disapproving look and you have me battling the pangs of a conscience I'd thought long stifled. Anyway, it's just that I need to keep Qizilbash happy, if only to stop him from calling in my debts – and my brother Taufeeq's. We'd be bankrupt if he did,' he added baldly.

Muzaffar swallowed. 'But if Qizilbash *is* guilty, I'll not have it swept under the carpet. You understand that.'

'*If* he is guilty. Yes, then I will let you call in Kotwal Sahib.'

'Good. And now: what happened?'

The nawab rubbed a hand along his jaw, absently feeling the close-trimmed beard. Muzaffar, accustomed to seeing a perennially unruffled Nawab Mukhtar Ali, looked on anxiously. 'I hosted a party here today,' the nawab replied. 'For a select few. It was to be an early dinner, because two of my guests leave for Lahore at dawn tomorrow. We began with some wine – and sometime during the party, Qizilbash must have slipped away. We didn't realize he'd vanished until it was time for dinner. Gulrez got some servants to search; they found him in the room you just saw. He was unconscious, and Abbas – the serving boy – was lying beside him, dead.'

He paused, and Muzaffar asked, 'Where were your other guests at the time?'

'At dinner. The two men who leave town tomorrow were restive, and I didn't want to delay dinner. I gave orders to Gulrez to serve the rest while the servants looked for Qizilbash.'

'And are any of your guests still here?'

'No; they've gone.' The nawab looked embarrassed. 'I did not think it wise to publicize Abbas's death. It would lead to unnecessary gossip.'

Muzaffar nodded, pensive. 'And do you remember where your guests were the rest of the evening? Before dinner?'

Nawab Mukhtar Ali mulled over the question for a minute or so. 'There were to be eight men at dinner, excluding me,' he said finally. 'Qizilbash was one. Two were delayed at the qila and arrived just as dinner was being served. Three others wished to see a new manuscript that I have acquired – a copy of the *Iskandar Nama* – so I took them to my library. I was in the library with them when Gulrez came to say Qizilbash was missing.' He paused. 'How many does that account for?'

'Six.'

'So there are two men still to be reckoned with. One was Mirza Mohammad Aslam – drinks so much, his hands shake, though he puts it down to palsy. He was deep in his cups when I went off to the library. He couldn't even sit down to dinner.'

'And the eighth man?'

The nawab chewed his moustache. 'Taufeeq, my younger brother.'

Muzaffar waited for him to continue, but when the nawab remained silent, Muzaffar asked, 'And? Where was Taufeeq during the party?'

Mukhtar Ali's voice was gruff when he replied. 'He was in the dalaan at the beginning – I remember him greeting the first guests. He sat with Mohammad Aslam for a while, and then…' His voice trailed away. 'There was a difference of opinion,' he sighed. 'Taufeeq and one of the guests. It blew up into a full-fledged quarrel and Taufeeq stormed out of the room.'

'And went where?'

The nawab shrugged. 'I don't know. It was all very awkward, so I brought up the topic of the *Iskandar Nama*. The man with whom Taufeeq quarrelled is interested in literature. I took him off, along with two others, to the library. I didn't see where Taufeeq went.'

Behind them, a discreet clearing of the throat announced the presence of the steward, Gulrez. As Mukhtar Ali and Muzaffar turned around, the man bowed. 'Huzoor, the hakim has attended to Qizilbash Sahib.'

Nawab Mukhtar Ali looked expectantly towards Muzaffar.

'We'd better go in,' Muzaffar said. 'I'd like him to examine the boy.'

The hakim was a short, bullet-headed man, brisk and efficient. He gave his diagnosis in a few clipped words as he washed his hands over the sailabchi held by a slave. 'Throttled. Bulging eyes, protruding tongue, mottled skin – and marks on his neck. Someone wrapped their fingers around his throat and squeezed hard.'

He reached for the clean square of cotton proffered by the slave and wiped his hands.

'And what's wrong with Qizilbash?'

The hakim's mouth twisted in a sarcastic half-grin. 'Ah. *Him.*' He handed the damp cloth back to the slave, and began to turn down the cuffs of his sleeves. 'Nothing much except for a dose of opium. I can't tell how long he'll remain unconscious, but you may have him on your hands for the night.'

Muzaffar's gaze flicked to the two cups, both now standing neatly beside the mattress where the hakim had placed them after a careful sniff. 'Yes,' the hakim said, as if replying to a question. 'There's definitely opium in the wine there. The empty cup could have been dosed too, but I'm not sure.'

He looked at Mukhtar Ali. 'If that is all, Nawab Sahib, I shall take your leave.'

The nawab, with Muzaffar's unspoken consent, dismissed the hakim and turned back to Muzaffar. 'What now? Do you think Qizilbash is responsible?'

Muzaffar grimaced, a mirthless chuckle of disbelief at the nawab's naïveté. 'It's too early to tell, Nawab Sahib.' He paused, glancing uneasily at the corpse – now laid out neatly, the slim legs drawn together, the arms folded primly over the abdomen, the trickle of blood wiped clean and the eyes closed. 'Tell your steward to have the body removed, and those two cups kept aside. I'll collect them before I leave,' Muzaffar said. 'And tell me about this boy.'

'I don't know if I can actually tell you much about Abbas,' Mukhtar Ali replied as they seated themselves in one of the smaller chambers adjacent to the dalaan. The servants were still tidying the dalaan, Nawab Sahib had explained apologetically – and had, the very next moment, winced in mortification as he realized that his reluctant guest had probably forgone his own dinner. Gulrez had been swiftly summoned, and even as Muzaffar settled back against a bolster, a procession of servants began threading its way through the arched doorway of the chamber, bearing covered dishes, platters, cups and pitchers.

The nawab watched silently as a serving boy placed a small porcelain bowl of pickled green mangoes beside Muzaffar's plate. The boy straightened and turned back to retrieve more relishes – wedges of lime, fine slivers of crisp ginger – from a tray held by another servant.

'I barely knew Abbas. A beautiful boy. Clever. Quiet and unobtrusive.'

At Muzaffar's elbow, the serving boy, leaning over with a bowl of yoghurt, sucked in an audible breath. Muzaffar glanced up, to see the youth's jaw tighten and his gaze fix momentarily on Nawab Sahib before his eyelids lowered again decorously. Muzaffar instinctively reached out to touch the boy's arm.

'Huzoor?' The whisper was breathless, half-afraid at being caught out, but the eyes staring up at Muzaffar held a trace of arrogance.

'You knew Abbas?'

Before the boy could speak, Nawab Mukhtar Ali ordered the other servants out. When the last of the serving boys had withdrawn, he gestured to the boy. 'Go on – Eqhlaq, isn't it?'

'Huzoor.' The boy stood still, hands clasped in front.

'Well? What –' Nawab Sahib's voice broke off in midsentence as a scream tore through the house. Even as Muzaffar and the nawab scrambled to their feet and ran towards the doorway, the sudden silence of the house struck Muzaffar as almost unnatural. A minute earlier, he had been vaguely aware of the buzz of distant conversation; muffled footsteps; the faraway clink of crockery; the sound of water flowing. Now, in the aftermath of that unearthly shriek, there was utter stillness, as if the house was waiting with bated breath.

And then the haveli erupted. A loud keening, spiralling into a hysterical crescendo, rang through the corridor. A man, his voice deep and irritated, yelled for someone – presumably the screamer – to shut up. A series of sharp thwacks resounded, followed by a dull thump. The keening changed to a petulant wail.

Muzaffar burst into the room where Abbas's body still lay. Pandemonium had erupted in the chamber. The Persian carpet had been rucked up at one end, the sheet covering the mattress pulled out, and one bolster flung clear across the room. A girl, all bony elbows and long hair, was clutching Abbas desperately, her face pressed into his neck. Gulrez crouched beside her, looking harassed.

'Get up, Sana,' he hissed, stubby fingers tugging at the girl's elbow. 'Get *up!*'

'What on earth is the matter?' Mukhtar Ali exclaimed.

At his words, the girl twisted around and up, her fingers still digging into the dead boy's shoulders. Her eyes were red and swollen, the sallow cheeks tear-streaked and plastered with damp strands of hair. 'He's dead!' She wailed. 'Oh, what will I *do*?' Behind her, Gulrez grew frantic, pulling desperately at her arm, pleading with her to go.

Muzaffar moved forward, gesturing to the nawab and his steward to leave the girl to him. He waited till the two of them – the nawab looking affronted, Gulrez embarrassed – had left. Then he lowered himself and sat back on his heels, forearms resting on his thighs, looking on quietly.

The girl's wails subsided into sobs, then sniffles. Finally, with a last unhappy sniff, she straightened up, and recoiled visibly. 'Forgive me, huzoor,' she whispered breathlessly. 'I did not realize –' She got to her feet, dragging her crumpled dupatta over her head. She was halfway to the arched doorway when Muzaffar said, 'Wait. I wish to ask you a few questions about Abbas.'

The girl stiffened and inched closer to the doorway.

'Were you fond of him?' Muzaffar asked, his voice soft, empathetic.

The girl lifted miserable, eloquent eyes to Muzaffar's face.

'Very much?'

'He was – my life, huzoor,' she mumbled. She looked past Muzaffar at the body on the mattress. Tears welled up in her eyes, but she blinked them away. 'He was wonderful, clever and witty. Bright and cheerful.' She took a deep, quivering breath. 'He wanted to marry me, take me away from here.'

Muzaffar blinked, taken aback. 'But Abbas was a slave, as are you. How did he intend to do that?'

Sana kept silent and retreated into her shell.

Muzaffar heaved a sigh. 'How long had you known him?'

She bit her lip, the gesture making her look younger than she was. 'Almost three years, huzoor,' she answered. 'When Nawab Sahib bought him.' Her eyes misted over. 'He was a good friend, and then – more. He was always giving me things. He even wrote poetry for me. I can't read, of course, but he told me what he'd written and I memorized it. I have a good memory.' She pitched her voice an octave higher and recited in a singsong falsetto: '*Ah love! Could thou and I with fate conspire, to grasp this sorry scheme of things entire, would not we shatter it to bits – and then remould it nearer to the heart's desire!*'

Muzaffar's eyes narrowed. 'Abbas penned that for you?'

The girl nodded. 'Yes, huzoor. He said he'd written it for me.' She swiped at her cheek with the back of her hand. 'He gave his poetry to me, to keep it safe. Just yesterday, when he returned from Qizilbash Sahib's haveli. I'll always cherish his papers. Perhaps someday he will be famous.'

'Perhaps. Tell me, do you know who would have wished Abbas harm?'

Her gaze wavered momentarily, but she did not say anything.

'Do you suspect someone?'

'I am no-one to express my opinions, huzoor.'

Muzaffar waited, still silent.

'Gulrez Sahib,' Sana burst out suddenly, her face contorting in fury. 'You saw how he spoke to me, huzoor – *you* were here. He wouldn't even let me grieve!' She paused for breath, then continued in a more controlled voice. 'He's vindictive; always hated Abbas, picked on him. Perhaps he was jealous; who knows? But he'd always be accusing Abbas of being lazy, disobedient. He beat him too. Once he thrashed him so badly, Abbas couldn't get out of bed for a week. Qizilbash Sahib was most unhappy.'

'Qizilbash Sahib? What say did *he* have in the matter?'

The girl flushed. 'He – he was very fond of Abbas. Ever since he saw Abbas at one of Nawab Sahib's parties.' She fidgeted with the edge of her dupatta. 'In the beginning, he'd simply ask for Abbas to wait on him at parties. But then I think he came to an understanding with Nawab Sahib, and Abbas would go and spend time with him occasionally. He took Abbas hunting a few times, then on a trip to Agra – and at his own haveli. I was scared he'd take Abbas away for good.' It suddenly seemed to dawn on her that Abbas *was* gone for good, and she began crying again.

Muzaffar decided it was time to leave the girl to her misery.

Just short of the doorway, he froze. Out in the corridor, the faint rustle of cloth was followed by the light slapping of leather sandals on a stone floor as someone sped away. Muzaffar sprang forward to see a lithe figure, white muslin jama and pyjamas flapping, racing down the corridor. With a muffled curse, Muzaffar followed, his longer legs allowing him to quickly gain on the eavesdropper. Despite the advantage, Muzaffar just about managed to make a grab for a thin shoulder before the momentum of his sprint carried both him and the other person down, crashing unceremoniously to the floor.

Muzaffar rolled off the squirming body below him. It was the serving boy, Eqhlaq.

'You still haven't answered the question I'd asked you,' Muzaffar said frostily as he got to his feet. He grabbed the boy by the collar and hauled him up too. Eqhlaq glared back defiantly.

'Well?'

'What question, huzoor?' The insolence in the boy's expression was unmistakable.

'What about Abbas? You knew him, didn't you?'

Eqhlaq's gaze wandered towards the doorway through which Muzaffar had chased him. 'Sana's already told you,' he replied bitterly. 'Isn't that enough, huzoor?'

'I want to know what *you* have to say.'

The boy grimaced. 'One should not speak ill of the dead.'

'Ah. So you *do* have opinions that differ from Sana's. Tell me. Even if it *is* ill.'

It looked for a moment as if the boy would refuse to answer; but he merely shrugged. 'As you wish, huzoor. You will probably hear it anyway, from everybody here except Sana. She was besotted with Abbas.' He spat out the dead boy's name with unconcealed contempt. 'Silly about him. She didn't even care that he was a bloody catamite, happily getting buggered by –' His voice had risen in his agitation, but he broke off suddenly. 'I beg your pardon, huzoor. I did not mean to offend.'

Muzaffar folded his arms across his chest and regarded Eqhlaq with interest. 'You do not appear to have liked Abbas much,' he remarked mildly. 'Why?'

'He wheedled Sana away,' Eqhlaq replied sullenly. 'She was mine, huzoor!' The words came out in an impassioned rush. '*Mine*. Before her mother died, she told *my* mother she wanted Sana to be my wife some day. Sana liked me too. But then Abbas came along, and that was the end of it. I hated the bastard,' he added viciously. 'I'm glad he's dead.'

Muzaffar pressed a forefinger to the bridge of his nose. 'And where were you during the party?'

Eqhlaq laughed mirthlessly. 'Oh, I didn't kill him, huzoor,' he replied. 'I was serving. You can ask Gulrez Sahib; he will confirm I was there all the time. Either in the kitchens, or in the dalaan, or somewhere between the two. Not in this part of the haveli at all.'

'I see. So Gulrez was there all the time, in the kitchens or the dalaan or in between?'

The boy squirmed. 'More or less, huzoor. If not him, then there are others who will vouch for me – the kitchen slaves, the other serving boys. *They* saw me. I did not come here.'

Muzaffar nodded. 'Take me to Nawab Sahib. I would like to speak to him.'

'I wish I'd taken your advice,' Muzaffar muttered, sitting down beside Akram at the qahwa khana and sipping tentatively from the cup of coffee a waiter had placed before him. 'I would have done well to have stayed away from Nawab Mukhtar Ali's haveli. Too much unpleasantness there.'

Behind him, a loud guffaw rang out, and Muzaffar glanced over his shoulder. It was just two hours past dawn and the coffee house was still relatively empty. A servant was using a twig broom to sweep desultorily around the few patrons who had already arrived. Motes danced in the bright sunshine pouring in through an open window.

'I was there when Mir Jumla arrived at the qila,' an old amir with pendulous jowls was saying. 'You should have seen the nazar he brought from the Deccan to present to the Baadshah. Made my mouth water.'

Another amir, his arm laid companionably around the older man's rounded shoulders, laughed again. 'Girls, eh? I've heard the women in Golconda are luscious.' His voice dropped as he leaned closer and whispered something that made the old man snigger. Beyond them, a thin young man leaned back against the wall, its original whiteness greyed by constant contact with greasy fingers and oily heads.

Akram slid a generous spoonful of sugar into his coffee and began to stir. 'Yes. I know Nawab Mukhtar Ali and his ilk. Sordid.' He sipped the coffee. 'Hmm. Not bad. Quite invigorating, in fact.' He put the cup down. 'So who do you think did it?'

Muzaffar shook his head in exasperation. 'I can't tell

at this stage. I'd thought it might be Eqhlaq – he hated Abbas, and with good reason. Couldn't be pleasant to have your girlfriend desert you for another.' He looked askance at three Persian merchants who were sitting across the room, discussing in loud voices their chances of an audience with the Emperor. 'That girl Sana was inclined to suspect Gulrez. She said he hated Abbas and used to beat him. But I asked around a bit: Nawab Sahib, the head cook, some serving boys. Gulrez is a highly visible figure. Someone or the other could vouch for him for every minute of the evening. And that goes for Eqhlaq too; I checked.'

'So it cannot have been either of them?'

Muzaffar shook his head. 'No. Oh, Gulrez admitted he couldn't stand Abbas. Said he was a lazy, slimy little bastard – but Gulrez said *he* has his hands full running the household. In essence, Abbas was too minor a worry for him to do more than rave and rant occasionally.'

Akram drank down the last swallow of coffee in his cup and beckoned to a waiter. 'More coffee, Muzaffar? Yes?' He placed the order and sat back.

Muzaffar rubbed his jaw reflectively. 'Abbas seems to have been Qizilbash's favourite. Everybody – Gulrez, Sana, Nawab Sahib – admitted that Qizilbash had more or less adopted Abbas as his own special lover. From what Gulrez told me, it seems Abbas was virtually living in Qizilbash's house.'

Akram grimaced. 'But why didn't Qizilbash simply buy Abbas off the nawab? That would have suited everybody.'

'He probably realized it was simpler to have Nawab Sahib bear the cost of housing and feeding Abbas. And Nawab Sahib's so deep in debt, he'd be unlikely to go against Qizilbash.'

The waiter came by to pour coffee for them. Akram waited till the man had taken himself off – to a pair of newcomers, merchants who had brought along their own coffee. Akram turned his attention back to Muzaffar. 'So who did it, if not Gulrez or Eqhlaq?'

Muzaffar shrugged. 'I don't know. I thought Sana, but she looks too fragile to have throttled him. And her grief was genuine enough. I wonder if it was Nawab Sahib's brother, Taufeeq. He appears to have disappeared for a while before dinner.'

'Why would *he* kill Abbas?'

Muzaffar sat back and rested the cup on his knee. 'I wonder. I need to talk to him: I didn't get the chance last night.'

Behind them, the three noblemen – the old man, his lascivious comrade and their thin friend – had now graduated to poetry. The thin man was reciting something in a surprisingly deep, pleasant voice.

Muzaffar chuckled. 'That reminds me. Sana said Abbas wrote poetry for her; she recited some of it. I hadn't known Abbas was Omar Khayyam.'

Akram grinned back. 'He wouldn't be the first one to try impressing a woman by passing off someone else's work as his own.'

'Yes, well.' Muzaffar downed the last of his coffee. 'But I don't think it makes sense to give copied poems to an unlettered girl.' He peered into Akram's cup, noted that it was empty, and got to his feet. 'It's time I was moving on,' he said. 'I have a few appointments to keep.'

Shafi Sahib, the quiet attaar who had his dingy little chemist's shop in a narrow lane off Khaas Bazaar, had news to impart. He had analysed the contents of the two cups Muzaffar had left at his house late the previous night. The results bore out the hakim's prediction. The empty cup had yielded traces of wine, and nothing but wine. The cup that still contained a swallow of wine had been dosed with opium. 'A small amount, though,' Shafi Sahib added as he wrapped the two cups in a square of unbleached cotton and handed the bundle to Muzaffar. 'Enough to knock a full grown man out for an hour or two. It couldn't have harmed him unless he was an invalid or very old.'

Muzaffar, with a puzzled frown, had thanked Shafi Sahib and ridden off towards Kabuli Darwaza, near which, according to Nawab Sahib, Naseeruddin Hassan Qizilbash had his haveli.

Muzaffar had expected opulence on a scale surpassing the nawab's haveli. But if Qizilbash possessed wealth, it was not reflected in his dwelling. The gateway was all peeling plaster and faded paintings; the garden in the central court wore an air of neglect, its roses scraggy and dripping wilted petals. And there appeared to be no servants around. Muzaffar wandered about, bemused, until he found a sharp-nosed clerk, hunched like a vulture over a stack of papers in a dusty office. He glanced at Muzaffar, put the papers aside and emerged from the office. 'Yes?' He was not hostile; merely wary, thought Muzaffar.

'My name is Muzaffar Jang. I would like to meet Qizilbash Sahib; Nawab Mukhtar Ali gave me to understand he would have returned here by now.'

The man had been rubbing a finger vigorously in his eye; he blinked. 'Nawab Sahib? But I'd sent word to Taufeeq Sahib that it would take time to redo the papers –'

He was cut off in midsentence by Muzaffar. 'Wait; I think you misunderstand me. I wish to speak to Qizilbash Sahib about what happened at Nawab Sahib's haveli last night.'

'Oh.' The man coughed, suddenly embarrassed. 'Do you mean the death of that –' his mouth twisted with contempt '– that simpering *boy*?'

'Abbas. Yes. Did you know him?'

The man snorted derisively. 'Everybody in this household knew him. He was here day in, day out, sidling up to Qizilbash Sahib. And he got encouragement too,' he added. 'Sahib coddled and petted him. Every wish was granted, every whim catered to.'

'I've heard Qizilbash Sahib was very fond of him,' Muzaffar admitted.

'And what does he get for it? That thieving little bastard had no compunctions about –' The man broke off. 'Will you wait? I shall see if Sahib is available.'

And leaving Muzaffar standing in front of the office, he walked off purposefully down the corridor.

Muzaffar watched him obliquely. Midway down the corridor, the man turned right, into another corridor of fluted columns marching towards the far end of the haveli. He stopped at the second doorway, a pool of dimness beyond a cusped arch that Muzaffar could just about discern behind the canopy of a weeping willow.

Muzaffar waited impatiently, his eye on the doorway through which the man had disappeared. A barbet, all vivid green and drab tan, flapped onto the top branch of the willow and glared suspiciously at Muzaffar before flying off. Muzaffar watched its flight across the garden, then stepped off the corridor, glanced sharply left and right, and ran lightly towards the willow.

The tree offered just enough shelter for Muzaffar to stand in its shadow and pretend an interest in the water channel beside it. More importantly, it was close enough to the room beyond for Muzaffar to eavesdrop on the conversation inside. The first voice he heard was an unfamiliar one, deep and authoritative.

'Look again in your office. I couldn't find a thing; not one bloody page.' There was an irritable grunt, then the voice continued in a malicious hiss. 'I'm beginning to wonder if he did steal anything. For all I know, *you* lost the papers.'

'Huzoor, please,' the clerk interrupted, part placatory, part impatient. 'What shall I tell this person?'

'Oh, send him in. Might as well get it over and done with.'

Muzaffar slipped back swiftly to the clerk's office. He was standing outside the little room when the clerk returned to announce that Qizilbash Sahib had consented to meet huzoor, and would huzoor be so good as to follow him?

Qizilbash's haveli may be a shambles, but the man himself put Muzaffar in mind of one of the more decorative hill pheasants, plump and with an incongruously small, elegant head. A monal, thought Muzaffar with a private grin. Yes, a monal, unabashedly opulent in its garb of iridescent orange, red, turquoise and emerald. Qizilbash's clothing – resplendent with gold thread and seed pearls – gleamed with every movement. The aigrette in his turban fluttered like a crest.

Only his voice, resonant and powerful, broke the illusion. 'You've come to the wrong man,' he said grumpily when Muzaffar had explained the reason for the visit. 'I was unconscious through all of it. Didn't Mukhtar Ali tell you I spent the night at his haveli?'

Muzaffar inclined his head. 'All I wished were a few details of what happened earlier… what was the last thing you remember before you lost consciousness?'

Qizilbash regarded his visitor balefully for a few moments. 'I had retreated from the main dalaan. It was getting stuffy, and I wanted some peace and quiet. So I took Abbas off to the other room. He poured a cupful of wine for me. I told him to have some himself; he looked as if he needed it. I must have sat there a few minutes, drinking and talking to him – and then I don't remember anymore.'

'What did you talk about?'

The man's ears, protruding below his shimmering blue turban, reddened. 'This and that,' he replied evasively. 'What he'd been doing all day long.'

And that, Muzaffar realized, was all the answer Qizilbash would provide. He admitted he had awakened in the dim hour before dawn, stayed on at Mukhtar Ali's haveli for an early breakfast, and then come home.

'I see. And did you see Taufeeq last night anywhere near the room, while you were there?'

Qizilbash frowned, puzzled. 'Not that I recall. Why? Do you suspect – but yes; perhaps you have cause to.' He looked pointedly away, as if discouraging further questions.

Muzaffar gritted his teeth and said quietly, 'It appears you have reason to suspect Taufeeq. Why is that, may one ask?'

A small, awkward smile flitted across Qizilbash's face. His gaze shifted to the garden outside. 'I wouldn't go so far as to say I suspect Taufeeq,' he murmured. 'It is just that Taufeeq was very *fond* of Abbas, you understand. I'd say he was jealous.'

'That sounds like ample reason for him to murder *you*,' Muzaffar observed drily. 'I cannot see why he would kill the object of his affections.'

'It takes the twinkling of an eye for love to turn to hate,' Qizilbash said sagely. 'Or at least for lust to turn to hate.'

Muzaffar, arriving at Nawab Mukhtar Ali's haveli half an hour later, asked to see the nawab's younger brother. Taufeeq, who was near Muzaffar's own age, entered the dalaan shortly after. His face bore a strong resemblance to that of his brother, but lacked the laugh lines, the twinkling eyes and the easy smile. This man, thought Muzaffar, would be embittered and harsh by the time he reached his forties.

His answer to Muzaffar's first question gave Muzaffar an inkling of how uncooperative Taufeeq was likely to be. 'Where was I just before dinner was served?' he murmured, his voice thoughtful. 'Why, Jang Sahib, I do not see what business it is of yours.' The words were accompanied by a sardonic smile, but Muzaffar, looking into Taufeeq's watchful eyes, wondered why the man was worried.

'I'm sure it is no business of mine,' Muzaffar concurred. 'But, unless you can provide a valid explanation for your disappearance, I will be compelled to assume you were up to no good.'

'And what if I was?'

'Then I will assume you had something to do with Abbas's murder.'

Taufeeq muttered an obscene curse and turned away, presenting a broad back to Muzaffar. 'Damn you, you won't give up, will you?' he grated. He took a deep breath and turned back, his face a little more composed. 'Very well, I'll tell you. But should this get out – if *anybody* in Dilli comes to know – I will personally, with my own hands, throttle you.'

Muzaffar did not respond.

'I had gone to the zenana,' Taufeeq said. The sentence hung in the still air of the dalaan. 'No, not to pleasure one of Mukhtar's concubines,' he added sarcastically. 'To meet a lady, a noblewoman who'd come to visit my sister.'

Muzaffar raised an eyebrow.

'She's my betrothed, damn it! And there was nothing even vaguely improper about it – my sister was there all the time: ask her if you don't believe *me*.'

'And why did you feel the need to meet the lady so urgently? Couldn't it wait?'

Taufeeq glared. 'You're like a dog worrying a rat,' he muttered. 'You won't let go till you've shaken the wits out of the poor creature.' He laughed ruefully. 'No doubt you've heard about the quarrel I had with one of Mukhtar's guests.'

'Yes.'

'The man is brother to my betrothed; her only living relative. Last night, I told him I wouldn't be able to pay the meher, the bride-price, which I'd promised at the engagement. He started calling me names right there, in the midst of the other guests. And I – well, I lost my temper too.'

'What does this have to do with your going to meet the lady? Did you want to tell her what had happened?'

Taufeeq nodded. 'Yes. I was so angry, I wanted her to choose there and then between her brother's household and mine.' He frowned. 'My sister nearly threw me out of the zenana, but my betrothed intervened. We talked a bit, and then I returned to the party. Dinner had already been served.'

'I see. Did you pass by the room where Qizilbash was, with Abbas?'

'No; it's in the opposite direction. The zenana lies on the other side of the house.' He looked narrowly at Muzaffar. 'Why? Haven't you been able to find any witnesses to what happened there?'

Instead of answering the question, Muzaffar responded with a question of his own. 'I'm puzzled by your timing. Why did you choose to discuss such a delicate matter with your betrothed's brother at the party? Why not earlier? Or why not later? I would have thought –'

He blinked and pulled back sharply as Taufeeq interrupted with a growl of rage. 'I would have thought that would be obvious! These are not matters one pushes under the carpet until a more auspicious time; I wanted to get it out of the way. Surely even you can understand that?!' He fell silent, looking sheepish about his outburst. 'I'm sorry; I didn't mean to let fly like that.'

There was an awkward silence, which Muzaffar finally broke. 'You still haven't answered the first part of the question,' he reminded Taufeeq quietly. 'Why not *earlier*?'

'Because Qizilbash spoke to me only when he arrived for the party.' Taufeeq noticed the bewilderment on Muzaffar's face, and explained. 'I was meaning to borrow money from Qizilbash to pay the bride-price. But before I could do that, Qizilbash said he wanted me to clear my previous debts. Within the week, too.'

Muzaffar stared vacantly at Taufeeq for a few

moments, then blinked. 'Ah. So that's why.' After a pause, he added, 'Just one last question: how well did you know Abbas?'

Taufeeq chuckled, a genuine sound of amusement that made Muzaffar wonder if he hadn't been wrong in his initial estimation of this seemingly dour man. 'And what is that supposed to mean?' Taufeeq said, his eyes twinkling. 'Tell me, Jang Sahib, are you looking for possible rivals for Qizilbash? If that's the case, you're barking up the wrong tree. Abbas may have been pretty, but he held no attractions for me, thank you.'

Muzaffar grinned back and, with a quick word of thanks, turned to go. At the doorway, he glanced back over his shoulder and asked, 'By the way, where could I find the girl Sana?'

'I have news for you, Nawab Sahib,' Muzaffar said an hour later to his host. Nawab Mukhtar Ali was seated in his own dalaan, the room where he had entertained his guests the previous night. It was a larger, more magnificent version of the room in which Abbas had been found dead. A room designed for ostentatious banquets, thought Muzaffar, not for tête-à-têtes such as this, with their voices echoing in the stillness of the vast hall. He and the nawab sat facing each other on one of the thick mattresses; Taufeeq sat beside them.

Muzaffar withdrew a sheaf of papers from the pocket of his choga. He smoothed them out and handed them over to the nawab, who stared down at the close-written sheets, his forehead wrinkling in bewilderment as he read on. When he had finished, he wordlessly handed over the sheets to his younger brother. Taufeeq was not as composed as Mukhtar Ali; less than a minute's perusal, and his head snapped up. 'What –?' he began indignantly.

Muzaffar lifted a hand to stall further questions. 'Yes,' he said. 'The accounts of your borrowings from Qizilbash. Fudged accounts, as you've probably gathered. Everybody – even those who had little reason to admire Abbas – admitted he was clever. That' – he indicated the papers – 'is proof of just *how* clever. Qizilbash, you see, made the mistake of allowing Abbas the run of his house. And Abbas discovered that Qizilbash had been duping all who borrowed from him. Sometime recently, I think the day before yesterday, Abbas stole *your* papers from Qizilbash's office. He smuggled them out of Qizilbash's haveli and brought them here, giving them to Sana for safekeeping. She couldn't read, of course, and he told her it was poetry he'd written for her.'

'I don't think Abbas ever meant to inform you of Qizilbash's duplicity,' Muzaffar said to Taufeeq. 'Qizilbash could drain you white for all Abbas cared. But he thought he, Abbas, could profit out of it by blackmailing Qizilbash. And Qizilbash, for all his fawning over Abbas, knew Abbas. He – or perhaps his clerk – guessed that Abbas had stolen the papers.'

'But he told me the papers were damaged,' Taufeeq interrupted, at a loss. 'His clerk sent a note to say there had been a minor mishap, but they were reworking the papers.'

'And what did Qizilbash say when he asked you to pay him back?'

Taufeeq frowned. 'He said the papers were being redone. He'd realized I owed him a large amount and he wanted at least the principal to be returned within this week.'

'Did he tell you the sum?' Anticipating Taufeeq's indignation, Muzaffar hastily added, 'I'm not asking how much it was. Just whether he told you what it was.'

Taufeeq nodded.

'And does it match what's written there?' Muzaffar tilted his chin towards the papers clutched in Taufeeq's hand. Taufeeq glanced down, riffled through the pages, and looked up. 'No,' he said in a low, puzzled voice. 'This sum is much more. What Qizilbash told me – and what I myself recall of my borrowings from him – is probably a fifth of this.'

'It would be. Qizilbash didn't know if Abbas had revealed anything to you, but he wasn't taking any chances. He certainly didn't need the money back soon, but he needed to let you think he was being honest with you. And the only way he could do that was to ask for the sum – the *correct* sum – back. If Abbas had passed on the papers to you and you'd confronted Qizilbash with them, he would probably have laughed it off. Said it was a joke, a forgery.'

'But he couldn't let Abbas get away with it, so he took the boy off into the other room on the pretext of a little privacy. I suppose he tried to get Abbas to return the papers or promise to keep quiet – but Abbas may have resisted, and Qizilbash ended up strangling him. Then he set things up to look as if someone had drugged *him* and murdered Abbas while he was unconscious. He probably uses opium now and then – it's the fashionable thing to do – so he slipped some into his cup and drank it down. Enough to knock him out for a couple of hours, after which he'd be alert enough to embark on a late night search for the papers. He didn't find them, but not for want of trying.'

The only sound in the room was that of Taufeeq's deep breathing as his gaze ran down the topmost page, his mouth turning down as he reread the entries. 'That bastard,' he rasped finally. 'The cheating, murdering bastard. I'll *kill* him.'

'Oh, I don't think you need bother,' Muzaffar said as he got to his feet. 'The men at the kotwali are working on him. Before the day is out, he'll be wishing he were dead anyway.'

The Bequeathed Garden

Zeenat Begum tucked a strand of greying hair under her muslin dupatta and said in a deliberately offhand manner, 'Nawab Shahnawaz Ali has finally died.'

Muzaffar waited for his sister to continue. Zeenat reached for her fan and twirled its carved stem between her fingers, running a thumb along the delicate filigree of the ivory strips – and studiously avoiding Muzaffar's eye.

'Aapa,' Muzaffar prompted, 'why does Nawab Sahib's death distress you?'

'Muzaffar!' Her eyes flashed fire, and Muzaffar was reminded of the innumerable scoldings of his boyhood. Zeenat, twenty-five years older than him, had been married and a mother when her little stepbrother entered a world his frail mother had shortly after exited. Eager, fond and sorry for the motherless infant, Zeenat had immediately taken him under her wing. Muzaffar's childhood had been spent in being alternately coddled and admonished by his elder sister – with the coddling being somewhat more frequent.

But Zeenat Begum was not kindly disposed towards Muzaffar at the moment. 'You're shameless,' she grumbled. 'You don't think before you speak.'

'I'm sorry; I didn't mean to offend. But I *really* didn't think Nawab Sahib's death was of any real consequence – to us, at least. Is it?'

Zeenat's grey eyes clouded. 'I know his widow; the second wife, Farzana Begum. I went today to offer my condolences, and she – she wept a lot.'

Muzaffar nodded encouragingly.

'There is trouble ahead, Muzaffar. Bitterness and bloodshed, if things aren't sorted out. Farzana needs your help.'

Her brother, immediately suspicious, raised an eyebrow. 'Why? Does she suspect murder?'

Zeenat's eyes widened. 'No, no. Of course not,' she replied quickly. 'It was a long illness. The hakims said he would not last till the next Id. No; there is no reason to suspect foul play. The problem is that he seems to have dealt with his sons most unfairly. He has three sons from his first wife, all soldiers like him, and he has bequeathed to them the best havelis and lands. The youngest – Farzana's son, Ejaz – was left a paltry wooden casket.'

Muzaffar stifled an unseemly shout of laughter. 'That couldn't have made him very happy.'

'He is furious. He was not there at the time of Nawab Sahib's demise, you see; he arrived late. Farzana handed over the casket to Ejaz, and he insists his stepbrothers have tampered with it.'

'If his mother gave it to him, I don't see how they could have done that. What was in it?'

Zeenat Begum shrugged. 'Odds and ends. Small things, some expensive, but negligible compared to what his brothers got. That is what angers Ejaz; he cannot believe Nawab Sahib treated him so shabbily. He's certain he's been cheated.'

'But is there any proof?'

'I do not know.' She looked miserable. 'But Ejaz is on the warpath, ready to do battle with his brothers. And Farzana is terrified that he will be the loser if it comes to that.' She looked appealingly at Muzaffar.

'Aapa.' Muzaffar groaned. '*Please*. I cannot even summon up a liking for Ejaz. He's insufferable. How will I bring myself to fight his battles for him?'

'Nobody's asking you to fight his battles, Muzaffar,' Zeenat murmured. 'Just a little help, that's all. For his mother.'

By the end of the hour, Muzaffar had resigned himself to his fate. Zeenat Begum had chiselled away at his resistance, using every weapon in her formidable armoury – from emotional blackmail to sheer persistence – and he had surrendered. A servant had been sent off to Nawab Sahib's haveli, with a polite request for a meeting with Ejaz Ali Sahib. From the haste with which the reply arrived, Muzaffar guessed that Ejaz had already been briefed by his anxious mother. Muzaffar was requested, in a terse and elegant missive, to honour the haveli with his presence as soon as it was convenient.

'The sooner, the better,' muttered Muzaffar, riding reluctantly towards Chowk Sa'dullah Khan. Halfway between the square and Faiz Bazaar was Nawab Sahib's haveli, and Muzaffar arrived shortly before sunset.

Ejaz, a stout young man with a wispy moustache and a tendency to sniffle, conveyed his mother's gratitude to Muzaffar. 'She is extremely emotional,' he explained, steering his guest towards the dalaan. 'It is very trying to have to look after someone so highly strung.'

Muzaffar, with a private snort of disgust, tried to change the topic. But Ejaz had begun a monologue on his many burdens, the innumerable jolts a vindictive fate had dealt to a mild-mannered, scholarly man. 'My brothers have never bothered to understand me,' he complained. 'No; they go about their own brutish, uncouth ways, caring for nothing except their own selfish selves. I tell you, Jang Sahib, you should thank Allah for sparing you such relatives –'

Muzaffar cut in. 'Where were you at the time of Nawab Sahib's death?'

'At an assembly in Mehrauli,' Ejaz answered, after a meaningful sniff. 'There was an interesting debate on the ramifications of fiqh. Islamic jurisprudence, you see, is a yet unexplored topic; most people, even the most highly educated ulema, skim the surface –'

'Who was at Nawab Sahib's deathbed, then?'

Ejaz glared. 'My brothers; they rode over from their camps as soon as they heard Abba was dying. Vultures flocking to a carcass,' he spat.

The metaphor may have been apt but it demonstrated a startling lack of filial feeling, thought Muzaffar. He decided he liked Ejaz even less than he thought he did.

'What happened the day of Nawab Sahib's demise? Why do you feel injustice may have been done?'

'Not injustice. If there was injustice, it would have been on the part of Abba – and I am certain *he* wanted nothing but the best for me. No; this was pure and simple thievery.' He gave Muzaffar a disconcertingly long, lugubrious look. 'Let me show you.'

He left the room, and when he returned, he held a wooden box, about the length of a man's forearm and half as wide. The whiff of sandalwood wafted on the air as he placed the box on the mattress and opened it, letting the lid fall back to reveal a strange jumble of objects.

Muzaffar stared, puzzled. 'May I?' he murmured, and at Ejaz's nod of assent, reached into the box and began retrieving its contents.

First out was a turban ornament – a sarpech – in the form of an exquisitely bejewelled peacock. Emeralds gleamed along the curving breast, and the tail was a shimmering cascade of sapphires, turquoise and diamonds. The head, with its crown of diamonds and gold filigree, was delicate and perfect in every detail. The only part that jarred was the peacock's feet: they were of brass, sadly tarnished.

Next was a small enamelled jewel case, shaped and coloured like a pomegranate. A fine pomegranate, painted over with flames that curled around its body. Orange, yellow and gold, the flames radiating from the stem of the pomegranate, and fading into the redness of the fruit.

Muzaffar frowned, then peered into the box and pulled out a small drawstring bag of black velvet – a bag that clinked as Muzaffar pulled apart the string and upturned the bag. A handful of coins tumbled out onto his palm.

Muzaffar gazed thoughtfully at the coins, raised an eyebrow, but said nothing. He let the coins slide back into the bag, and then withdrew from the box the last of its contents. The turban ornament and the jewel box Muzaffar could imagine as a meagre but reasonable bequest. But what he now held was totally bizarre. Nestled in a small muslin handkerchief were a pistachio and a tiny shrivelled onion.

Ejaz was regarding Muzaffar with a longsuffering and self-righteous air. 'You see. Would any father leave such junk for a son?'

If the son is of your stamp, certainly, thought Muzaffar. He bit down the urge to let fly at his host, and contented himself with asking, 'And this was all? Was there nothing else?'

Ejaz shook his head. 'He left the garden to me, but that's it. And who wants a garden, anyway? I have neither the time nor the inclination to potter about amidst flowers and fountains.'

A garden – and this junk. Muzaffar frowned. 'Is the garden part of this haveli?'

'No, it's near the Qutub Minar. What on earth am I to do with it?'

Muzaffar replaced everything in the box and closed it, his hand resting briefly on the carved surface of the lid. He looked down absently at the inscription on the lid, the curving Persian letters beautifully polished, but still not quite part of the lid. The smoothness that comes of many years of being handled, by the frequent lifting and closing of the lid, by absent caresses – that glossy, fine-grained finish was missing.

'"*If you wanted thy father's inheritance, acquire his knowledge.*"' Muzaffar read the inscription and glanced enquiringly at Ejaz.

'Sa'adi,' Ejaz said. 'Abba was devoted to his poetry. It's all over the place.'

Muzaffar nodded. Yes, the verse was familiar.

He rose to his feet. 'I think it may help to see this garden. Would tomorrow morning be suitable? Say, after the first namaz?'

It was a pleasant garden, charming and quiet. The only sound was the gurgle of a stream flowing from the baradari, the open pavilion at the far end of the terraced garden. The water rippled along the two levels down to the gate through which they had entered. Paved paths hemmed in the stream and divided it at the centre of the garden, into four branches of water that shimmered in the sunlight. The four quarters of the charbagh were pleasingly symmetrical: the same star-shaped parterres of red sandstone, the same masses of flowers – pink roses, fragrant white jasmine, tuberoses – and the ubiquitous mango tree, its canopy spreading dark and cool above a grassy platform.

'If you think this is a passable legacy, allow me to correct you,' Ejaz said grumpily. 'I cannot imagine why Abba wasted so much money –'. He broke off abruptly. 'Have a look if you want to.'

He led the way along a path, up half a dozen steps to the upper terrace. At the centre of the garden stood a pavilion of white marble, its flat roof supported on fluted columns. From below the pavilion, the stream gushed out, forming a chaadar – a miniature waterfall – over the carved marble slope below. A pool of water bubbled white and silver at the foot of the chaadar before flowing on to the four sides of the garden.

Ejaz made his way to the second pavilion, a smaller, less ornate one at the far end of the garden. This too straddled the stream, but instead of a chaadar, here was a tiny pool of water, and a quaint bit of garden symbolism. Majnun, the weeping willow with its drooping branches, reached longing arms in vain towards its beloved, Laila, the water lily floating on the surface of the water.

'As you can see, nothing,' Ejaz muttered. 'Nothing except water and flowers.'

Muzaffar bent and looked closely at the base of the pavilion. A strip of white marble, four inches high, spanned the front edge of the structure. It was decorated sparingly with a pattern of carved vine leaves; but in the centre was a small lozenge on which, instead of the foliage, was an inscription. Muzaffar slipped off his choga and gathered the edges of his muslin jama in one hand. Gripping the corner pillar of the pavilion with the other hand, he leaned out over the water.

'"*Words have a head, O shrewd man, and a tail,*"' he read. '"*Do not insert thy words between the words of others.*"'

'Sa'adi,' Ejaz volunteered.

'So I see.'

He looked at Ejaz, his eyes expressionless. 'My work here is done for now,' he said abruptly. 'We can leave.'

They walked in silence towards the gate, its single cusped arch made of mellow red sandstone, inlaid with arabesques in white and black marble. Muzaffar followed his host outside, to where a servant stood guarding their horses.

'I had a question,' Muzaffar said as he mounted. 'Did Nawab Sahib leave a document willing the garden to you?'

'Of course not,' Ejaz huffed. 'He was too weak. He told my mother, when he gave her that box for me.'

'And what exactly did he say when he told Begum Sahiba you were to have the garden?'

Ejaz stared, perplexed. 'I don't know. I can ask her, if you like. But –'

'If you would.' Muzaffar inclined his head briefly and lapsed into a forbidding silence that effectively silenced Ejaz.

They arrived at the haveli near Chowk Sa'dullah Khan shortly before lunch. Muzaffar had no desire to linger, but waited nevertheless for Ejaz to return from the zenana after talking to Farzana Begum.

'Abba said, "Tell Ejaz the garden is his." That is all.'

Muzaffar nodded, still looking preoccupied. 'I see. Would it be possible, do you think, for me to meet your brothers? It might help.'

Ejaz made a face. 'They have returned to their camps. They went back the day after Abba's funeral.'

'Very well.'

With that cryptic utterance, Muzaffar took his leave and headed home. Halfway through, he changed his mind and turned his horse towards Kotwal Sahib's haveli. The purdah, he mused, was best pierced by a woman. The wife of the kotwal, the sister of Muzaffar Jang, would, with tutoring, perhaps learn more than a bookish, self-centred son. Yes, it was time to enlist the help of Zeenat Begum.

The next day, when Muzaffar returned to his sister's haveli, Zeenat was looking dejected.

'It sounds straightforward,' she sighed. 'Farzana was there when Nawab Sahib died. She had been sitting beside him all day, and most days since he took to his bed. He had been ailing the past eight months, and in the last few weeks he became too weak to even sit up.'

'His death was no surprise, then.'

'No. In fact, a week before he died, Nawab Sahib himself instructed Farzana to send for his sons. The two eldest, Isaam and Imaad, were at Fatehpur Sikri, and their younger brother, Husaam, was on his way to Lahore. Messengers were sent after them, and all three men made it back in time. Husaam arrived on the last day, but even then…' Her voice trailed off and it took an encouraging murmur from Muzaffar for her to continue.

'Ejaz was not at home, and by the time he came, Nawab Sahib was dead. Farzana gave him the box that Nawab Sahib had bequeathed, along with the message. The three elder sons had been given deeds by Nawab Sahib himself for the havelis and lands they inherited.'

Muzaffar rubbed his jaw. 'And was Begum Sahiba present when Nawab Sahib handed over the deeds?'

Zeenat nodded. 'And she admits she found nothing suspicious in the entire proceedings. She was surprised that Nawab Sahib seemed distressed that Ejaz was taking so long to come.'

'Surprised?' Muzaffar scowled. 'I would think any father would be distressed at the thought of dying without bidding farewell to a son.'

His sister flushed unhappily. 'From what I gather, there was no love lost between father and son.' She gathered her dupatta about her shoulders. 'Ejaz was scornful of the fact that Nawab Sahib and his three elder sons all chose to be men of the sword. He was ashamed that his own father was a soldier, not a scholar.'

'But Nawab Sahib was erudite in his own way,' Muzaffar muttered. 'A lover of Sa'adi's work. Ejaz told me, while we were at the garden.' He blinked suddenly, as if a thought had struck him. 'Aapa, did Begum Sahiba tell you exactly what Nawab Sahib said about the garden?'

'Yes, of course. "Tell Ejaz the garden –"'

'I know, I know,' Muzaffar interrupted hastily. 'Ejaz told me that. What I wanted to know was, what word did Nawab Sahib use? When he spoke of the garden, did he call it a bagh or a gulistan?'

Zeenat looked puzzled; but her answer was prompt. 'Gulistan. Should that matter?'

But she had lost her audience. Muzaffar had sprung up, and after a quick farewell, had gone rushing out into the corridor, shouting to a servant to have his horse fetched.

'If Nawab Sahib was so very fond of Sa'adi's work, then surely it is plausible to assume that he would own a book or two…?'

Ejaz stared, glassy-eyed.

'More specifically, *Golestan*. Have you ever come across, in your late father's possession, a copy of Sa'adi's *Golestan*?'

'I don't see what possible bearing this could –'

'Please. Yes or no?'

Ejaz scowled. 'Yes. An illuminated copy. Though why anyone should be so excessively fond of Sa'adi, I cannot imagine. Some verses in *Golestan* are downright outrageous –'

But Ejaz was not destined to complete a sentence in his impatient guest's presence. 'Could I have a look at it? Now, if you please.'

It took Ejaz a quarter of an hour to unearth the book. When he finally returned, disdain written all over his face, he was carrying a large package wrapped in white silk. Whoever had been looking after Nawab Sahib's belongings since his death had neglected their duties: fine dust billowed as Ejaz unwrapped the book.

Muzaffar took the tome from Ejaz and, his fingers moving gently, opened it. It was a beauty; Muzaffar could well understand why it could have been a prized possession for Nawab Sahib. The calligraphy, elegant and curving, was superb; the paintings accompanying the verses were airy and light. On one page, the court of a king was depicted in all its opulence; in another, a busy, bustling marketplace came alive. Not every verse was illustrated, but there was enough here, not just in the splendid poetry, but also in the delicacy of the art, to hold captive a lover of books.

'Well?'

'It is beautiful. May I borrow it for today? I would like to examine it before I can offer an opinion.'

Ejaz's eyes widened with sudden interest. 'Do you think there is something there? A hidden will?'

'I do not know. I doubt it, but if you wish to satisfy your curiosity, you are welcome to look through it before I leave.'

Ejaz took the book from Muzaffar with unseemly haste, and began riffling through the pages with such brutal swiftness that Muzaffar flinched. Ejaz flung the book back disgustedly less than five minutes later. 'Take it. Do what you want; I have no use for it.' And – in an unforgivable display of rudeness – he strode from the room, leaving his guest to make his way out by himself.

But Muzaffar smiled a sarcastic little smile, and said nothing as he rose and walked out, the very picture of dignity.

Muzaffar studied Nawab Sahib's copy of *Golestan* through much of that night. Early the next morning, he sent a servant off to request Ejaz's presence at the garden. Ejaz, the note implied, could possibly profit by arriving at the garden an hour before noon. That, thought Muzaffar, would give both him and Ejaz enough time to reach the garden. It would also give Ejaz four hours to stew over the reason for the rendezvous. That, decided Muzaffar with a mischievous grin, may do Ejaz a world of good.

An impatient Ejaz was pacing in front of the garden gate when Muzaffar arrived. He heaved an exaggerated sigh of relief and came rushing over to Muzaffar, who dismounted leisurely and handed the reins to Ejaz's servant. 'Why have you called me here? What have you discovered?'

Muzaffar willed himself to keep a straight face.

'*Well?*'

'Come. We shall enter the garden,' Muzaffar said. 'Are there any gardeners around right now?' His gaze swiftly wandered round the charbagh. 'Ah, there is one. Good; he is certain to have a pick, or a spade, or something similar.'

Muzaffar strode off, and was back a few minutes later, a solid pick clutched in one hand. 'You have an excellent man there,' he remarked cheerily as he hefted the pick, feeling its weight absently as he looked around the garden, his eyes keenly searching.

Ejaz, watching him suspiciously, heard Muzaffar mutter under his breath. 'Away from this door… which door? One of the pavilions? No; that is – ah!'

He whirled around and started walking towards the lower end of the garden. A few paces away, he turned. 'I assume you want to see your inheritance? Come along, then.'

He stopped just inside the gate, and looked up at the pietra dura inlay. His eyes narrowed, and then, before Ejaz could say anything, Muzaffar had gone out through the gate. He returned almost immediately, leading his horse by the bridle. Muzaffar positioned the stallion under the gate, and with a swift, graceful movement, mounted the horse and stood on its back, while he examined the inlay on the gate more closely.

'Will you be so good as to pass me the pick? Thank you.' With firm, steady hands, Muzaffar worked the pick, loosening a section of the pietra dura. Ejaz frowned, perplexed, as fragments of what appeared to be white marble fell to the ground. 'You aren't hitting it hard enough to break marble,' he observed.

'No, I'm not,' Muzaffar answered. 'It isn't marble; it's plaster. That's why it's breaking off. There's a cavity behind it…'

Ejaz was bending to pick up one of the fragments, but he straightened, suddenly all attention. 'Yes? What is it?'

Muzaffar flung the pick aside and lowered himself carefully until he was sitting astride his horse. He held a slim rosewood box in his hands. 'Here you are. Would you like to open it?' He passed the box to Ejaz and dismounted.

The box was not as ornate as the sandalwood casket Nawab Sahib had bequeathed. This was a slender one, just a hand's breadth across, and three fingers deep. Ejaz regarded it with disappointed eyes. 'Abba could hardly have left me a treasure in this,' he mumbled dismally. But curiosity, ever a strong motivator, proved more powerful than Ejaz's despondency. His hands were prising up the lid even as he spoke.

The box fell open, and Muzaffar drew in a sharp breath. Nestled inside was another, slimmer box, of white jade inlaid with a floral pattern of rubies. Tiny tendrils of gold outlined the petals and traced the stems. Fine slivers of gold leaf suggested curling leaves, and a delicate gold hasp held down the lid.

Ejaz lifted the box out of its wooden casket, and summarily handing over the wooden box to Muzaffar, opened the lid of the jade case. The inside was carved into three sections, with the necessary tools for a calligrapher's work. The first cavity, long and slim, held the handle of a stylus. The second, broader and shallower, housed a sharp knife, with a jade handle – used, as Muzaffar well knew, to trim the reed pens that would be fitted into the handle of the stylus. In the third section lay a tiny spoon, with a jade handle and a golden bowl. A spoon to measure and mix the ingredients for the ink.

'It's lovely,' Muzaffar murmured. 'A treasure.'

Ejaz shut the box with a sudden snap and slid it into the pocket of his choga. 'A pen set. Expensive – but nevertheless a mere pen set. It is nothing compared to the lands –'

Muzaffar looked away in disgust, and found himself looking at the lid of the wooden box Ejaz had handed him. On it, in one corner, was carved a strange little icon. A tiny turban with a minuscule feather curled jauntily above, and below it a tiny symbol: an upright, inclined almost imperceptibly to the left, with a right-curving crescent blossoming from the top left. A Persian digit, four.

Muzaffar stared, then turned to his horse. He rummaged through the saddlebag and finally drew out the *Golestan* he had borrowed from Ejaz. 'Let us see,' he said, as he balanced the book on the horse's saddle. His fingers moved gently through the first few pages of the book, stopping after some six or seven leaves had been turned. 'Here we are. "*A tree which has just taken root...*" That should not be difficult in a garden.' He closed the book and handed it to Ejaz.

'We may yet have need of it,' he said curtly and walked on. Five paces down the path, he asked, 'When did Nawab Sahib lay out this garden?'

Ejaz shrugged. 'Years ago. I was a child. I remember Abba bringing me here to see the mango trees being planted.'

'Yes. The trees,' Muzaffar said. He looked slowly around, his eyes wandering methodically from the gate, clockwise along the wall, round the periphery of the garden – and back again. 'Were any trees planted recently?'

'I do not know,' Ejaz answered sourly. 'You could ask the gardener. He seems fascinated by your antics.'

The gardener squatted beside a parterre. His sleeves were rolled up to expose dark sinewy arms, and his hands moved absently among the flowerbed he was ostensibly weeding. A curious man, his eyes alight with interest.

Muzaffar made his way towards the gardener, who rose respectfully. His forehead creased in concentration as he listened to Muzaffar's question, and it was some time before he replied. 'The last tree Nawab Sahib got planted was the one near the pavilion at the end – the weeping willow. Nawab Sahib himself came to supervise the planting, though he was already very ill. Would that be the tree huzoor is interested in…?'

'There is none other you can think of, planted in the past year – or less?'

The man shook his head emphatically. 'No, huzoor. Of that I am sure.'

And so it was to the weeping willow that Muzaffar made his way, the morose Ejaz trailing in his wake.

'It does look young. I should have noticed that before,' Muzaffar said, gazing critically at the drooping branches of the tree, its pale slender leaves reflected in the ripples below. 'Well, Ali Sahib? Would you like to try your hand at uprooting it?'

'Uprooting it? But why?'

'To humour me?' Muzaffar could not suppress a grin. 'Hardly. But Nawab Sahib seems to have wanted you to. Perhaps there is something interesting here.'

It took a lot of effort – much of it on the part of the brawnier Muzaffar – to loosen the soil around the base of the tree. The weeping willow looked deceptively frail, but its roots clung tenaciously to the earth. Clods of soil crumbled and fell away from the tangle of roots only after much striking with the pick, and by the time Muzaffar straightened, his hands were grimy and his back ached. But the melon-sized cube he held in his hands was proof that his quest had not been in vain. Muzaffar held out the cube – another box, but this one of some dark metal, possibly gunmetal – to Ejaz.

'It could well contain an inheritance,' Muzaffar chuckled when Ejaz took the box. 'Open it; I'll wash my hands in the meantime.'

He bent to rinse the earth off his hands in the pool beside the downed tree. Poor Laila, thought Muzaffar as he gazed at the water lilies. Majnun sacrificed for the avarice of an unworthy nobleman.

Behind him, Ejaz uttered a curse, low and muffled.

Muzaffar glanced over his shoulder. Ejaz held a dark green sphere, about the size of a large apple. The polished surface glowed emerald, with a hint of underlying black – all of it carved over in a pattern of entwined leaves. The short, delicately tapered neck of the flask ended in a gold ring topped with a gold lid, attached by a dangling gold chain. A lovely little piece of work, this inkwell with its heavy base and fine carving.

'An inkpot!' Ejaz snorted. 'He left me an inkpot!'

'It is a beautiful piece,' Muzaffar retorted. 'Nephrite jade, if I am not mistaken.'

'Hmmph. It doesn't interest me,' Ejaz turned away with a petulant shrug of one shoulder, holding out the inkwell to Muzaffar.

It was cool, both from the dampness of the earth in which it had lain entombed, and from the inherent coolness of the stone itself. A cool, elegant inkwell, fit for an emperor – though an emperor would have probably had diamonds set in that gold lid, instead of a somewhat rough engraving of a cap.

Muzaffar stared, suddenly intent. This was no turban, flamboyant and feathered. This was rounded and serviceable; a dervish's cap. And below it were the Persian numerals for three and nine. Thirty-nine.

He smiled. So Nawab Sahib had more up his sleeve. But how much more?

Ejaz had seated himself on the edge of the pavilion. The book – *Golestan* – lay forgotten on the white marble beside him. Muzaffar placed the inkwell beside it, then picked up the book and opened it about halfway through. He flipped quickly but carefully through the pages and then, finding what he was looking for, frowned to himself, trying to make sense of what he read.

A man must receive into his ears
The advice although it be written on a wall.

'But which wall?' Muzaffar muttered as he stood, gazing contemplatively down at the grass. Ejaz, hunched unhappily, fidgeted with the inkwell. The only sound that broke the silence was the gurgle of the water. A soothing sound, thought Muzaffar, soothing and conducive to thought.

He turned so suddenly that Ejaz shied like a frightened horse. 'What did you do that for?' He scowled. 'You gave me a fright –'

But Muzaffar was busy taking off his choga and rolling up his sleeves. When he was done, he bundled the choga and placed it on the floor of the pavilion, before tugging off his boots and lifting the pick. He handed it to Ejaz. 'Give this to me when I ask for it,' he said tersely, and without further explanation, stepped onto the narrow, slippery ledge below the pavilion, one hand gripping a pillar for support. The stream washed over his bare feet up to the ankles. Ejaz shuddered delicately but leaned dutifully over the edge of the pavilion, ready to hand over the pick.

Muzaffar reached the centre of the ledge, to where the inscription had been carved. 'Put that pick down and give me your hand,' he instructed. 'I need to see this more closely.' His left hand wrapped itself painfully round Ejaz's bejewelled fingers as he examined the inscription. After about half a minute, his right hand was extended next to his left, and he said, 'The pick.' His voice was muffled, the words obscured by the gurgling of the water. Ejaz put the pick into the outstretched hand, and shortly after, the sound of blows striking the marble drifted upward.

An agonizing ten minutes later, a dripping hand, clutching a thin oblong panel of white marble, flung itself over the edge of the pavilion. A moment later, Muzaffar – drenched in sweat and water – appeared and hauled himself over the edge. Ejaz, caught between sniffing distastefully at Muzaffar's appearance and thanking him for his efforts, took the easy way out. 'So this is what you found? It doesn't look like a treasure to me.'

Muzaffar, too far gone for manners, gave him a murderous look. 'It seems to be all that Nawab Sahib has left – other than the pen box and the inkwell. And this, if I am right, is all there is.'

Ejaz glared suspiciously down at the marble, with the inscription they had read the other day. *Words have a head, O shrewd man, and a tail. Do not insert thy words between the words of others.*

'Why?' he asked. 'Why do you think this is all?'

Muzaffar heaved a sigh of resignation. 'Turn it over. Look at the other side.'

The other side, which had been glued to the lower edge of the pavilion, was also, surprisingly enough, carved. And that too with an inscription. A single line, part of a verse.

Because this property of his may be spent in ten days.

'The second line of what was inscribed on the wooden box that Begum Sahiba handed over,' Muzaffar said quietly. 'The first line of the verse – "*If you wanted thy father's inheritance, acquire his knowledge*" – began it, and the second line ends it.'

Ejaz gaped at him, and Muzaffar looked away, his shoulders beginning to shake with ill-suppressed humour.

'Nawab Sahib was a soldier *and* a scholar,' Muzaffar said. 'And Ejaz may be a scholar, but he's also a fool. An arrogant, mulish one. It's a lethal combination, Aapa. Don't do this to me ever again, please.'

'Stop smirking, Muzaffar,' Zeenat Begum admonished, only to have Muzaffar's lopsided grin grow wider still.

'I cannot help it,' he said. 'You should have seen him, clutching his legacy – the pen box and the inkwell, even that tiny slab of marble. He forgot *Golestan* simply because my choga had landed on top of it and by the time I retrieved it, he had ridden off.'

His sister looked down at the book in her lap. Her fingers caressed it reverently as she opened it to the first page, an almost luminous depiction of a rose garden. 'Lovely,' she murmured. 'This is a treasure in itself.'

'For someone who values its worth. Not for a self-centred moron like Ejaz.'

Zeenat contented herself with a sharp glance. 'So how did you unravel the mystery?' she asked. 'I thought that silly box was all that Ejaz got.'

Muzaffar smiled a slow, lazy smile. 'If Ejaz used his brains a little, he could probably have worked it out all by himself. He couldn't see beyond his own petty animosities; couldn't imagine that Nawab Sahib had actually meant him to have just that single wooden box – as a starting point, at least.'

'Did Begum Sahiba show you the box, Aapa?' he asked.

'Yes. It *was* strange, wasn't it? I wondered why Nawab Sahib would have even bothered to leave Ejaz such a collection of odds and ends.'

Muzaffar nodded. 'And when I discovered that Nawab Sahib had handed over the box to Ejaz's own mother, I ruled out the notion of the evil stepbrothers. They hadn't even been around when Nawab Sahib became seriously ill; all three of them had to be fetched. And though they made it in time to bid farewell to their father, Begum Sahiba was in that room all the time. What is even more telling is that right after Nawab Sahib's funeral, Ejaz's stepbrothers went back to their camps. They didn't even stay to gloat over their inheritances.'

'Which seems to indicate a lack of interest in material things,' observed Zeenat. 'It would be illogical, I think, to assume that they have no love for the riches of this world. But it would appear that they probably *do* have more values than Ejaz credits them with.'

Muzaffar's mouth curved into another grin. 'And Nawab Sahib apparently did not lay much store by Ejaz's wits. He left clues by the bushel, Aapa.'

He leaned back against the brocaded bolster. 'At first, I couldn't make head or tail of it – the contents of that wooden box were baffling. It was a series of facts that, when I considered them all together, pointed me to a possible clue.'

'Which was?'

'Sa'adi. A verse of his was carved on the lid of the box. "*If you wanted thy father's inheritance, acquire his knowledge.*" What was more, it had been recently carved on a box that was obviously much older than the inscription itself – as if it had been carved there with a purpose. And Ejaz mentioned that Nawab Sahib had been extremely fond of Sa'adi's writings.

'Then there were the odds and ends inside the box. A lovely little peacock, but with feet that were horribly ugly; a pomegranate painted in flames; a pistachio, tied up along with an onion. And *counterfeit* coins. The sarpech and the pomegranate could have had some intrinsic value, but the pistachio, the onion, and the coins?' He shrugged. 'They could only have been there because they were meant to convey a deeper meaning. And when I learnt that Sa'adi was a favourite of Nawab Sahib's, things fell into place.'

He broke off. 'This is going to take long, Aapa. Could you send for some sherbet?' He smiled winningly at Zeenat.

The sherbet was ordered, and Muzaffar leaned back. 'Everything in that box pointed to Sa'adi. Do you not remember the verses, Aapa? "*What wilt thou purchase, O vainglorious fool, On the day of distress with counterfeit silver?*" – and, "*The peacock is for his beauteous colours by the people Praised whilst he is ashamed of his ugly feet.*"'

Zeenat Begum blinked. 'Allah,' she breathed, her eyes suddenly wide. '*Golestan*.'

'Precisely. "*And branches with pomegranates upon them: Fire suspended from the green trees.*" And, of course – that verse you flung at me every time I praised someone merely because he was wealthy –'

'"*Who appeared to thee all marrow like a pistachio, Was but skin upon skin like an onion,*"' his sister murmured. 'Of course. When you look at it that way, it seems so obvious.'

'And all of it points to *Golestan*,' Muzaffar added. 'As does the inscription on the box. And as do Nawab Sahib's words for Ejaz. Tell Ejaz the garden is his.'

Zeenat Begum's eyes lit up, just as a servant entered with the sherbet. 'So that was why you wanted to know exactly what Nawab Sahib said.' She smiled.

Muzaffar waited till the servant had left the room. 'Yes. The garden was pleasant enough, and I suspect was in any case supposed to be given to Ejaz, but it was *Golestan* – the book – that Nawab Sahib bequeathed. And it was *Golestan* that contained the clues.'

He took up the book and moved closer to Zeenat. 'I wondered if there was more to the contents of the box than that they all pointed to *Golestan*. I wondered if Nawab Sahib had wanted Ejaz to look at specific portions of the book. So I borrowed it and searched out those four verses… here we are,' he added, with a note of satisfaction. '"*What wilt thou purchase*" – but no illustration.'

'Should there have been?'

'I suppose not. I couldn't find any signs of any leaves being torn out of the book. And the verse that should appear after this one *is* there on the next leaf. I matched the sequence against my own copy.'

He showed his sister the other three verses, the one for the peacock and the one for the pistachio and onion also lacking an illustration, but the fourth – the last one – splendidly illuminated with a painting of a garden. An exquisite garden, similar to the one Ejaz had inherited, but also different. The snow-capped mountains of the backdrop were reminiscent of Kashmir, thought Muzaffar. The cypresses were probably much like what Sa'adi would have seen in his native Persia, but the pomegranate trees bore strange, flaming fruit. *Fire suspended from the green trees.*

Tucked away in the bottom right corner of the page was something that had been added to the painting after it had been polished and finished. A reed pen with a fine nib had been used to draw a tiny round cap. Below it was written, in equally tiny digits, the number forty-eight. Muzaffar pointed out the strange little notation to his sister, and she frowned. 'What is that?'

'You tell me,' Muzaffar smiled indulgently.

'A cap? Labelled forty-eight?' Zeenat Begum glanced sceptically at Muzaffar.

'Not just any cap, Aapa. A dervish's cap. "The Morals of Dervishes". Remember?'

Zeenat Begum nodded. *Golestan* was divided into sets of chapters: 'On Rules for Conduct in Life', 'On the Effects of Education', 'On Weakness and Old Age': eight sets in all, like the eight entrances of paradise. But among the most popular were the first two sets of chapters: 'Manners of Kings', and 'The Morals of Dervishes'.

'Story forty-eight from "The Morals of Dervishes",' said Muzaffar quietly. 'Would you like to see what it is?' He watched with affection as Zeenat Begum fumbled slightly, turning over the leaves carefully with thin, trembling fingers.

'Here it is,' she whispered finally. '"*Unlucky is he who turns his head; Away from this door for he will find no other door.*"' She turned to Muzaffar, bemused. 'But there is no illustration here, no indication about how to proceed.'

'No, there isn't. Because Nawab Sahib shifted the rest of the clues to a physical place: the garden. The door is the actual gate of the garden.'

'The gate? But – how?'

Muzaffar sipped his sherbet. 'That mystified me too. I tried everything I could, but nothing made sense. There are no marks like the dervish's cap, either on this leaf or any of the leaves immediately next to it. There is nothing to indicate, as you said, how to proceed – except the words themselves. The meaning is straightforward: there is no way but through this door, through here. And if you ignore this, you will be the unlucky one.'

'It could be a metaphor,' Zeenat suggested, with little conviction.

'Possibly. But the clues that led to this one were *not* metaphors. They were clear, unmistakable, literal signs. So I guessed this was meant to be literal too.'

He paused. 'And you already know the rest,' he added. 'There was only one door – one gate – and it contained a clue to something buried under a young tree. Which held one more clue, and that to the end of the trail – and, interestingly enough, completing a neat loop. What began on the wooden box, ended on that marble strip.'

'"*If you wanted thy father's inheritance, acquire his knowledge. Because this property of his may be spent in ten days.*" A neat slap on the wrist for Ejaz. He never hid his contempt for his father's and his stepbrothers' chosen profession; for him, a man of the pen is infinitely superior to one of the sword. He seems to have pushed Nawab Sahib just a little too far.'

Zeenat tried to hide a smile, but failed miserably. A mischievous dimple sparkled in her cheek as she murmured, 'So Ejaz gets left a scholarly inheritance

– a pen set, an inkwell, an illuminated copy of Sa'adi. Ah, Muzaffar, what have you done? Farzana will never welcome me into her household again.'

'Which,' concluded Muzaffar, 'is probably all for the best.'

Author's Note: *Muslih-ud-din Mushrif-ibn-Abdullah, Sheikh Sa'adi (1210–90) was a native of Shiraz in Persia. His works – such as* Bostan (The Orchard) *and* Golestan (The Rose Garden) *– were much admired in Mughal India.*

The Hand of an Artist

The first thought that came to Muzaffar Jang was that the dead man had bled a lot. The very next moment, he realized that it was not the profusion of dried blood that was so unsettling; it was its stark contrast against the gleaming white marble of the floor. A reddish-brown streak ran almost right across the room, like a gory brushstroke.

An apt simile, thought Muzaffar. He had never before had the privilege of visiting one of the imperial ateliers, and he looked around it with interest.

The atelier was a hall large enough to seat at least fifteen men comfortably. Mattresses covered with white sheets lay on the floor. Two walls were lined with marble shelves while a third was pierced by screens of filigreed white marble. Beyond lay a small garden, part of it visible through a large square window in the centre of one of the screens.

Inside the room, the shelves and mattresses bore witness to the fact that this was the workplace of some of the most accomplished – certainly some of the most prolific – artists of the realm. Along one of the screens lay drying sheets of wasli, thin layers of paper glued together with a floury paste of layee to form the base for the paintings. Stacked on the shelves were sheets of prepared wasli, brushes of squirrel-tail hair, jars of gum tragacanth, and large seashells, to be used as palettes. And most important of all, there were the jars and bowls of pigments and the raw material used to create them: copper, to be steeped in salt water to produce the vivid green of verdigris; indigo, for the most exquisite of blues; pungent-smelling yellow, distilled from cow's urine; lampblack; and vermilion.

But the most jarring colour was the huge splotch of dried blood marking the back of the man crumpled over a workplace at the far end of the hall. Basheer Ghiyas, thirty years old, an apprentice of the aging master Bichitr himself. Stabbed in the back in the middle of the night, with no sign of the weapon anywhere and no witnesses.

Farid Khan, the perennially overworked kotwal of Shahjahanabad, turned to look at his young brother-in-law.

'Come on over, Muzaffar,' he said.

The hakim who was bending over the body glanced up, his eyes flicking over the new arrival with interest. Muzaffar accorded him a brief salaam, and the hakim, after a courteous nod of acknowledgment, turned back to Kotwal Sahib.

'Stabbed in the back with a knife or dagger,' he pronounced confidently. 'With a blade at least six inches long – you'll see it went right through him.'

Kotwal Sahib frowned. 'Would that imply considerable force being used by the assailant?'

The hakim rose to his feet. 'Not necessarily. A heavy blade – a surprise attack – and the deed could have been done by anyone. As it is, he doesn't seem to have been a sturdy creature.'

The trio gazed down speculatively at the dead man. Basheer may have painted beautiful pictures, but he was no vision himself. His cheeks were sunken and unshaved, his beard was straggly, and his face wore an expression of distaste, as if death had been more a matter of disgust than surprise.

Muzaffar glanced back at the trail of blood that led across the floor. 'Would he have died instantly?'

'No, but he couldn't have lived more than a few minutes.'

'Enough to drag himself some ten feet or so?'

The hakim's eyes widened. 'You think he dragged himself?'

'I do not know. All I want to know is if he could have done it.'

The hakim shrugged. 'It's difficult to say. Anything is possible.'

'And how long has he been dead?' Muzaffar asked quietly, his deep voice echoing in the silence of the atelier.

'Just over four hours,' replied the kotwal. 'He was discovered almost immediately by the guards outside. They broke down the door and entered when they heard a scream. This happened at about three in the morning.'

Muzaffar raised an eyebrow. 'There are guards here, Khan Sahib?'

'Two of them.' The kotwal's lip curled. 'Though I have my doubts about their efficiency. They should be around outside. I'd given orders for them to stay back for questioning.'

Muzaffar gathered up the sides of his muslin jama, and going down on his haunches, began to carefully inspect the dead man. There appeared to be nothing in the wound – either in the back or the chest – that could be considered much of a clue. A heavy dagger, at least six inches long... There must be hundreds – no, thousands – of such knives in Dilli, thought Muzaffar unhappily. And there was a good chance that the one they sought was already at the bottom of the Yamuna.

There was, however, something interesting: a large bloodstain on the dead man's right thumb.

'Did you move the corpse?' Muzaffar asked.

'I had to,' the hakim answered, instantly defensive. 'How else could I have examined him?'

'Of course.' Muzaffar's voice was soothing. 'I do not blame you. All I want to know is how you found him – assuming, of course, that the guards hadn't already moved him about by the time you arrived...?'

Kotwal Sahib intervened. 'They hadn't moved him. They said it was obvious he was beyond help, so they let him be.'

The hakim had got back down on the floor and rearranged the corpse as best as he could; the limbs had already begun to stiffen. 'That should be it,' he finally said, getting to his feet.

Basheer now lay prostrate, his legs trailing on the floor, his torso on the mattress, and his right arm bent near his head. Muzaffar stood still for a minute, his face expressionless. Then he said, more to himself than to the others, 'And I assume that painting was there too, since it bears his mark.'

He indicated, with a quick gesture, a picture that lay on the mattress. It was a striking work, with sharp lines and luminous colours. The artist had depicted a nobleman's wedding procession in all its grandeur. Pipers and drummers sat on richly caparisoned elephants, preceded by bearers of gilded lamps and carriers of waterskins. Wealthy noblemen, clad in heavy brocades and bedecked with jewellery, rode mettlesome stallions, and commoners stood along the edges of the scene, watching the spectacle. It was a lovely painting, though a little too flat for Muzaffar's liking.

It was marred by a streak of brownish red about half an inch wide that had obscured the face of one of the bystanders in the right corner of the picture.

The hakim's face was pensive. 'Yes,' he said after a moment's thought. 'I suppose that *is* his mark. His hand was definitely very close to that part of the painting. He could well have died in the act of pressing his thumb down on it.'

Muzaffar smiled, the gravity of his face suddenly changing to a handsome boyishness. 'Thank you,' he said. 'You have been most helpful.'

The hakim gone, the kotwal swiftly briefed Muzaffar. The atelier, it transpired, consisted only of the master painter Bichitr and his four apprentices. 'Bichitr and two apprentices are out of town currently,' Kotwal Sahib said. 'Bichitr is in Agra, working on a painting commissioned by Jahanpanah Baadshah Salamat. The two apprentices have gone to Kashmir with the Prince Dara Shukoh and his household, who are holidaying in the Valley.'

'Which implies that these three people can probably be safely excluded from the list of suspects – at least as far as the actual wielding of the dagger goes. Who's the third apprentice?'

'Mukhtar. I've sent for him. He's the senior apprentice. He was summoned by the guards as soon as they discovered Basheer.'

Mukhtar, when he arrived a couple of minutes later, proved to be a sturdy young man in his mid-twenties, with an anxious face and a tendency to fidget. His story was simple enough. He lived in the quarters adjacent to the atelier, and had been woken by the agitated guards with the news of Basheer's death. Mukhtar had accompanied the guards back to the atelier, where he had taken charge of the situation. One guard, Rafiq, had been sent off to the kotwali, while the other, Shamsuddin, had taken a lamp and searched the garden.

'The garden? Why so?'

Mukhtar shrugged. 'Where else would the murderer have gone? Rafiq and Shamsuddin entered the room within a few minutes of hearing Basheer scream, and they saw nobody inside. The room has no doors other than the one through which they entered, so obviously the murderer had escaped through the window. And the window leads into the garden.'

Shamsuddin was bleary-eyed, and sweated profusely in his heavy leather tunic and helmet, but valiantly clutched his lance. He insisted that the garden had been empty. And although he had peered over the low wall enclosing the garden, he had seen nobody in the vicinity either. Muzaffar inspected the garden, but could find no trace of any intruders – no footprints, no bloodstains, no discarded dagger.

'And where is your colleague – Rafiq?' Muzaffar asked Shamsuddin.

'Home, huzoor. I think to inform Rehana. He will be here soon.'

'And who, pray, is Rehana? His wife?'

'No, huzoor. His sister. She is the maidservant at the atelier. She'll be coming along any minute now to begin cleaning up.'

'I see.' Muzaffar sighed. 'When she arrives, keep her outside for the time being. It's not a pretty sight; if we can spare her, we may as well do it.'

He turned to the kotwal. 'A word with you, if you would step in, Khan Sahib.'

Compared to the stillness of the atelier, the kotwali was a busy place. An officer in the chamber adjoining Kotwal Sahib's office was conducting an interrogation, and further down the corridor, someone was shrieking accusations of bribery, rape, theft and fratricide. From the open window at Muzaffar's elbow, sounds drifted up from Chandni Chowk: the clip-clop of hooves, the cries of palanquin-carriers, the merry chatter and laughter of the hundreds who flocked to the market to buy brocades, jewellery, glass hookahs, slaves – everything.

Muzaffar turned to Kotwal Sahib. 'Do you mind if I think aloud?'

'Be my guest.' Kotwal Sahib sipped from the goblet of sherbet in his hand. 'If you can make head or tail of the affair, you're welcome to do just about anything you want.'

Muzaffar nodded absently. 'From what your man reported, it seems none of the chowkidars in the area noticed anybody moving around.'

'That's hardly surprising, Muzaffar,' the kotwal observed. 'At three in the morning, the city is dead. And any murderer fleeing the scene of crime would keep to the shadows. Especially a murderer who was cool-headed enough to pull the knife out of the victim and carry it away.'

Muzaffar glanced up, his gaze suddenly keen. 'That's a thought,' he murmured. 'But do you really think the murderer had enough time to get the knife out of Basheer's back? It isn't an easy thing to do. *I* wouldn't have the nerve to attempt it, not when I could hear a couple of fully-armed guards hammering away at the door.'

He straightened and reached out an arm for a slim packet of leather that lay on the mattress. 'And I, like a fool, did not think of asking either of the two guards if they'd found the knife in Basheer's back or not.'

Kotwal Sahib frowned. 'They said they hadn't touched the body.'

'Hmm.' Muzaffar was lost in thought as he untied the cord that bound the packet, and drew out the painting that had been found next to Basheer's corpse. He held it to the bright sunlight streaming in through the window and examined it closely. 'I personally prefer the old school, Khan Sahib,' he remarked, 'but I suppose most people would say this is a fine piece of work. Complete in every detail.'

'And?'

'And I'm wondering whose face lies below the bloodstain.' He handed over the painting to the kotwal, who scrutinized it. 'I see no reason for the murderer to drag Basheer across the room – and if the guards found him where they say they did, then one can only assume that Basheer managed to summon up the strength to drag himself there.'

'In order to point a dying finger at his slayer?'

'It would appear so. But there's more to this picture than just Basheer's blood, Khan Sahib,' Muzaffar added, replacing the painting in its leather wrapping. 'Questions that perhaps the great Bichitr himself may be the best person to answer. But for that I suppose I shall have to wait till tomorrow, when he returns to Dilli.' He rose to his feet. 'I will take your leave,' he said formally. 'I intend to call at the atelier tomorrow, to question Bichitr. If you would care to be present, I would be honoured.'

And so it was that the atelier, its floor now a spotless white, saw the arrival of the kotwal and Muzaffar the following day. Lunch over, the master and his remaining apprentice were back at work. Bichitr, a greying and gnarled man of seventy, sat hunched over a painting of a hunt. Mukhtar was seated near the window, his hand moving in assured strokes across the paper on which he was drawing a scene of two lovers seated on a swing. Nothing original about that subject, thought Muzaffar; but the young man's talent was undoubted: this would develop into an impressive painting.

'There was a time when our art was well rewarded,' Bichitr grated. 'When the Baadshah's father – may the gods grant him peace! – was alive, and even through much of the Baadshah's time, we could take pride in our work. But things have changed.' He sighed. 'Who knows how much longer we can survive?'

There was an awkward silence, broken only by the sudden appearance on the threshold of a woman. Muzaffar, looking at her with watchful eyes, estimated her to be about his own age: twenty-five or so. She was tall, fair-skinned and beautiful, with hair that hung in a heavy plait down to her waist. Large kohl-rimmed brown eyes regarded the gathering in the atelier with indifference. From her clothing – a simple kurta of blue cotton embroidered in white, with churidars and a white dupatta – it was apparent that she was by no means rich. Her only jewellery was an enamelled bracelet on her right wrist.

Muzaffar's gaze had wandered surreptitiously to the two men sitting in the atelier. Bichitr, absorbed once again in his work, ignored the woman. But Mukhtar was sitting rigidly straight, his drawing forgotten as he stared unblinkingly at her.

She stepped into the room, and the spell was broken. Mukhtar, catching Muzaffar's eye, reddened perceptibly and returned to his work. The woman made her way to the far corner of the room and reached under the lowest shelf to draw out a twig broom, with which she began sweeping the floor. Rehana, realized Muzaffar. The maidservant who was sister to the guard Rafiq.

Muzaffar glanced back at the kotwal and inclined his head in a silent, eloquent gesture. Kotwal Sahib cleared his throat and addressed the artist. 'I think a break would be in order. Shall we step out into the garden? It seems to be exceptionally pretty.'

The artist's old eyes regarded the kotwal with a disconcerting keenness. 'You think so? Perhaps; I wouldn't know. I rarely feel the need to wander off from my work.' Carefully and unhurriedly, he rinsed his brush, placed it next to the painting, and using the bolster for support, got to his feet. 'But let us go.'

The garden was *not* exceptionally pretty. It was not even passably pretty. There were a few bushes of jasmine and roses, but that was all. Dead leaves from a gulmohar tree floated in the fountain; and it had been a while since the lawns had been trimmed or the paths swept. Bichitr grinned wryly and turned to his two visitors, a look of enquiry on his face. 'Well?'

Muzaffar was ready with his question. 'Tell me about Basheer. His family, what sort of man he was, what sort of artist – everything you can think of.'

'Everything I can think of?' The old man looked down meditatively at his long, shapely hands, stained with lampblack and vermilion. 'That would be a lot indeed. A man of thirty years – and whom I have known for more than fifteen years now – has a lot that can be said about him.'

Muzaffar waited patiently, silently.

Bichitr folded his hands decisively behind his back, and with a sudden lifting of his grizzled chin, said, 'But yes, one can make a start somewhere. Basheer didn't have any family that I know of. He was an orphan, and was brought here when he was thirteen years old. Not a brilliant artist by any means. Mukhtar is the brilliant one here; ah, that boy has magic in his fingers! Had Jahanpanah Baadshah Salamat commissioned the *Padshahnama* now, Mukhtar would have been invited to contribute to it.'

'Basheer was not original,' Bichitr continued, after a ruminative pause. 'Probably because he didn't begin young – thirteen is not a good age to begin learning art, especially when you have little innate talent. But he could, with some effort, copy. We used him mainly in that capacity – as a copyist. He wasn't much good at anything else, and I think he realized it.'

'Was he not jealous of the others? Of Mukhtar?'

'Wouldn't you have been?' Bichitr said wearily. 'I think he was. It's only human, after all.'

Muzaffar nodded. 'I suppose so.' He undid the cords of the leather packet he had been carrying, and carefully drew out the painting he and Kotwal Sahib had examined the previous day. 'I want you to see this,' he said, handing it to Bichitr. 'And tell me what you think of it.'

The old man took the painting and looked at it critically for a few minutes, before handing it back. 'Not bad,' he said. 'But I would have expected better of Mukhtar.'

'You are sure this is Mukhtar's work?'

'It certainly looks like his. Basheer was incapable of such finesse, and the other two have been away since the past one month. And this is a recent painting, no more than a week old – see, even the polish has not mellowed yet.' He noticed the puzzled look on Muzaffar's face, and explained, 'Each painting is polished with alabaster once it is complete. The older the painting, the more mellow the polish. This one has been polished recently.'

'One last question. What was Basheer like – as a man?'

Bichitr's eyes widened, and then he laughed in genuine amusement. 'That is a question you would do well to ask Rehana, my friend,' he said, his shoulders shaking.

Muzaffar flushed. 'I meant – what sort of person was he? How was he to deal with? If you'd known him these many years, you'd have formed an opinion of him.'

'What is any man like? Not black, not white. Many shades of grey. He could be kind and helpful. But he could be rude, selfish, unsociable – and who is not?'

'Of course. Thank you.' Muzaffar swept an aadaab to the elderly painter, who nodded and made his way back into the atelier.

Muzaffar walked about in the garden with the kotwal for a further ten minutes before returning to the atelier. Khan Sahib took his leave of Bichitr, but Muzaffar stayed on, to examine the paintings executed by Basheer over the past few months. Mukhtar, instructed by Bichitr to attend to Muzaffar, rummaged about among the shelves and emerged with a stack of paintings, which he lowered carefully onto the mattress. 'Basheer's work, huzoor,' he said, in a barely audible whisper. Muzaffar responded with a brief word of gratitude, but glanced at Mukhtar only when the young apprentice had gone back to his work. There was a paleness about him, and – unless Muzaffar was imagining things – his hand was not quite steady.

Muzaffar spent the next half hour looking through the paintings. Bichitr had been right; Basheer's talent was close to non-existent. But Bichitr had been wrong, too: for Basheer, it appeared, had begun to hone whatever little skill he possessed. The resulting work was not as fine as that of Bichitr or even Mukhtar, but there were definite signs of art as it should be – good composition, fine brushstrokes, intricate details. Muzaffar frowned, perplexed. Then he rose and made his way to Bichitr.

'I have two questions to ask of you,' he said quietly. 'And that, hopefully, will be all.'

The old man looked up, waiting patiently for Muzaffar to continue.

'Firstly: what did you mean by saying that I would do well to ask Rehana about Basheer?'

'What do you think I meant?' Bichitr dipped his brush into the pool of liquid gold in the seashell he held. In a swift, curling stroke, he outlined the flowing peshwaaz of a dancing girl twirling on a carpet. 'He was a young man, after all – a young man who spent most of his time cooped up here. Rehana was one of the few women he ever got to see; it was inevitable.'

'And apparent?'

'Oh, they were discreet; I grant them that.' The brush moved, embroidering curving leaves and delicate tulips on the rosy ground of the peshwaaz. 'But I have eyes, like anybody else.'

Muzaffar waited for him to say more, but when he did not, Muzaffar began his second question. 'I had shown you the painting that was found next to Basheer's body. One of the figures in that painting had been smudged by a bloodstain. I want you to tell me if you know whose figure that could be.'

Bichitr put down his brush. 'Show it to me again.'

He looked long and hard at the painting, then returned it. For a long while he did not say anything. Only the abstracted expression and the restless hands revealed the turmoil in his mind. When he finally looked up at Muzaffar, his eyes were worried and his voice hoarse.

'That bloodstain is where the artist would generally paint himself in a picture.'

Muzaffar frowned, but did not say a word. Then, with a word of thanks, he went out, leaving behind him an atelier that was silent as the grave.

'Mukhtar?' Kotwal Sahib's voice was incredulous. 'An innocent, Muzaffar; I'd never have imagined!'

Muzaffar nodded. 'I know. But everything seems to point to it. Bichitr says that the painting appears to be his; and if the smudged figure is the artist's – then it could mean that Basheer was trying to indicate that Mukhtar was his murderer.'

'Speculation. An intelligent – and informed – guess. But that's all.'

Muzaffar groaned. 'I know.'

Kotwal Sahib heaved a sigh. 'The person I feel sorry for is Basheer's bride. Poor child; it's hard on her. Barely married, and now this.'

Muzaffar's eyes narrowed. 'He'd been married recently?'

'Last week, from what I hear.'

Muzaffar chewed meditatively on his lower lip. Then he rose and said, 'I take back my words, Khan Sahib. Mukhtar may not *definitely* have something to do with it. But I need time – a day, maybe two – and then I shall return to you, hopefully with something more substantial than mere suspicion.'

As it happened, the kotwal did not have to wait two days. The very next day, Muzaffar's servant arrived at the kotwali with an urgent request for Kotwal Sahib to reach the imperial atelier along with a few soldiers in tow. 'Jang Sahib shall reach before you do, huzoor,' he said. 'He was already riding towards the atelier when I started off.'

The small retinue from the kotwali reached the atelier to find Muzaffar's stallion tethered to the post and the young man himself pacing impatiently along the path. He turned as Khan Sahib dismounted, and came striding up to the older man. 'Leave two of your men here, and bring the other two inside,' he said softly. 'I haven't gone in yet, but they know I'm here. And now that you've arrived, we can expect someone to suddenly lose their nerve and try to run.'

Kotwal Sahib instructed his men accordingly, but caught Muzaffar's sleeve before he could enter the atelier. 'No, you don't,' he said. 'Not without telling me what's happening. I refuse to go in looking like an ignorant fool, without the least idea of what you've unearthed.'

'We don't have time, Khan Sahib,' Muzaffar replied, his voice placating. 'All you need to know right now is that Basheer was a much better painter than Bichitr thought. And that Rehana has more admirers than just the unfaithful Basheer. Come along inside; it's time to reveal a few sordid secrets.'

The kotwal, his mind struggling to make sense of Muzaffar's words, followed him in. Two of the soldiers trailed in behind, lances at the ready.

The atelier was much as it had been the day before: Bichitr and Mukhtar at their work, the woman, Rehana, at hers. The two artists and the woman looked up simultaneously at the men entering the room; and all three stopped their work at once. Watchful, waiting.

Kotwal Sahib could not quite recall later how it all

happened. One moment, Muzaffar was whispering a command to the two soldiers to block the doorway. The next, he was strolling casually but pointedly towards the single window, to position himself in front of it. When he began speaking – and when the woman began shrieking and protesting her innocence – Kotwal Sahib found himself floundering to keep abreast of the swiftly-changing situation. There was a sudden flurry of activity: Bichitr, rising to his feet and saying that this must surely be all a mistake; Mukhtar, his eyes wide and his face a mask of terror, babbling incoherently that he knew nothing. And above it all, Muzaffar's voice, calm and powerful, commanding the soldiers to stay where they were.

'It took some work, Khan Sahib,' Muzaffar said later, when they were back at the kotwali. 'And it is you that I must thank for giving me a clue to the whole affair. Had you not mentioned Basheer's wife, I would never have guessed at the motive.'

He once again placed the painting – still smudged with Basheer's blood – on the mattress in front of the kotwal. 'Have a look at that,' he said. 'A good, close look.'

Kotwal Sahib obeyed. 'Well?'

'Do you notice the woman shown next to the artist? You may not recognize her face, but she wears a rather unusual piece of jewellery – an enamelled bracelet identical to Rehana's.'

Muzaffar sat back, resting his broad shoulders against the bolster behind him. 'I spent a lot of time peering at that painting. If Basheer made the effort to crawl across the room and pull out a finished painting – one already polished, mind you – in order to mark a particular figure on it, then that painting merited close inspection.'

'And when I *did* examine it more closely, I found something interesting. The woman's face is *not* polished.'

Kotwal Sahib stared, uncomprehending. Then, very cautiously, he said, 'It was painted on after the rest of the painting had been completed.'

Muzaffar grinned.

'And then there were all the other paintings, made by Basheer, that Bichitr got Mukhtar to show me. I doubt if Bichitr had ever seen them himself; if he had, he probably wouldn't have had such a low opinion of Basheer. You see, Khan Sahib, those paintings showed a marked improvement in style over time. Basheer may have been a mediocre painter to start with, but years of copying had probably imparted some skill. His paintings were getting progressively better – I saw specimens with my own eyes – and the curious thing about them was that each of them was in Mukhtar's style.'

He paused. 'And you would recall that Bichitr was critical of this painting, when I showed it to him the other day in the garden. He said he'd expected better of Mukhtar.'

Kotwal Sahib nodded. 'Go on.'

'This painting was never made by Mukhtar. It was Basheer's work. Not as good as Mukhtar's, but good enough to confuse even Bichitr. And the artist had, according to convention, painted himself into the picture – alongside his beloved, Rehana.'

'Wait, wait.' The kotwal gestured frantically. 'You're saying things that don't make sense. If Basheer was the artist – and if he's painted himself there – why did he mark himself with his own blood? Surely he was not trying to indicate that he'd committed suicide?'

'Basheer was dying, Khan Sahib. He had spent nearly all his remaining strength in dragging himself across the room. By the time he got to the other end of the room and pulled out the painting from wherever he'd kept it, he'd be close to his last breath. In such a situation, it's hard to imagine him being able to bloody his thumb and put it on the exact spot where his murderer appeared in the painting.'

'Which means?'

'Rehana was the one he was trying to point to. But his thumb never quite made it to the woman he had painted – it fell across his own likeness. He branded himself by mistake, and died in doing so.'

'Basheer, as you informed me, had married very recently. He had been in love – or had at least been infatuated – with Rehana, and it is easy to understand why she encouraged him. She was after all a mere maidservant, with little hope of marrying well; and here was a man employed in the imperial atelier. Most certainly a fine catch – until he dumped her and married another.'

'So she killed him? Muzaffar, how on earth did you come to that conclusion?' Kotwal Sahib stared in frank amazement.

'I couldn't be sure, of course,' replied Muzaffar, 'but the fact that Basheer had been stabbed in the back was a factor. Most women would not take the chance of attacking a man head-on, even were he a puny creature like Basheer. A man, on the other hand, may – or may not. But then there was also another point to be considered: how did the attacker enter the atelier, and then get out? At least one of the two guards would have been likely to spot the intruder. It seemed to me, therefore, that either Rafiq or Shamsuddin had something to do with it.'

'And Rafiq is Rehana's brother,' added Kotwal Sahib quietly. 'He could have contrived somehow to get her in.'

'Precisely. He may not have known her motive for entering the atelier at such an unearthly hour, though I hardly think he imagined she was there for a legitimate purpose. But he probably let her in – or at least diverted Shamsuddin's attention while she was entering – and then, when Basheer was discovered dead, did what he could to help. Rehana had already escaped through the window, and she made her way out of the garden while the two guards forced their way into the room.'

'There's a problem with your story, Muzaffar,' interrupted the kotwal. 'If you say she escaped through the window, where did the dagger vanish? The guards began trying to beat down that door as soon as they heard Basheer scream. I can't imagine Rehana struggling with the dagger, trying to pull it out of Basheer's back, with the guards threatening to break in.'

'*And Basheer still alive and dragging himself to the painting,*' added Muzaffar, with a grin. 'No, Khan Sahib; I hadn't forgotten that. And that is what brings me to the second part of the story. Because I spoke to both Rafiq and Shamsuddin, you see, and asked them separately whether they remembered seeing a dagger in Basheer's back when they first entered. Rafiq denied it vociferously; he was willing to swear on his sword, his honour, his very faith, that there hadn't been any weapon to be seen anywhere. But Shamsuddin, when he thought about it, recalled that there had indeed been a dagger, its handle sticking up out of Basheer's back. He'd seen it when they entered the atelier, but he couldn't remember whether it was there when they brought Mukhtar back to the room. At any rate, by the time your men arrived on the scene, it was gone.'

'Rafiq? Mukhtar? Who?'

'Mukhtar. Rafiq and Shamsuddin went together to fetch him, so neither of them could have had the opportunity. And Mukhtar got plenty of opportunity after he'd seen what had happened. He sent Rafiq off to the kotwali while Shamsuddin was sent to search the neighbourhood. While both of them were away, he got rid of the evidence. He pulled out the dagger, probably wrapped it in paper or cloth and slipped it into his pocket to be thrown away later. And he showed himself for the skilful artist that he was: in the short time that he got, he got together his paints and changed the face of the woman in the painting.'

Muzaffar looked, with his head tilted slightly, at the painting. 'He was intelligent enough to realize that the very fact that Rehana's face appeared in the painting would make her a suspect. So he gave the woman a new face. Unfortunately, he made two blunders.

'The first was that he overlooked the distinctive bracelet painted on the woman's arm – and from which I eventually identified her. The second, which may well have been a result of sheer lack of time, was that he did not polish the area he had just painted over. That was what first alerted me to the fact that the painting had been meddled with recently, you see: all of it, except for the woman's face, is polished. The woman's face, since the paint hadn't dried, couldn't be polished – and unpolished paint looks very different from the gleaming finish of the rest of the painting.'

Kotwal Sahib reached for the painting, and holding it up to the light, regarded it with wonder.

'And all for the love of a woman who wouldn't even look at him,' he murmured.

He handed the painting back to Muzaffar, who silently and carefully wrapped it in the leather packet in which it had originally come. Muzaffar tied the cords, then glanced up at Kotwal Sahib, a twinkle in his eyes. 'Come, Khan Sahib,' he said. 'Now that we've got this blood and gore out of the way, maybe we should have some sherbet.'

'Certainly,' Khan Sahib replied. 'Until another murder comes along?'

Author's Note: *Bichitr (active 1615-1650, possibly till 1660) was one of the foremost painters during the reigns of the Mughal emperors Jahangir and Shahjahan. He* *was one of the many artists commissioned by Shahjahan to create works for the manuscript known as the* Padshahnama, *which chronicles the first twenty years of Shahjahan's reign.*

The Tale of a Traitor

'Yusuf Khan Chaghtai is not alone in this conspiracy,' said Abdul Munim Khan gravely. 'And I want to net all the fish at one time.' His hands, the veins thick and blue under parchment-thin skin, fluttered indecisively above the goblet of lime juice near his elbow.

'And, Allah forbid, he should make an attempt on the life of – *Why can you not understand?*' Ismail Begh sat back, barrel chest heaving, the scar on his cheek as livid as the day it was slashed twenty years back. 'There should be no mercy for a traitor. You cannot condone his treachery.'

Abdul Munim Khan lifted the goblet and drank slowly. The lime juice had become tepid, its coolness evaporated in the heat of the waning day.

He glanced at the men around him. Watchful eyes stared back from faces that showed an inclination to side with Ismail Begh. These may not be the wealthiest or most powerful omrah at Shahjahan's court, but they were men of experience, wisdom and a fierce loyalty to the Emperor. Abdul Munim Khan sighed and put down the goblet. 'Very well. So what do you suggest?'

'I can send half a dozen men,' volunteered

Mohammad Khan Ansari, a taciturn man with a flowing white beard. 'They will find him.'

'My men are ready, too,' said Ismail Begh. 'Ten men, twenty – however many you say. They can leave within half an hour.'

'They will bring him back?'

'Yes,' Ansari and Begh spoke in unison.

Abdul Munim Khan looked one last time at the others. There were nods, murmurs of assent. Finally, reluctantly, he nodded. 'As you will. You can each send five men. Ten should easily subdue Chaghtai's five. And tell your men to take care; we want him alive.'

Ismail Begh rose to his feet. 'Do we?' he murmured derisively. 'Turncoats like Chaghtai are no use alive.'

Abdul Munim Khan looked up at him with a faintly sarcastic smile. 'I thought you were a friend of his,' he said mildly, as the other men began to leave the tent.

The scar flared red again. 'A friend of Chaghtai's? I don't fraternize with scum like that.'

He strode out, leaving Abdul Munim Khan alone with Ansari. 'I don't like this,' Khan Sahib confessed. 'But if your men go with orders to capture rather than kill, I think we will manage.'

Ansari nodded. 'Yes. Begh seems to be in a ferocious mood.'

They stood in the tent, talking quietly for a couple of minutes before Ansari took his leave.

Outside, the camp teemed with over a thousand people – omrah, sweepers, cooks, soldiers, water-carriers, clerks, mahouts, grooms and men from the farrashkhana, the imperial department that handled the needs of the travelling court. They were on their way from Dilli to Agra, moving at a leisurely five kos a day, a long, impressive caravan of camels, military elephants, horses, palanquins and men on foot. By the evening, when the nobility halted, their servants, and those of the Emperor, had set up shop. One set of equipment – embroidered tents, heavy carpets and furniture – would already have travelled on, with its accompanying slaves and servants, ten miles ahead. The cleaning of the chosen campsite and the setting up of the tents would begin by the time the royal entourage left *this* camp in the morning.

It was tiring, complained many omrah. Tiring to set off every day for the next halt; tiring to be on the road for days on end. Few, if any, even gave a thought to how exhausting it must be for the servants who had to set up camp every day, and dismantle it the next, in time to hurry ahead and set it up all over again.

Abdul Munim Khan heaved a sigh of irritation and stood still, listening absently to the noise filtering in through the thick fabric of the tent. Someone at the camp bazaar was extolling, in loud and raucous tones, the virtues of the textiles he sold. Someone – in a cultured, mellifluous voice – was advising the man to save his breath.

And someone, in a voice that Khan Sahib recognized instantly, was shouting for the guards, for there had been a murder.

The guards had managed to push back much of the crowd that milled around the entrance to Ismail Begh's tent. Some tenacious souls still hung hopefully around, ears open for a whisper of floating gossip. The rest, less patient or more occupied, had wandered away. Nobody had bothered to send for a hakim; the man sprawled outside the tent flap of Ismail Begh's dwelling was obviously far beyond human aid. His leather tunic was smart, the chain mail recently cleaned, the helmet fitting snugly on his head. A fist clutched a lance with a grip that even the dagger slicing through the man's throat had not loosened.

There was a lot of blood, and Abdul Munim Khan, despite his many years on battlefields far gorier, turned away hurriedly. He gestured vaguely to Ismail Begh to follow him.

'When did this happen?'

'How do I know?' Ismail Begh's temper was notoriously short, and anxiety had only made it worse. 'I came back here and nearly stumbled over him. Nobody else was around; they were all away, wandering around the camp, gossiping, in the bazaar – wherever. Bastards!' He spat viciously.

Ansari Sahib and the others who had met in Abdul Munim Khan's tent had gathered around. And with them, elbowing his way through the crowd, came a debonair young man, immaculately attired, glittering with jewellery and elegantly perfumed. Khan Sahib winced. He loved his son, but Akram's inability to see beyond the gold-embroidered edge of his own fine choga was taxing at the best of times. And this was not the best of times.

Akram jostled his way to the front and stared wild-eyed at the corpse spread-eagled on the ground. He looked dazedly around until he spotted Abdul Munim Khan.

'Abba huzoor,' Akram made his way forward. 'I heard there had been a murder –'

'This is no concern of yours, Akram,' Khan Sahib replied briskly. 'This is a matter for *us* to investigate.'

'Yes, of course,' Akram nodded vigorously. 'That is why I came. I know just the man – and Allah is merciful, is he not? – he is here right now, in the camp!'

'Allah is everywhere, son,' Khan Sahib said in a flat, toneless voice.

Akram scowled. 'The *man* you need is here, Abba. Mirza Burhanuddin Malik Jang's son, Muzaffar. He's a good friend of mine, and very clever. You will see; let me fetch him.'

Muzaffar's first move was to politely but firmly disperse the crowd outside the tent. Only Ismail Begh, Abdul Munim Khan, Akram and two of Ismail Begh's servants were allowed to remain.

Muzaffar glanced swiftly around at the people left standing around him. It was hard to tell whether Ismail Begh was angry, impatient or simply contemptuous of Muzaffar. Abdul Munim Khan was obviously unhappy, and just as obviously squeamish. The two servants looked uncomfortable.

And Akram was plain curious. 'What is it, Muzaffar?' he asked eagerly.

Muzaffar sat back on his heels after a swift, careful

inspection of the body. 'Murder, of course,' he said crisply. 'Not an accident. His throat has been slit very neatly.'

He glanced at the two servants. 'Did you know this man? You did? What was his name?'

'Salim, huzoor,' one responded in a hesitant voice. 'Salim Qadir.'

'How well did you know him? Do you know where he was from, whether he had a wife and children?'

The servant looked dazed. He turned momentarily to his colleague as if for encouragement, then ran a nervous tongue over dry lips. 'We did not know much about him, huzoor. I think he was from somewhere near Lahore.'

'Family? Friends? Anyone here who would know?'

The man shook his head. 'I doubt it, huzoor. He kept to himself. I don't think anybody really knew him.'

Muzaffar looked down pensively at the dead man, whose grey eyes stared unseeingly up at Muzaffar. Eyes that contrasted jarringly with the sun-darkened skin and brownish beard of a man less than Muzaffar's age. He had died a long way from home, a hideous death.

Muzaffar turned to Abdul Munim Khan. 'No doubt a hakim will perform an autopsy, huzoor. I have finished, however; we may have the body removed.'

Khan Sahib nodded. The sooner a corpse – and that too one so gruesome – was removed from the scene, the better.

The imperial camp was preceded on its travels by a camel laden with shrouds of white cotton. The sole task of the men accompanying the animal was to scurry ahead and cover up any corpses, human or animal, that lay along the road. The imperial gaze should not be offended by a sight that was unholy or unhealthy.

And the sight of Salim's slashed throat was undoubtedly offensive.

One servant was sent off to collect a shroud and bring a couple of slaves to carry away the body. The other was left to keep watch until his comrade returned. The four omrah went into Ismail Begh's tent.

The interior of the rectangular white tent was much like that of the other noblemen's tents. It was nowhere close to the fifty thousand square metres of the Baadshah's own tent, but it was sizeable nevertheless. A chintz canopy stretched overhead for fifty metres, hand-painted in an intricate pattern of irises and curving leaves, in soothing shades of sunset red and moss green. The green was echoed in the carpet and in the bolsters that lay on the white-sheeted mattresses.

Lamps illuminated even the farthest corners of the tent, and in their golden light, Muzaffar glanced swiftly around. On the far left stood an elaborately carved wooden chest with gleaming brass handles. Beside it on a low stool rested a hookah, pipe coiled neatly around the globular body of the vessel. On the right, next to the mattresses, stood a pitcher of sherbet with a set of four glasses – all made, noted Muzaffar, of rock crystal decorated with red enamel. Alongside it was a bowl of pomegranates, and in the centre of the tent was a shallow bowl of water, in which floated five blushing lotuses.

Muzaffar frowned. A man who could afford fresh fruit and flowers while travelling was either very rich or very resourceful. Or both. And rich men tended to make enemies. But did their servants also necessarily end up making enemies, and murderous ones at that? Salim's death was a puzzle, and his obscure past made Muzaffar's task tougher.

'Did you send out your men after Chaghtai?' Abdul Munim Khan asked abruptly. 'I know Ansari Sahib sent his men off.'

Muzaffar looked up, startled out of his thoughts. But the question was addressed to Ismail Begh, who responded in his usual brusque style. 'Of course. I ordered the captain of my men before I came back here.'

Khan Sahib suddenly seemed to recollect that Muzaffar and Akram were not privy to Yusuf Khan Chaghtai's conspiracy. 'Akram,' he said briskly, 'Do not breathe a word of this to anyone. You too,' he added, glancing at Muzaffar. 'Nobody must know.'

Muzaffar inclined his head in acquiescence. 'You have my assurance, huzoor. I do not know, however, what it is you would have me hold my tongue about.'

Ismail Begh guffawed, a sharp, unpleasant laugh that rang in the tent. 'Chaghtai is a bloody traitor, that's what. A villain who has sold himself, his honour, his fidelity – *everything*. He's prostituted himself; no more, no less.'

Abdul Munim Khan blinked at the viciousness of his colleague's harangue; Begh was oblivious. 'I need my hookah,' he muttered abstractedly, walking across the tent. 'Anyway,' he added as he bent down to lift the hookah. 'Chaghtai has little chance of escaping now –'

His voice trailed off and he stood still, the hookah, now forgotten, clutched in one hand. His face was tense, the jaw rigid and the scar vivid in the fitful light of the lamp. Muzaffar watched with growing curiosity as Ismail Begh placed the hookah on the ground and reached for the ornate brass lock on the chest. He gave it a sudden, sharp tug, and it came away in his hand. Ismail Begh flinched visibly.

He threw the lock aside, flung up the lid of the chest, and with a muttered oath, started rummaging about inside. Heavily embroidered chogas, gossamer-light muslin jamas, silk turbans and pyjamas came spilling out as Ismail Begh's hands worked feverishly through the layers of neatly folded clothing. He straightened up after a minute or two, and turned back to his guests.

There was a moment of silence.

'My seal is missing.' Ismail Begh was tight-lipped, his eyes bright with suspicion. 'Someone has stolen my seal.'

Khan Sahib spoke. 'Can it not be that you have not searched properly – that it is somewhere other than that chest?'

Ismail Begh shook his head. The man looked disturbed, and no wonder. The value of an amir's seal – and that too of a man as powerful as Ismail

Begh – was immeasurable. The seal, stamped in ink on a document, was a personal endorsement. An edict, a will, a testimonial: the worth of each derived from the seal that turned it from a piece of paper into something far beyond. A seal could turn a man from a pauper to a prince or vice-versa; it could give life and take it away; it could be the undoing of one and the making of another. A simple object, small enough to fit in a fist, but with a potent power all its own. And a seal in the wrong hands could wreak havoc.

'When did you see it last? And – if it is not impertinent to ask – what did it look like?'

Ismail Begh looked as if he thought Muzaffar insufferably impertinent for asking. When he replied, it was with ill-concealed impatience. 'It is carved from a single piece of pale green jade. A circular seal, with my name inscribed on it. The handle has a pattern of grape leaves.'

He had walked over to the mattresses on which the three men sat. 'As to when I saw it last... just over two hours ago. I wrote to one of my clerks back in Dilli, and used my seal on the letter.'

'And what did you do with the seal when you had finished with it?'

'I put it back into the chest and locked it. Here, the key is still with me.' He reached into the pocket of his choga and drew out a large brass key. He waved it before Muzaffar, then replaced it in his pocket. 'In any case, you can see a key hasn't been used – the thief broke the lock.'

Muzaffar stood up. 'I would like to have a closer look at that lock, huzoor. Have I your permission?'

Ismail Begh nodded; Muzaffar inclined his head in a silent gesture of acknowledgment and went to the chest. He picked up the lock and scrutinized it carefully. 'Yes,' he said after a moment's thought. 'The thief does seem to have smashed the lock.'

There was a lull, then Muzaffar said, 'I would think the thief is also the murderer. If I am not mistaken, the guard was killed simply to get him out of the way.'

He picked up the hookah absently, then replaced it and stood ruminating for a while. Finally, he addressed Khan Sahib. 'Huzoor, I do not think I can be of any assistance at the moment. This is all a blur to me – I can make neither head nor tail of it. Perhaps if I were to return tomorrow morning…?' He looked apologetically at the older man.

Akram interrupted, disappointment showing clear on his face. 'We will be on our way to the next camp by tomorrow morning, Muzaffar,' he said. 'And who knows what will have happened by then?'

Before Muzaffar could answer, Ismail Begh interjected. 'I will not say that the loss of my seal or the death of one of my men does not bother me; but, yes, I do not expect miracles of any man. And Jang Sahib is human, after all.'

Muzaffar Jang withdrew after a courteous salaam and a brief request to Akram to follow him whenever possible. Akram stood, looking indecisive and unhappy, before striding out in the wake of his friend.

The night sky was a clear, shimmering spread

of stars and the imperial camp glittered with an illumination fit to rival the stellar. The mehtabi – the tent of the moonlight – where the Baadshah held a nightly audience of his most trusted omrah, sparkled with lamps. A steady stream of lamps and torches, flickering gold and orange, wove its way through the camp, carried by slaves lighting the way for their masters. The camp was at its busiest. The nobility were roaming the camp bazaar, gossiping, eating, sleeping – living life as they knew it. The rank and file were hard at work, serving, sweeping, cleaning, cooking, washing, guarding… getting killed.

Akram caught up with Muzaffar as they reached the lamp hanging atop a pole in the centre of the camp. Muzaffar was looking up at the lamp, a quizzical expression on his face. He turned when Akram placed a hand on his shoulder.

'That lantern's supposed to light the way,' Muzaffar said. 'So nobody gets lost in the camp.'

Akram looked up at the lamp, then askance at Muzaffar. 'Yes,' he admitted hesitantly. 'So what?'

'So I should not be getting lost either. But I am.'

Akram stared unhappily at Muzaffar. 'You mean you don't know what to make of it?'

A corpulent amir passed by in a gorgeously enamelled palanquin borne by six sweating slaves. On the left trotted two slaves, vigorously fanning the nobleman with iridescent peacock tail fans, all emerald, deep blue and gold. Their lord and master reclined, eyes half-closed, chewing meditatively on a paan. As he passed by, he leaned out and with unerring aim, spat into a silver spittoon that another slave, hurrying along the other side, held out just in time. Muzaffar gazed distastefully at the busy little procession. 'The flower of Mughal aristocracy,' he murmured with the sarcastic lift of an eyebrow. 'How refined.'

He noticed the look on Akram's face, and took a deep breath. 'How well do you know Ismail Begh?'

'A passing acquaintance. Abba knows him, but is no friend. In fact,' Akram added after a pause, 'I doubt if Ismail Begh is friend to *anyone*. I once thought he was a close friend of Chaghtai, but from what I heard today, I suppose not. Begh isn't a pleasant character.'

Muzaffar nodded. 'Yes. Unfriendly; extremely wealthy; careless of his belongings; what else?'

Akram shrugged. 'Unlucky?'

'I don't know,' Muzaffar replied. He chewed thoughtfully on his lower lip, gazing into space. Then with a sudden decisiveness he said, 'I'm going to find out where they took that guard's corpse. And if a hakim hasn't had a look at it yet, I'm going to arrange for that. Coming?'

Muzaffar and Akram were still on their quest for Salim's body when a servant, panting and anxious, caught up with them. He was Abdul Munim Khan's oldest servant – one who had helped bring up Akram – but it was Muzaffar he addressed.

'Huzoor, Khan Sahib sends word that you need trouble yourself no longer with the problem that was posed. Huzoor says the mystery has been solved; you may rest easy.'

'It is obvious,' said Abdul Munim Khan, his face more haggard than it had been an hour earlier. 'Yusuf Khan Chaghtai is the one behind all of it. Not just treason, but theft and murder too.'

'You seem very certain, huzoor,' Muzaffar said gently. They were sitting, along with Akram and a smug Ismail Begh, in Khan Sahib's tent. The tent was much as it had been during the meeting Abdul Munim Khan had hosted in the evening. But the lamps burnt lower and the lime juice had been replenished, a chilled goblet now sitting within easy reach of Akram's father. Other than that, there were few changes – except for the heavy saddlebag lying between Ismail Begh's feet. It was of good brown leather, with solid, heavy seams; but long use – and rough – had taken its toll. There were scuffed patches on the bag, and the cords were frayed in places.

Abdul Munim Khan sipped his lime juice, then glanced at Ismail Begh. 'You better tell him.'

Ismail Begh looked more than happy to be recounting the downfall of one whom he obviously regarded as a public enemy – and possibly a private one too. 'Five of my men rode out, along with five of Mohammad Khan Ansari's, to arrest Chaghtai. They caught up with him and his men about six miles from here. There was a skirmish; some of my men were wounded, and all of Ansari Sahib's men perished. There were no prisoners. All of them, including Chaghtai himself, were killed. My men returned less than half an hour ago.'

He heaved a deep, satisfied sigh. 'And this,' he added, lifting the saddlebag in one large, calloused hand, 'is what they found on Chaghtai's horse.'

Muzaffar gazed at the saddlebag with polite interest, but said nothing.

Ismail Begh huffed in annoyance. This was a man, thought Muzaffar with a private smile, who liked his audience to be appreciative and encouraging.

But if Ismail Begh was a vain man, he was also an impatient one. Waiting for a slow-witted audience to ask the right questions was not his cup of tea. He tugged at the cords of the saddlebag with obvious irritation, and upturned it onto the mattress. An assorted collection of odds and ends tumbled out. A small pouch of muslin, containing a handful each of dried dates and walnuts. An exquisite tasbih, a rosary of amber beads. A prayer mat, rolled into a compact cylinder. A tiny crystal bottle of fragrant attar of roses – rooh gulaab. A scroll, bound with a silken cord.

And a circular seal, crafted from pale green jade, its handle carved in a pattern of vine leaves. Muzaffar, before he could stop himself, had reached out and picked up the seal. It was cool in his hand, the curlicues of the carving smooth under his fingers. His thumb stroked across the inscription of Ismail Begh's name, and his forehead creased fleetingly as he did so.

Ismail Begh was looking triumphantly at the booty. 'You see, Jang Sahib?' he purred. 'The seal that was stolen. *My* seal. Found among Chaghtai's belongings.'

Muzaffar replaced the seal. 'And why do you

suppose Chaghtai would want to steal it? What could he possibly stand to gain?'

In response, Ismail Begh merely reached into the heap of items on the mattress. He picked out the scroll, untied it, and handed it over to Muzaffar without another word.

The scroll was of stiff paper, serviceable and sturdy. An untidy, unsophisticated form of nastaliq calligraphy covered most of the page. It was a letter, and it said, in so many words, that Yusuf Khan Chaghtai had but to say the word, and both the writer and his men – more than five thousand well trained, fully armed soldiers – would be at his disposal. To side with the rebellious prince Aurangzeb in his increasingly frequent snatches at the imperial throne. To oust the Baadshah and his proclaimed heir, Dara Shukoh, from the ranks of the rulers. To, in essence, contribute wholeheartedly to treason.

At the bottom of the letter was the imprint of the seal, in black, of the man who had authored the letter. The seal was that of Ismail Begh.

'You see?' Ismail Begh said. '*Do you see*? This is how he used my seal. To brand me a traitor, like himself. I have only Allah to thank that Chaghtai's evil ways led him nowhere but to his own death.'

Muzaffar stared fixedly at the letter, as if he could not bring himself to believe the duplicity of Chaghtai. Then he nodded and handed it back. 'Yes,' he admitted. 'I see.'

Five minutes later, he begged leave of the two older men, and Akram followed him out into the moonlit night. The camp was quieter now, but still busy enough.

'Well,' Akram said awkwardly, 'so that's that. A sordid tale, but at least all of us can sleep in peace now. No chance of getting murdered in our beds, is there?' He laughed self-consciously.

Muzaffar strode on. After a few paces, he stopped and turned to Akram. His eyes were keen, but his voice betrayed no emotion. 'I need to visit the stables as soon as I possibly can,' he said. 'And then I need to complete the errand we'd set out on, to have a look at Salim's body.'

Akram's jaw dropped in inelegant and spontaneous reaction. 'The stables? And the corpse? But why? We know what happened; it's clear enough. We know Chaghtai – or one of his men – killed Salim and stole the seal. And we know the reason. Then why...?' His voice faded away, perplexed.

Muzaffar was standing, head lowered, hands clasped behind his back. He looked up at Akram and said, 'Sealing wax had obscured part of the inscription on the seal; but the imprint of the seal on the letter was clear. Clear and readable.'

Akram stared stupidly.

'Never mind. Come now, we have no time to lose.' And without waiting for Akram to acknowledge the summons, Muzaffar walked off.

The stables were a hive of activity. The odour of sipand, the wild rue burnt at the entrance to ward off the evil eye, hung in the air. Mingled with it were other, earthier, smells: sweat, manure, grass, molasses, ghee and hay. The imperial horses, reflected Muzaffar wryly, were fed better than the stable boys who cleaned out the stables. The akhtabey – the chief stablemaster – was an amir, but the men under his charge were by no means privileged. At the moment, most were busy attending to the horses and their equipment. Some were cleaning the chintz padding on the saddlecloths; others were polishing bridles or filling feed bags for the next day's march. One of the men directed the two visitors to the far end, where the horses belonging to Ismail Begh and his men were stabled. A few servants were rubbing down the horses; and it was to one of these, a slim youngster with an amiable twinkle in his eyes, that Muzaffar made his way. The boy was combing out the mane of a handsome grey Turcoman mare, but his work obviously did not require his full attention. He straightened expectantly when Muzaffar stopped beside the horse. 'Huzoor?'

Muzaffar smiled serenely and shook his head. 'I did not mean to disturb you. Go on with your work; I came only to admire Begh Sahib's horses.'

The boy rubbed a proud hand down the glossy neck of the mare. 'She's a beauty, huzoor, but she's not Begh Sahib's, really. This one belongs to one of Begh Sahib's soldiers.'

'Ah.' Muzaffar looked suitably impressed. 'Very brave men, I believe. I heard a party of them gave a good account of themselves in a clash today.'

The boy's eyes widened with interest. 'The fight with Yusuf Khan Chaghtai, huzoor? Yes, that was something to be proud of.' He ran his fingers through the mare's mane. 'This one was there too, huzoor. I heard it was bad; many men died. But I thank the gods this one is back in one piece.'

Muzaffar nodded and reached out a hand to stroke the mare. 'That's true.'

'I was worried about her,' said the boy. He seemed a garrulous sort, grateful for a captive audience. 'She was one of the first six that went, and I feared it was too small a number. I was very relieved when Begh Sahib ordered the reinforcement. The reinforcement got back sooner than the first party, but at least nobody was killed. Ansari Sahib's men were singularly unlucky, huzoor – not one survived.'

This time, Muzaffar did not say anything; he merely looked puzzled.

He spent a few minutes chatting with the lad, then wandered around to the other horses – all of which, his new friend assured him, had been of the party that pursued and killed Yusuf Khan Chaghtai. The grey mare was the young stable hand's favourite, and so he had attended to her first. Other horses stood, each in its own stall, waiting patiently to be rubbed down. Muzaffar wandered along, stroking each of them, keeping up a desultory, one-sided conversation all the time with a bemused Akram, who could make no sense of Muzaffar's sudden interest in horses.

He could also make little sense of the questions that Muzaffar asked of the irritable and sleepy hakim whom they tracked down, just before midnight, in a far corner of the camp. The man admitted that he had subjected Salim's body to a cursory examination, but had not conducted an autopsy. A mere soldier, it appeared, did not merit a post-mortem; the slit throat was too obviously the cause of death. The only thing unusual was that the dead man's mouth seemed strangely bruised. 'It almost looks as if somebody slapped him in the mouth,' the hakim said peevishly.

It was past midnight by the time they wandered back to the centre of the camp. Much of the camp slumbered; the guards and some servants were on duty, but that was all.

Abdul Munim Khan, roused by a son as bewildered as himself, was initially reluctant to give up his sleep for what threatened to be a wild-goose chase.

'But I don't know, Abba,' Akram protested. 'Muzaffar insists he will tell only you and Begh Sahib, and that too *now*.'

'And it would help if your guards were to accompany us to Begh Sahib's tent,' added Muzaffar quietly from the shadows. 'After all, we want no harm to come to anybody present.'

He did not say anything more, not until the three of them were standing inside Ismail Begh's tent – the man was too incensed at this intrusion to offer his uninvited guests a seat – and Abdul Munim Khan had, in a resigned voice, announced that Jang Sahib had something important to say.

'At this hour of the night?' Ismail Begh rasped. 'When anybody who's sane is fast asleep?' He spat the words out, so angry that Akram flinched and glanced pleadingly at Muzaffar.

But Muzaffar was not distracted; neither by Akram's silent entreaty, nor by Ismail Begh's raging. 'Sanity is not the only requisite for a sound sleep, Begh Sahib,' he replied. 'So is a clear conscience.'

Before Ismail Begh could explode, Abdul Munim Khan interrupted. 'It would perhaps be advisable to let Muzaffar tell us why he thought it necessary to talk now, and not wait till morning. Once he has given us his reasons, if you still feel that you have been imposed upon – well, we'll see about that later.'

It was a lame remark, and passed in a timid, tired voice; but it calmed Ismail Begh enough for him to growl an impatient 'Very well. Hurry up and say what you want to. I cannot see what possible reason there could be for barging in at this hour.'

'The reason is closely connected to you, Begh Sahib,' said Muzaffar quietly. 'It concerns the murder of your guard and the theft of your seal.'

'Both of which were solved to my satisfaction. I know who killed Salim; I know who stole the seal. We all knew Chaghtai to be a traitor; it has now been proven that he was also a thief and a murderer.'

Muzaffar seemed to have been listening intently; but his next words were unconnected to what Ismail Begh had been saying. 'You are a wealthy man, Begh Sahib,' he said. His gaze wandered purposefully around the interior of the tent. 'So prosperous that you can pay your men well enough for them to ride Turcoman horses.'

Abdul Munim Khan stared. 'I fail to see –' he began, but was cut short by Ismail Begh. 'So? I am not the only one. Many land owners are good paymasters.'

'True. But a man who can pay his soldiers so well usually has servants to prepare his hookah for him.'

Involuntarily, all three men listening to him turned to look at the hookah, as if expecting some strange revelation.

'And,' continued Muzaffar, 'I do not think I have ever come across a horse, no matter how impeccable its bloodline, that could cover twelve miles in just about two hours. One such horse would be a boon indeed to its owner; but *five*? And five of Ansari Sahib's too? A miracle.'

'You aren't making sense, Muzaffar,' Akram muttered nervously. Ismail Begh had, surprisingly enough, calmed down. Though his scar throbbed red and angry, his voice was level enough. 'I fail to see the significance of this. What are you trying to get at?'

Muzaffar rubbed his jaw thoughtfully. 'Just the mere fact that the ten men sent out after the meeting with Khan Sahib could not possibly have caught up with Chaghtai six miles from here, killed him and returned, all within the space of a couple of hours. Even if they could, their horses would have been in a lather. I checked your horses, Begh Sahib; those horses *were* ridden, but not hard. *They* could not have met Chaghtai six miles from here. So who did meet him – and kill him? And who, then, fought with the ten men so that not a single soldier of Ansari Sahib's remained alive?'

Ismail Begh shrugged and stood staring into a lamp near the wooden chest. The wick was dying out, and the flickering flame threw eerie shadows across the scarred face of the man. 'And what does that imply?' he asked mildly. 'Are you saying my men are guilty – of what?'

'Perhaps of just obeying orders,' Muzaffar answered. 'The second thing that bothers me,' he continued, 'is that the imprint of your seal on that incriminatory letter was clear – whereas your seal itself is partly obscured by a splotch of sealing wax. Your seal, Begh Sahib, would leave a distorted mark, not a clear one. Unless, of course, the letter was stamped *before* the seal was obscured.'

'Or Yusuf Khan Chaghtai spilt sealing wax on it *after* he had used it.'

Muzaffar lifted an eyebrow. 'Chaghtai was on the run. If he stole your seal and used it on the letter before he fled, he would hardly have had the time to fiddle with the seal much. It could have been an accident, of course – but so many coincidences, one on top of the other? I wonder.

'And there is the matter of the murdered guard. To kill an armed man in broad daylight requires not mere daring, but also desperation. Or the assurance that one will not be caught red-handed.'

'The other guards were not there at the time,' said Abdul Munim Khan hesitantly. 'They were at the camp bazaar or something. I remember Ismail Begh being very annoyed at their absence.'

'Of course he would be,' murmured Muzaffar.

'As guards, they're expected to be on duty. But why did none of them turn up when Salim's body was discovered? The world and his wife were crowding around; where were the guards?'

'This is getting convoluted,' Khan Sahib sighed. 'Where does it all end?'

'In that Salim was armed – well armed, may I add – with a lance and a sword. He may have had to draw his sword from the scabbard, but his lance was in his hand. He was clutching it, ready to defend himself. Yet he did not. He stood there, lance in hand, and let himself be stabbed in the throat. Why?'

Before any of the others could react, he continued in a voice that Akram, through long association, had come to recognize as dangerous.

'Because Salim didn't see his attacker approach. The man who slew Salim came at him from behind – slapped a hand across Salim's mouth, and drew a blade across his windpipe. Swift, soundless, and very effective.'

'I don't understand,' Akram interrupted. 'Salim had his back to Begh Sahib's tent; then how could his attacker come from the back?'

'From inside the tent,' Muzaffar said quietly. He spoke to Akram, but he was watching Ismail Begh all the while.

Abdul Munim Khan turned to Ismail Begh, his eyes anxious. 'There is something terribly wrong here,' he said. 'From what Muzaffar tells us, it seems Yusuf Khan Chaghtai, or someone of his camp, has corrupted your men. You may be in grave danger –'

Muzaffar chuckled despite himself. 'I doubt if Begh Sahib is in any danger at all,' he said. 'Unless it is the danger of getting caught.'

'*How dare you!*' Ismail Begh lunged forward, his hands reaching for Muzaffar's neck. Muzaffar sidestepped neatly, and moved swiftly to stand across the entrance of the tent.

'It's really your own fault you got caught,' he said quietly. 'You chose the wrong way to draw my attention to the broken lock on the chest. You pretended you wanted to smoke your hookah – but your hookah was stone cold; it hadn't been prepared. And you, Begh Sahib, are not a man to prepare your hookah for yourself. You put up a show for my benefit, so that I could be a witness to your discovery of the theft.

'That letter in Yusuf Khan Chaghtai's saddlebag was not forged by Chaghtai earlier today with your stolen seal. No; Chaghtai had that letter from you some time back. And today, by the time you came to Khan Sahib's tent, you knew that Chaghtai had been exposed as a traitor, and had fled. You also knew he possessed a letter that could mean death for you, so you decided to cover your tracks. Before you went to Khan Sahib's tent, you sent off six of your guards to chase after Chaghtai, with orders to kill him and bring back all his belongings. During the gathering in Khan Sahib's tent, you denounced Chaghtai to the point of going overboard – because some knew you to be a friend of his.'

He cleared his throat. 'Unfortunately for you, Ansari Sahib offered his men first – and you guessed that if his men ran into the six you had already sent off, your cover would be blown. So you decided to send your five men too, just to keep Ansari Sahib's men in check – and to ensure that the all-important letter was brought to you, not to anyone else. I imagine your men were ordered to ensure that none of Ansari Sahib's men returned to report the truth. Unfortunately for your men, the encounter with Chaghtai *did* take place six miles from here. Towing back the bodies of both Ansari Sahib's men and Chaghtai's would be impossible for just five men, especially since some were wounded. They could not bring the bodies back, so they left them out there, six miles out.

'You sent off your men, then came back here, pocketed the seal, and on your way out of your tent, silenced Salim so that he could never claim that you were the only one who had entered the tent. After that, of course, you raised a hue and cry so that the murder and the theft could be discovered. And when your men returned with Chaghtai's body and the saddlebag, all you had to do was slip the seal into the bag and take it dutifully to Khan Sahib.

'Most ingenious, I must admit. But the horses, the sealing wax and the very fact that you were so eager to get rid of Chaghtai – no, Begh Sahib, not a good way to cover up.'

Khan Sahib was already shouting for the guards outside; Ismail Begh was screaming obscenities at Muzaffar, at Chaghtai, at Abdul Munim Khan – at anybody connected with his downfall.

Muzaffar heaved a sigh, deep and thoughtful.

Then, with a brief grin, he said to Akram, 'I trust I have redeemed myself. It is not morning yet, and when we break camp, I will not be burdened with two unsolved crimes on my conscience.'

The Stolen Gifts

Muzaffar had never quite known when the rains had disappeared. Before he realized it, the clouds had melted away into a blue sky, leaving behind days that were shorter, sunsets that came earlier, and evenings that were beginning to turn chilly. Autumn – that ephemeral, never-quite-there season for Dilli – was here, pulling yellowing leaves off the trees and giving the city a few days of pleasant weather before the winter set in.

Muzaffar had spent an invigorating day watching the birds that had begun to arrive from colder climes for the winter: the shovelers, ducks, teals and cormorants that were now bobbing and squawking, diving and quacking on the Yamuna. It had been a fascinating sight, and despite the peevish protests of his boatman friend, Salim, he had enjoyed himself. Now, entering his own haveli, he was looking forward to a quiet evening at home.

But it was not to be. Akram Khan, impeccably dressed and bejewelled as always, was hovering impatiently in the dalaan, and came bounding out as soon as he heard Muzaffar approaching in the company of the steward, Javed, who was in the process of informing his master that an unexpected guest had been sitting in the dalaan for the past quarter of an hour.

'Where on earth have you been, Muzaffar?!' Akram grabbed Muzaffar – even in his distress, he took care to hold not the sleeve of his choga, but the exposed wrist – and pulled his friend into the dalaan. 'I've been waiting for you such a long time, and your household could tell me nothing but that you'd gone for a joyride down the Yamuna!'

'Which I did. But something appears to be bothering you. What is it?' Muzaffar waved Javed away and invited Akram to seat himself.

'No, no! You have to come with me, Muzaffar. *Immediately*. There's no time to be lost. Allah knows, enough time has been wasted already. I tell you, I haven't seen anybody behave in such a completely mindless fashion; it makes my blood curdle to think I'm related to them!'

'And what, may I know, has happened?' asked Muzaffar as they mounted their horses at the gate of Muzaffar's haveli. 'You have raved and ranted all this while, but with no indication of where we are going or why.'

'To the haveli of my uncle, Moinuddin Khan. His son, my cousin Feroze, is getting married five days from now. He got engaged a week ago, to one of Rahmat Ali's daughters – do you know the man? Never mind. It's not important; he's an oily creature, obsessed with wealth and power, and not likely to lay his hands on either this side of Paradise, that is if he ever gets there… where was I?'

'Rahmat Ali? Your cousin Feroze? Your uncle?'

'Ah, yes. Sorry. Feroze. *And* my uncle. You'll never believe the half-witted way in which my uncle has behaved. I hadn't visited them since just after the engagement, and when I go there today, guess what I find? That there's been a theft. And no small thing, either. A large sum of money, a few pieces of heavy brocade, and some jewellery that Moinuddin Khan's household were to give the bride's household. Two days from now, the family is supposed to go to Rahmat Ali's house, taking gifts for the household. Only, the gifts in question have vanished.'

'And when was this discovered?'

'Five days ago! That's what made me hit the roof, Muzaffar. My moronic uncle has been blundering about all this while trying to do an investigation of his own. And Feroze has been too weak-kneed to protest. They've turned the house upside down millions of times and bullied all their servants in an effort to force a confession out of someone. But will they take the matter to the local thanedar? No, they won't, because people will laugh at them. They'll say that Moinuddin Khan's house is so ill-guarded, anybody can walk in and help themselves to what they like. I ask you –!'

Muzaffar interrupted, his face grim. 'Five days is a long time, Akram. I cannot possibly hope to find any clues now, especially after – as you've said – the house has been searched again and again. What can I hope to achieve?'

'Don't worry about that; I've already told my uncle that you're good at detecting, not at working miracles.

He's more or less accepted that all that money is gone forever… but this is a last-ditch effort, Muzaffar. If you can find it, well and good. If you can't – well, nobody can blame you.'

But Muzaffar, entering Moinuddin Khan's haveli half an hour later, found himself prey to misgivings. As in any house where a wedding was imminent, the haveli had been illuminated with hundreds of pretty earthenware lamps, and musicians were playing on drums and pipes. There was music, there was light; but there was none of the spontaneous gaiety, the laughter and the excited bustle of a house celebrating.

Moinuddin Khan, fluttering and flapping like a nervous hen, was by turn apologetic and despairing. Feroze was merely silent, looking as if he wished he were anywhere but home.

'I don't think anything can be done now,' he finally said in a dull voice. 'If you'd listened to me, Abba, we might have been able to salvage some of it. Now there's –'

He was cut off abruptly by his father, who exploded. 'At what cost?! At what cost, I ask you? To have all the neighbours snigger behind our backs? I would rather –'

He was, in turn, interrupted by Muzaffar, who said quietly, 'Khan Sahib, I would suggest we get down to business immediately. It might be best if you took me to the room from which the items were stolen.'

The chamber was a nondescript one in the men's apartments of the haveli. The polished plaster walls, dulled with age and neglect, had a few niches, all bare. The wall facing the sole doorway was pierced by a window. It was a large one – perhaps three feet high and two feet wide – but except for a twelve-inch square opening in the centre, the rest was in the form of a border of carved sandstone.

Against the left wall was a mattress covered with a sheet. In one corner stood a takhat, a low stool – and that was all. It was a humble little room with no pretensions to grandeur and no ambitions of ever playing host to any guest.

It took Muzaffar less than a minute to take it all in. 'Well, Khan Sahib,' he said, 'you had better tell me what happened. Where had the stolen items been kept?'

Moinuddin Khan winced, as if the mere mention of the stolen wealth distressed him. He glanced at Feroze, and it was Feroze who answered. 'On the mattress. There was brocade, wrapped in unbleached cotton and stacked in piles. One large wooden sandook with all the jewellery – necklaces, bangles, nose rings, earrings, whatever. There were cane baskets full of nuts. The nuts were the only thing that were left behind,' he said bitterly.

'And how did it happen? The room was guarded, I suppose?'

'Yes, it was guarded. A servant stayed here, all the time. And if he had to leave, for his meals for instance, he would lock the door' – Feroze tilted his head towards the thick wooden door with its formidable bands of iron, an unusual fixture in a Mughal dwelling, which typically relied on heavy curtains rather than doors – 'and bring the key either to me or to Abba.'

Muzaffar stepped out into the corridor and swung the door back, examining the lock. It had not been broken or damaged in any way, but with his limited knowledge, he could not tell if someone had tampered with it. 'And on the day the theft occurred?'

'Some of the men of the family had gathered to celebrate. We were all in the dalaan, eating and drinking; there were musicians, a few dancing girls. This was in the evening, shortly after sunset. Suddenly, the servant who was supposed to be guarding this room came into the dalaan, wanting to speak to Abba. He was very agitated. He told Abba that the jewellery and the brocades had been stolen. He said he had his back turned to the door and was trying to light the lamp when someone entered and knocked him unconscious. When he came to, the room had been emptied of everything.'

'Except for the nuts,' Akram added helpfully.

None of the men paid any attention to his comment. Muzaffar said, 'Who was the servant guarding this room?'

'Yaqub,' Moinuddin Khan said. 'He's a good man; been with the family for donkey's years. Very dependable – I would trust him with my life. I told him this morning that we had decided to send for you, and he was all praise for the decision. He's a good man, that one.'

Muzaffar nodded. 'Send for him, please. I would like to ask him a few questions.'

So Yaqub, a prematurely stooped man with a nose like a beak and a prominent Adam's apple, was summoned. He salaamed his masters and the guests, listened carefully to what Muzaffar had to say and thought long and hard before answering.

'I cannot say, huzoor. I was bent over the lamp, trying to light it, when someone must have come in through the open door behind me.'

'Didn't you hear anything? Footsteps? The rustle of clothing?'

'No, huzoor. The music was very loud; much louder than it is today. I did not hear a thing.' Yaqub had a point, thought Muzaffar; the cacophony of kettle drums and pipes was enough to drown out softer sounds like footsteps. To carry on a conversation at a normal volume was possible, but just about.

'When did you come to? And what did you see?'

'I do not know when I came to, huzoor. It was already dark, you see; I could not tell how much time had passed. A few minutes, I suppose. The room was just as it had been, except that the cloth and the sandook were gone. I was lying on the floor with the lamp beside me. My head was throbbing and so was my entire body – the thief had thrashed me terribly. It still hurts.' He grimaced, eliciting a look of profound sympathy from Moinuddin Khan, who whispered, 'Yes, yes, Yaqub. Not much longer; then you can go on back to your bed and get some rest.' He looked at Muzaffar and added in an apologetic tone, 'The entire household has been in such an uproar, Yaqub didn't even tell us how badly he'd been beaten. Only today I saw how awfully he's been beaten. Bruises all over his back and limbs. He must be in excruciating pain.'

'Of course. Tell me, Yaqub: you said you came to with the lamp beside you. Was it lit?'

The man shook his head. 'No, huzoor. Allah be thanked I had not had the time to light the lamp before I was attacked. Who knows what would have happened if the burning lamp had fallen on the floor? The house may have burnt down.'

'And what did you do when you discovered the theft?'

'I rushed to the dalaan to tell my master. We came back and searched the room and all over the house, but nothing could be found.'

'And that is what you have been doing ever since?' Muzaffar asked Moinuddin Khan. 'Searching again and again, hoping to find it?' He waved away the protest rising to the other man's lips. 'Never mind. I'm sure you had your reasons. But you found absolutely nothing? Not even a scrap of brocade or a single small trinket that may have fallen from the booty as it was being lugged away?'

Moinuddin Khan shook his head.

'What about the other rooms in the vicinity? This room is at the end of a corridor; which rooms lie along the corridor?'

'There are a couple of guest rooms – currently occupied by members of the family who have come from afar for Feroze's wedding. There is Feroze's room, my own room, a small room that we sometimes use as a study, the dalaan… and the qutb khana at the far end.'

'Was anybody present in any of these rooms at the time of the theft?'

It was Feroze who answered. 'Except for the dalaan, no. Abba and I were with all the guests in the dalaan. The other rooms were empty.'

'Let us see the place, shall we? I would like to know the layout of this part of the haveli.'

Moinuddin Khan sent off Yaqub with a solicitously whispered instruction to look after himself, before he guided his two guests out into the corridor. Muzaffar, on his way to the room where the theft had taken place, had paid little attention to his surroundings. He recalled doorways leading off the corridor, but he had not bothered to find out where they led. Moinuddin Khan now pointed out the rooms that lay off the corridor: the guest rooms, the chambers of the men of the family, the tiny room that he said was used as a study. Except for the study, all were more spacious than the room where the gifts had been stored. More spacious, somewhat more ornate, but following the same basic plan: plastered walls, a single doorway, and one large window, with a foot-square opening in it surrounded by carved stone filigree. There was no other exit off the corridor till beyond the dalaan. There, the corridor forked: to the right was a narrow corridor that Moinuddin Khan pointed out as leading to the kitchens. The main corridor stretched on a few more feet, ending at the qutb khana. Between the dalaan and the qutb khana, the corridor was flanked on either side by the garden that surrounded the building.

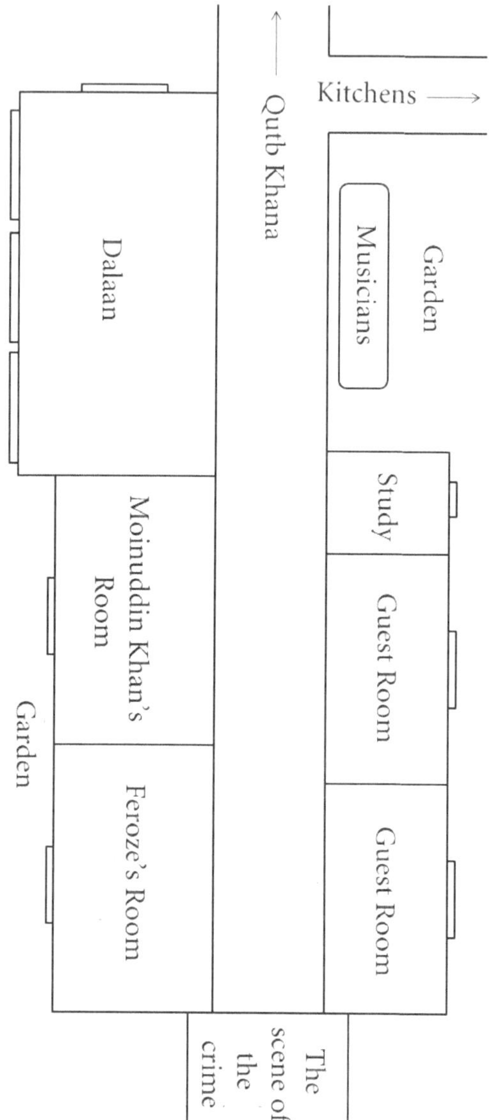
Kitchens
Qutb Khana
Garden
Musicians
Dalaan
Study
Guest Room
Guest Room
Moinuddin Khan's Room
Garden
Feroze's Room
The scene of the crime

'How large and how heavy were these items?' Muzaffar asked as they walked down the corridor and past the arched entrance to the dalaan. A group of musicians was seated opposite the archway, playing a tune in which the sonorous notes of shehnais dominated. They perked up at the appearance of Moinuddin Khan and started playing with even greater vigour, almost drowning out Muzaffar's voice. Feroze gestured to the men to pipe down, and with a last disappointed toot, the little orchestra fell silent.

'What did you say?'

'I asked how heavy and large the stolen goods were. Would a man be able to conceal them under a heavy shawl or if he had a blanket wrapped around him?'

Feroze looked thoughtful. Finally, he shook his head. 'No, I'm pretty sure that would be impossible. The sandook was large – about ten inches across and half that deep and high. *And* it was heavy. A man could carry it under his arm, but it would be a bit of a strain. And if he had to carry the cloth along with it – well, *I* wouldn't be able to do it. The brocades aren't as heavy as the sandook, but they're bulky.'

'So someone carrying the sandook or the brocades would be conspicuous? Were there servants here in the vicinity who might have seen someone coming down the corridor?'

'The servants were coming and going, from the dalaan to the kitchens. We questioned them, but they hadn't seen anyone. The musicians were sitting where they are now, right opposite the dalaan. They insisted they hadn't seen anyone coming down this stretch of the corridor.' He paused. 'If somebody had come down that corridor, the musicians would have noticed, since all of us – Abba, me, our relatives – had entered the dalaan well before. The only one left in that part of the house was Yaqub.'

'But you, Khan Sahib and the guests staying in those two guest rooms would have servants who may have had good reason to visit your rooms while you were in the dalaan. To clean up, or to perform some other chore. Did the musicians see any such men? Who went down the corridor is as important as who came up it.'

Feroze did not know, and neither did his father. The musicians, when questioned, said they did not recall who had gone down the passage that day, a long week ago. But there certainly had been traffic, probably servants who had errands to run or, as Muzaffar had guessed, chores to perform. 'But you do not recall anybody who came out of the corridor, down this way, carrying anything especially large or bulky? A sack? A large cooking pot? Anything capacious enough to hold the stolen goods?'

No, the leader of the musicians insisted. They would have remembered that. Nobody had gone by with anything that could have matched that description. A pitcher of water, a folded garment, newly washed; a small vase of flowers... those were the sort of things that had been carried down the corridor and into the rooms. Nothing large, nothing that could have held a small fortune in its belly.

Muzaffar heaved a sigh. 'Then,' he told Moinuddin

Khan, 'I think I had better go home and mull over this. I would have liked to have had a close look at the garden, but it's too dark for that now. I'll come tomorrow morning, if that suits you, three hours after the first namaz of the day.' He turned to Akram. 'Would you like to come home with me? We could discuss this business over dinner.'

'I can't make head or tail of it,' Akram said. He had picked uneasily at dinner, barely tasting either the spinach with fennel or the delicious khichri of rice and lentils that Muzaffar's cook had dished up. He had not even touched the kashk, a dish of lamb cooked with crushed wheat, onions, ginger and spices, that he had so admired on a previous occasion. Now, his hands washed, he fiddled with a pear that he had picked up from the silver salver placed on the white sheet in front of them. 'How could the thief have spirited away the stuff without taking it down the corridor? I suppose the brocades could have been taken one at a time, maybe tucked away inside someone's clothing. The same with the jewellery – individual pieces, a few at one go. But the sandook?'

'And that method would, in any case, take an eternity,' Muzaffar pointed out. 'Either the musicians missed something utterly obvious or utterly subtle, or the material wasn't taken out through the corridor at all. Or at least not past the musicians.'

Akram's eyes widened. 'One of the other guests, you mean? The occupants of one of those two rooms?'

'Oh, I'm not insinuating one of the guests is behind the theft. As it is, your uncle and cousin confirmed that all the relatives were in the dalaan at the time. I'm suggesting that the thief stole the sandook and the brocades, then instead of going down the corridor loaded with the goods, simply went into one of the rooms – Khan Sahib's, Feroze's, one of the two guest rooms, or the study – and hid the things there for the time being, intending to return later to collect them.

'If that's what happened,' he continued, 'I'd think the two guest rooms would have been the likeliest candidates for a good hiding spot. They're close to the room at the end of the corridor, so one would have to spend less time in the corridor, and therefore run less risk of being caught red-handed. Khan Sahib's room and the study are too close to the dalaan, where a passing servant or one of the musicians could have seen anyone ducking in. And the bridegroom's room? I don't know if that would have been a good hiding place... though,' he conceded with a grin, 'it might have been the ideal place: nobody would think of searching there.'

Muzaffar's conjectures, however, came to naught. The next day, at Moinuddin Khan's haveli, he learnt that the first rooms to be searched – barely a couple of minutes after Yaqub had come blundering hysterically into the dalaan with the news of the theft – had been those abutting the corridor. 'There was nothing to be found there, Jang Sahib,' Khan Sahib said. 'We turned everything upside down. Fortunately, both rooms were occupied by very close relatives: my brother and his son. Both helped in the search, but it was futile.'

Muzaffar's visit to the garden outside proved equally disappointing. He got down on his haunches and peered hopefully at the lawn just under the window that looked into the room from which the gifts had been stolen. The grass grew almost till the base of the wall, separated from it by a six-inch strip of bare earth. The imprint of a leather sandal, the toes facing the window, was to be seen in the soil; but that was all. And that, decided Muzaffar, could have happened any time in the past one week. Even early this morning.

'What are you looking for?' Akram asked. 'Nobody could have got out through the window. A very thin child, perhaps, but surely no-one else.'

Muzaffar turned to look up at Akram, and his gaze wandered past his friend to the far corner of the garden. A thin figure, bent over almost double under a large bundle, was walking rapidly across towards the rear of the buildings. It was a familiar figure, and one that Muzaffar thought he recognized. 'Isn't that Yaqub?'

'Yes, that's him,' said Feroze, glancing over his shoulder. 'Taking the laundry to the washerman, I think.'

His father chuckled. 'And preparing to settle down to a long gossip session with the washerman. I would have kicked any other man out, but not Yaqub,' he added. 'He's been around so long, he deserves a bit of leeway.'

'Is he feeling any better now? You said yesterday that he had been badly beaten by the thief.'

'Yes, yes – I saw the bruises myself. Horrible. I cannot understand why the man kept quiet so many days. But I sent for my own hakim last night; he prescribed something to ease the pain. An ointment, I believe. Allah be willing, Yaqub will soon be better.'

Muzaffar got to his feet. 'I think I'll have a brief chat with Yaqub,' he announced. 'Would you like to come along with me, Akram? And you, Feroze?'

Feroze looked taken aback, but did not comment on this unseemly desire to fraternize with a mere servant. Moinuddin Khan murmured something about it being more convenient to have Yaqub come to them instead of them following him to the washerman, but Muzaffar paid no attention. Akram and he strode off in the wake of that strange figure, its bloated top half balanced precariously on spindly legs, already disappearing around the corner of the building. Feroze hurried after his cousin, while Khan Sahib, with a resigned shrug, made for the dalaan to brood over the embarrassment that would ensue if the stolen gifts were not recovered.

Yaqub, large bundle and all, proved to be faster on his feet than Muzaffar had imagined. He had already reached the washerman's hut and was seated cross-legged on the ground outside when Muzaffar, Akram and Feroze arrived. The bundle – a vast heap of jamas, pyjamas, cummerbunds, turbans, handkerchiefs, and whatnot – had been untied, its yards of muslin, silk, chintz and cotton spilling out in a riot of colours and pristine whites. The washerman was apparently just starting to sort through the clothes; he was holding a very long strip of cloth in his hand, pulling it through his fingers and searching for the end, when the three omrah arrived.

The sound of their footsteps made Yaqub turn. He rose to his feet immediately, ducking his head in a salaam. The washerman dropped the cloth in his hands and was beginning to follow Yaqub's example when Muzaffar motioned to him to keep sitting. 'Go on with your work; all we need to do is ask Yaqub a few questions.'

The man sat down again and Muzaffar turned to Yaqub. 'I hope you are feeling better now,' he said. 'Khan Sahib had been telling me yesterday about how badly you had been beaten.'

Yaqub said nothing; he simply stood in front of Muzaffar, head bowed, eyes lowered, fingers clasped below his waist.

'Bruises all over, is that right?'

This time, Muzaffar's words elicited a reaction. It was wordless, but there was no faulting the sheer drama of the gesture: Yaqub raised his hands over his head, gripped the collar of the kurta he was wearing, and pulled it up over his head, the sleeves sliding up his arms. He did not need to remove the garment completely; even half-clad, his condition was shocking enough to cause Feroze and Akram to flinch. Muzaffar, staring at the purplish-brown splotches marring the man's arms and back, raised an eyebrow over suddenly narrowed eyes, but did not say anything immediately. After a few moments, he nodded, signalling to Yaqub to lower his kurta.

'I see. That must hurt terribly.'

Yaqub satisfied himself with an inarticulate murmur which Muzaffar took to mean that yes, it did hurt terribly, but he was being manly and bearing up with it.

Muzaffar noticed out of the corner of his eye that the washerman was now making a mere pretence of continuing with his work. He had been pulling aside clothing, pushing it back, and was now aimlessly stirring a bowlful of brownish-black liquid. His eyes were wide, staring into space; his hand moved mechanically, round and round, holding what looked like a small wooden spoon, its bowl engulfed by the liquid.

Muzaffar looked lost in thought for a few moments. Then he said to Yaqub, 'You said the thief knocked you out while your back was turned, which was why you could not see who it was. But if you were already unconscious and incapable of recognizing the thief, what possible reason could he have had for thrashing you so?'

Yaqub had returned to his usual pose, hands clasped loosely, head down, eyes hooded. Muzaffar thought the man stiffened at his words, but it was almost a minute before he spoke. 'I dare not guess, huzoor. Perhaps anger? Or perhaps he had been meaning to kill me, just in case I had seen him.'

'Yes, maybe you're right.' Muzaffar sighed. 'That is all for now. You may go, Yaqub. Thank you.'

Yaqub was moving off when Muzaffar reached out and caught him by the upper arm. 'No, wait. *We* will go. *You* were talking to the washerman.'

And with that he led Feroze and Akram away, Akram following obediently but with bewilderment written all over his face.

'What is happening, Muzaffar?' he said when they had reached the dalaan. Feroze had excused himself, and a servant had arrived bearing glasses of freshly squeezed limes, diluted with chilled water and sweetened. Muzaffar waited for the man to place the glasses and take his leave before he answered Akram's question.

'I am not certain,' he said. 'I think I know who was responsible – or at least partly responsible – but there are things about the case that puzzle me, because I cannot fathom how it could have been done.'

'If only *some* things about this case puzzle you, you're lucky. I don't understand a bit of it, and you're being deliberately mysterious. What is this all about?'

Muzaffar stared down into the glass of lime juice in his hand. He swirled it around once and took a long, deep swallow before replying. 'Yaqub is involved in this.'

'Yaqub? But he's an old and very trusted servant of my uncle's –'

'Which is the perfect situation to be in if you want to get away with a fortune large enough to keep you and your family well-fed for a few years. I would think Yaqub would right now be preparing to suddenly abscond, disappear into the teeming thousands of this city – or even go further, out into the countryside where nobody will ever find him. He's involved in it, all right. But I'm not quite sure who his accomplice is. The washerman, perhaps.'

'Ya Allah, Muzaffar, you can't just go about accusing people on a whim!'

'A whim? No, it's not a whim. There's a lot about the entire episode that doesn't fit together – unless one assumes that Yaqub is in some way part of it all. For example, the musicians insisted that nobody came out of that corridor, from towards the room, carrying anything large. Your uncle and your cousin say that all those rooms, including the guest rooms, were searched right after, and nothing was found in them. The only other conclusion possible is that the items – the brocade and the jewellery – were removed from the room through the window.'

'The window? But it's too small!'

'Not for the sandook. Remember what Feroze said? The sandook is about ten inches across and five deep and high. It could have gone through the window, handed out to someone who was standing outside. You were there when I discovered that footprint in the soil outside the window. It could have been a new print, of course, but still: it *was* there. As for the brocades, it's not that difficult to separate pieces of cloth, fold them and slide them through the window. There wouldn't have been any need to try and push the entire bundle through the window at one go.'

Akram looked doubtful. 'You think Yaqub did that.'

'Yes.'

'Then how do you account for his story that

someone sneaked into the room behind his back while he was lighting the lamp?'

'It doesn't ring true. First, if you remember, when Khan Sahib summoned him last evening, he said that he had been in the middle of lighting the lamp when he was knocked unconscious. And when he came to, the lamp was still unlit, and the room was dark. But he says he saw that the gifts – the brocade and the jewellery – had been stolen. I ask you, Akram: would you wait till it was nearly dark before you lit a lamp? Just about everybody lights a lamp before it gets too dark to see. Even if we assume that Yaqub *did* wait for it to get dark before lighting the lamp, how could he – in the darkness – see what had been stolen?'

'That's flimsy, Muzaffar, and you know it. Some people *do* wait for it to get dark before illuminating a room. And some people *do* have excellent eyesight; they can see fairly well, at least enough to make out shapes, even when it's dark.'

Muzaffar grinned. 'Yes, especially when it's not yet night. And when the item in question is wrapped in pale unbleached cotton. If it was just that, I'd have given Yaqub the benefit of doubt. But there are things that don't make sense. Why did the thief beat Yaqub? If I were a thief, wanting to steal the sandook and those brocades – which mind you, would have taken time to unwrap and push out of the window – I wouldn't want to waste time thrashing someone who was already unconscious. If I feared I'd been recognized by the man before he passed out, I'd have strangled him or suffocated him – something quick and easy and effective. Beating him in the hope that he will die of a thrashing is pure stupidity.'

'But we saw the bruises on him, Muzaffar! Those huge splotches of black and blue and whatnot – that wasn't pretence. That man was definitely thrashed. And badly, too.'

Muzaffar ignored the interruption and continued as if Akram hadn't spoken. 'Do you remember what Khan Sahib had said last night? That Yaqub hadn't said a word about the bruises before yesterday? Your uncle was inclined to believe that it was out of a misguided sense of duty or stoicism or something; I don't think so. I think Yaqub decided to be a little dramatic and show that he had suffered terribly in the incident. A precaution, a way of deflecting suspicion should it fall on him.

'And,' he added, '– though I can't see how it's possible – but it seems those bruises don't hurt Yaqub all that much after all. If *I* was so badly bruised, I'd probably end up in bed for a few days. But this man seems to go about his work as usual. Even when I grabbed his arm – and I made it a point to grip him hard – he didn't even wince. There's something about those bruises, Akram; something *very* fishy. Almost as if they weren't bruises, after all. It's as if someone had painted them on.'

He stood up. 'I must go and meet someone. Shafi Sahib. You remember him, don't you? The attaar. I need to pick his brains a bit.'

'I'll come with you. It'll be better than sitting around here, being pestered by my uncle.'

Two hours later, Muzaffar and Akram returned to Moinuddin Khan's haveli, bringing with them a tall and taciturn man of indeterminate age. It had been a busy two hours for the two young men; they had ridden all the way to the shop of the attaar, the chemist Shafi Sahib, only to be told that he had gone out on business to a house near the Kashmiri Darwaza. Muzaffar, too impatient to wait, had bullied Shafi Sahib's servant into accompanying them to find his master. They had arrived at the Kashmiri Darwaza to find Shafi Sahib already on his way back to the shop. Muzaffar had waylaid him and dragged him into the shade of a small khirni tree. 'Tell me, Shafi Sahib,' he had said after the briefest of greetings, 'can there be any such thing as a false bruise? Something that looks like a bruise – say, a few days old – but isn't really a bruise?'

Shafi Sahib had looked amused, then the amusement had faded away into perplexity. 'A false bruise? What colour was it?'

'*It*? *They* is more like it. I've met a man whose back and arms were covered with what looked like week-old bruises. He claims to have been soundly thrashed, possibly with a view to killing him, about a week back. I think he's lying; and he apparently doesn't feel any pain in what he otherwise says are painful bruises. What could it be?'

'Don't you think you should ask a hakim, Jang Sahib? Why me?'

'Because you sometimes know as much as a hakim. And perhaps – just *perhaps* – there is a chemical or something that will create an effect of a bruise. Think, Shafi Sahib, please.'

The older man had looked up meditatively into Muzaffar's face, but his thoughts had obviously been far away. Finally, with a regretful shake of his head, he had said, 'No. I cannot think what could cause that. But if you are willing to let another man ponder the problem, I can take you to him. This man is a hakim, of vast experience and much skill, and he has seen many strange and unusual things that I cannot even begin to imagine. He may well be able to help.'

So Muzaffar, Akram, Shafi Sahib and Shafi Sahib's servant had proceeded to the hakim's house, near Akbarabadi Masjid.

The man had listened carefully to what Muzaffar had to say; then, after a few moments' thought, he had asked Muzaffar, 'Did you get a close look at these bruises you talk of, Jang Sahib? Were you near enough to see whether or not the skin had blistered?'

Muzaffar had turned to Akram, who was, like Muzaffar, looking puzzled. 'Blisters?' he said. 'I – yes, I think there were. But I can't be sure. Do you recall, Akram?'

Akram had shaken his head. 'I wasn't close enough. I was standing further away, you know, beside the washerman. I just caught a glimpse of Yaqub's back –'

The hakim had interrupted then, his eyes suddenly alight. 'A washerman? Was there a washerman in the vicinity?' He waited just long enough for Muzaffar's nod of assent, and then burst into a cheerful grin. 'And is this washerman a good friend of the man you suspect? He is? I thought so. Come, Jang Sahib, I think we can rout out this criminal of yours fairly easily. Wait; I will get my knife – I do not think I will need it, but it is a good tool with which to threaten people.'

And so, having said goodbye to Shafi Sahib and his servant, Muzaffar and Akram had gone to Moinuddin Khan's haveli with the hakim. Khan Sahib, by now certain that Muzaffar would not be able to recover his wealth, was teetering on the brink of mental collapse. Feroze was a little more composed, but Muzaffar could see the strain showing in the younger man's face. It turned to blank surprise when Muzaffar said, 'Can you send for Yaqub, please? We have brought a hakim to have a look at his bruises. But don't tell him that.'

Yaqub was sent for, and entered the dalaan a short while later, his eyes watchful as he bent in a low salaam to the men assembled there.

The hakim said, to no-one in particular, 'Ah. So this is the man who was beaten so terribly, is it?' He moved forward to face Yaqub. 'I am a hakim. I have been told you were subjected to a horrendous beating. A week ago, was it?'

Behind him, Moinuddin Khan drew in a sharp, impatient breath. 'We've been over this dozens of times. Yaqub's injuries are the least of our worries right now. Can this not wait?'

'I fear not. Yaqub's injuries are very much a cause for worry. Go on, Yaqub; tell the hakim sahib how long ago you were beaten.'

Yaqub nodded. 'A – a week ago.' He was hoarse, barely audible.

'May I see your bruises? Please roll up your sleeves – or no, better still, take off your kurta. That'll be easier.' The hakim waited for Yaqub to shed his kurta, a fumbling manoeuvre that took a bit longer than the swift doffing that Muzaffar had witnessed near the washerman's hut earlier that day. When Yaqub was bare-chested, the hakim reached out, grasping the man's arm in one hand, and lifting it so that he could examine it more closely. He then moved around to look at the servant's back. 'This is terrible, indeed,' he muttered. 'Your back is blistered, you know. You should put something on it; a salve, perhaps.'

'But those blisters couldn't be so bad, could they?' Muzaffar added, coming to stand in front of Yaqub. 'Nowhere as painful as a beating.' He paused, and then said, 'But then, you never *were* beaten, were you, Yaqub? The hakim sahib here tells me that washermen use the juice of a nut called the bhela – they use it to put identification marks on clothes. The bhela's juice leaves an indelible mark, and interestingly enough, it also stains skin. In fact, it leaves a mark that looks very much like a week-old bruise. Isn't that so, hakim sahib?'

Yaqub was looking positively ill now. He was staring up into Muzaffar's face, eyes wide and mouth struggling to form words. 'I – I didn't, huzoor. These are bruises, they hurt – I swear by all that's holy! You can ask my master, huzoor. He knows that I have always been loyal – he will tell you. Huzoor –'

'Jang Sahib,' the hakim said conversationally, 'did

I mention, there is a way to tell whether a bruise is a true one or a false? In a true bruise, the flesh below the skin will show signs of bleeding: that is what causes the discolouration on the surface of the skin. If the bruise is false – if, for instance, the juice of the bhela nut has been used to stain the skin – the flesh below the skin will be clean and healthy. All I need do is make a few incisions, and we will know for sure whether this man is telling the truth or lying.' He smiled, a gentle smile of all-embracing benevolence, his eyes resting on Yaqub.

'To confess was the only option left,' Muzaffar told Feroze later that day, as he escorted Muzaffar and Akram to their horses. Yaqub had spouted out the entire story: his collusion with the washerman, the passing of the stolen goods through the window, the story about Yaqub being knocked out by the thief. The brocades and the jewellery, smuggled out by the washerman in a load of laundry, had been recovered nearly intact, and Moinuddin Khan had been touchingly, even obsequiously, profuse in his thanks to Muzaffar. Muzaffar had been invited to all the festivities surrounding Feroze's wedding; he had been told that he would have the place of honour at Feroze's side during the wedding banquet; and on the day of the hennabandi, when the bridegroom's hands and feet were daubed with a reddening paste of henna leaves, Muzaffar would be the first man to apply the henna. That he was not invited to stand by and watch the consummation of the marriage was a source of infinite relief for Muzaffar.

'Yaqub had not expected that you would call in someone to investigate the case,' Muzaffar explained. 'He knew Khan Sahib well enough, I think; he guessed that your father would not inform the kotwali, or even the local thanedar, for fear that people would laugh at him. And Khan Sahib had such immense faith in Yaqub's loyalty, he wouldn't dream of even suspecting that Yaqub could have had a hand in the affair.

'Then, a week after the incident, Khan Sahib announced that I would be coming to look into the matter. Yaqub panicked, and in his panic, made the mistake of going too far. If he hadn't changed his story – if he hadn't then said that he had been beaten severely – I may not have suspected him quite so much. But he thought he would be more convincing as the poor, put-upon servant, nearly killed in the performance of his duty, if he had enough bruises to sport. I suppose sometime in the past his friend the washerman had told Yaqub about the effect of bhela juice; or maybe it was simply the washerman's idea. They must have smeared it on to Yaqub's body when they learnt that Khan Sahib was calling me in, knowing full well that by the time I had a look at him, he'd look exactly as if he'd been thrashed a week back.'

'And he couldn't afford to have the hakim cut into him and discover he wasn't bruised after all,' Feroze observed.

'In any case, there was no point going through the pain of the incisions just to be proven guilty anyway,' Muzaffar added. He reached for the bridle Moinuddin

Khan's groom was holding out for him, and swung up into the saddle.

'I feel a bit sorry for Yaqub, come to think of it,' Feroze said. 'To be caught so securely between the devil and the deep blue sea cannot be a pleasant feeling.'

Muzaffar grinned. 'Then I will leave you to your sympathy. Goodbye, Feroze, and may Allah grant you a long and happy married life.'

Author's Note: *Semecarpus anacardium, the bhela nut, is also known in English as the 'marking nut', because its juice is traditionally used by washermen to put identification marks on clothing. The juice is also an effective means of creating artificial bruises that look startlingly similar to actual bruises.*

One Night in Winter

Muzaffar Jang reined in at the gate of the Begum ki Sarai and glanced appreciatively at the imposing sandstone facade of the building, the towers at its four corners mere shadows in the shifting mist. Less than two hours had passed since dawn, and the winter sun was still too weak to dispel the morning's gloom. The chill penetrated right through Muzaffar's thick choga, dew had formed on his boots, and his hands were like ice.

'Huzoor?' Of the four soldiers ranged across the gate, one stepped forward, the eldest of the lot. He was a barrel-chested man, with pendulous jowls above the leather tunic and battered mail of his uniform.

'Kotwal Sahib sent for me,' Muzaffar replied, dismounting. One of the younger soldiers moved forward to take the bridle from the young nobleman. 'My name is Muzaffar Jang.'

The older man's eyes, watchful all this while, cleared. He grinned briefly, showing a glimpse of teeth stained brick red with paan. 'Kotwal Sahib is inside the sarai, huzoor,' he said. 'If I may –?' He gestured to a colleague to open the wide wooden leaves of the gate, and ushered Muzaffar into the gloomy gatehouse beyond.

The gatehouse opened into a large square courtyard, hemmed in on all four sides by double-storeyed rows of chambers. The side opposite the gatehouse was pierced by another, smaller gateway, beyond which Muzaffar could just about see a small, scrubby field, bounded by the high wall that surrounded the sarai. On either side of the gate, the ground floor was occupied by the warehouses that were rented out to resident merchants. The other rooms, from the bales of cloth, bundles of grass and faggots of firewood that he could see piled in the verandas, seemed to have been given over to the permanent residents of the sarai: the tailors, the barbers, the physicians, the sellers of wood and fodder. Some of the rooms, thought Muzaffar, were probably occupied by dancing girls and musicians, a fixture in the larger sarais.

Muzaffar followed the soldier across the quadrangle, past the inevitable mosque and well. Beyond the well, in the centre of the court, was a garden with a fountain surrounded by trees and sandstone parterres. The grass was yellowing and harsh, the parterres empty but for a single crimson rose that bloomed in one corner. Muzaffar heard the distinctive call of a lapwing somewhere nearby.

Despite the early hour, the sarai was brimming with life – probably a result of the incident that had prompted Kotwal Sahib to summon Muzaffar. Wealthy Persian and Uzbek merchants huddled in tense knots, fringing the verandas. A few dancing girls stood at the well, making eyes at passing soldiers. Some slaves were busy cleaning the verandas and rooms; others hung about, looking on.

Muzaffar's guide led him off to the right, through a scattered group of Uzbek merchants. One of the men, almost snarling with rage, called out an obscenity as Muzaffar and the soldier passed by. The soldier reddened, but did not react; instead, he muttered a quick apology to Muzaffar. 'You know how it is, huzoor. The gates have remained shut ever since the theft was discovered. Many of the merchants are getting impatient.'

Muzaffar nodded silently. He was well aware of the practice of closing the gates of a sarai at nightfall, and opening them only the next morning – or, if a resident reported a theft, until the stolen goods had been recovered. With sunrise, the porter would have called out thrice, loud and clear for all the occupants of the sarai to hear, that the gates were going to be opened. Muzaffar wondered if that was when the alarm had been raised.

'Kotwal Sahib is upstairs, in the merchant's room,' the soldier said as he led the way up a steep, narrow flight of stairs built into the corner between two perpendicular blocks of rooms. Muzaffar followed him up the dark stairs, which opened out onto a narrow veranda stretching along a row of rooms. There were fewer people here. An elderly merchant, his skin parchment-like in its translucence, sat on the threshold of his room, gurgling complacently at a hookah. A slave swept the veranda with a twig broom, and a trio of soldiers stood outside a room at the far end. One of the soldiers, seeing Muzaffar approach, dipped his head in recognition and disappeared into the room, emerging a few seconds later behind Farid Khan, the kotwal of Shahjahanabad.

Kotwal Sahib was his usual unflappable self, but undoubtedly relieved to see his young brother-in-law. He wrapped a brawny arm around Muzaffar's broad shoulders and drew him aside. 'Thank you for coming, Muzaffar,' he said. 'My men are searching the warehouses, the merchants' rooms and their personal belongings, the rooms of all the local residents – *everything*. Nothing's emerged so far. I have a nasty feeling this is going to require more than just a routine search.'

Muzaffar frowned. 'But why are your men conducting the search? Surely that's the responsibility of the sarai's officer and his soldiers?' Each sarai had its own contingent of soldiers, headed by an official responsible for maintaining law and order. By rights, the officer in charge at the Begum ki Sarai should have been conducting this investigation, not Kotwal Sahib or Muzaffar.

Khan Sahib huffed in annoyance. 'Of course it is. They conducted a search last night, but found nothing. And the merchants here have been threatening to complain to Begum Sahib if the gates aren't opened soon.'

Muzaffar chewed on his moustache, pensive. It was a known fact that Begum Sahib, the princess Jahanara, favourite daughter of the Emperor Shahjahan, had built the sarai to cater to the cream of the overseas trading community that came to Dilli. Only the wealthiest stayed at the Begum ki Sarai. Some of these men probably had more than a nodding acquaintance with Begum Sahib herself. With her annual stipend of ten lakh rupees, and an added income of perhaps twenty lakhs from other sources, Jahanara Begum could well demand nothing but the best. No doubt many of these men, trading in raw silk, wool, leather, carpets and other fine goods from faraway lands, were purveyors to the princess herself.

'So what happened?' Muzaffar asked.

'You'd best ask Abdul Hassan himself,' answered Khan Sahib. 'He's a Persian merchant, deals in leather and wool, some raw silk. He's the one who was robbed. Come along in.'

The room into which he led Muzaffar was modest in size but richly painted, its plastered ceiling and walls covered with a pattern of flowers and curling tendrils in muted shades of red, blue and ochre. The mattress on the floor was at least two inches thick and topped with a white sheet, now crumpled and dirty from the unforeseen traffic in the room. At the far end of the chamber stood a bedstead, its length parallel to the door, the only entrance, through which Muzaffar had come in. Arrayed around the room was a motley collection of items, some the usual appointments of the room – a low stool, a serviceable prayer rug, a large earthen pitcher of water – and some the personal effects of the merchant: a heavy wooden chest strengthened with iron bands, a gleaming hookah, a square-sided bundle wrapped in faded green cloth, some odds and ends.

Two middle-aged men were sitting in the room,

deep in low-voiced conversation. They looked up when Muzaffar and the kotwal entered, and one of them – a tall, very thin man, almost cadaverous, with sharp grey eyes – got to his feet. He was dressed conservatively, but the rich brown wool of his choga and the heavy leather of his boots were ample proof of his wealth. He moved forward, and behind him, the other man rose. This one was in stark contrast to his companion: a rotund, red-faced man, short on inches and wearing a brilliantly embroidered green choga that swished about his booted ankles.

Kotwal Sahib made the introductions swiftly. The thin man was Abdul Hassan; the other was his friend and fellow merchant, Ismail Hyder. Abdul Hassan bowed briefly. Ismail Hyder bobbed his head and murmured something about it being a bad business.

'So what was stolen?' said Muzaffar when the four men had seated themselves.

Ismail Hyder looked taken aback at Muzaffar's forthrightness, but Abdul Hassan merely nodded. 'Of course.' He paused briefly, as if to mentally inventory his losses, then cleared his throat and continued in a monotone, 'A coat made of fine blue wool, embroidered in gold and pearls. An aigrette of diamonds and emeralds, set in a starburst pattern. An illuminated copy of the *Khamsa* of Nizami. A bejewelled dagger with a blade of Damascus steel, its hilt studded with rubies.' He looked fixedly at Muzaffar. 'Four items, packed together in a wrapping of red silk and destined to be presented to the prince Dara Shukoh. Only the silk is left.'

Muzaffar looked grim. 'A gift for the prince. So the loss is more than merely monetary.' It was common for the wealthier merchants to present gifts to members of the imperial household in an attempt to win royal favour, concessions, special privileges – and a loyal, extravagant clientele. The loss of such a gift could mean that Abdul Hassan would find himself deprived of the royal patronage he sought.

The Persian did not bother to express agreement, and Muzaffar continued with another question. 'When did you discover the theft?'

'Last night, when I returned to this room after dinner. Thc package was lying here' – he pointed at the end of the bed, where a scrap of red silk peeked out from under a bolster – 'tucked under the bolster. I could see the silk beneath the bolster, more or less as it is now. I did not realize then that the silk was all there was. When I was preparing for bed, I moved the bolster aside and discovered what had happened.'

Muzaffar glanced towards the bolster, made as if to get up, then changed his mind and turned back to Abdul Hassan. 'You said you *returned* here after dinner. Where did you have dinner, may I ask? And when did you leave this room for dinner?'

Abdul Hassan, decided Muzaffar, liked to think out his words before he spoke. He closed his eyes briefly now, his lips pursed under his moustache. A moment later, his eyelids fluttered open, the eyes bright. 'I had dinner in the room of a friend, Shahnawaz Ali. Ismail' – he glanced towards the man – 'was with me, as was another friend, Jalaluddin Hassan. Jalaluddin is my cousin. We left together for Shahnawaz's room, I think about an hour after sunset, was it, Ismail?' He looked at Ismail, who nodded.

Muzaffar gestured, as if to make Abdul Hassan slow down. 'Wait,' he said. 'Please. I do not understand. Who *left together*? Was Hyder Sahib here with you?'

Abdul Hassan shook his head. 'Not just Ismail, also Shahnawaz and Jalaluddin.' He noticed the bemused expression on Muzaffar's face and heaved a deep sigh. 'All four of us are good friends, you see. We have journeyed between Persia and Hindustan countless times now. We travel in the same caravans, stay at the same sarais, face the same bandits. More binds us together than the mere fact that we are all from Isfahan, or that we are all merchants.'

Muzaffar smiled in immediate understanding. 'You have travelled the same road. Khan Sahib here told me you trade in leather and wool. Do your companions trade in the same wares?' He glanced at Ismail Hyder, who was absently caressing the front of his choga. Ismail shook his head, but before he could answer Muzaffar's question, Abdul Hassan spoke. 'Jalaluddin and I come from a family that has been trading in leather, raw silk and wool for over three generations now. Ismail here is a horse trader – the best Arabian steeds anywhere. And Shahnawaz's specialty is carpets.'

Muzaffar nodded. 'Very well. And what happened yesterday?'

'Ismail and Shahnawaz were supposed to leave today for Agra. Last evening, therefore, we planned a small celebration.' The man coloured perceptibly as he continued. 'A dancing girl had come to me in the afternoon, offering to entertain the company. I told her to come along after sunset.'

'She was late,' Ismail Hyder pitched in indignantly. 'We sat about for a good quarter of an hour before she came, and even then she couldn't begin, because the musician wasn't ready.'

'He came along with the girl,' Abdul Hassan explained. 'But we never actually got around to seeing her perform, because she had some sort of fit while the musician was still tuning up.'

'A fit?' Muzaffar blinked. 'Right here, in this room?'

The two men nodded, their heads wagging vigorously. For a moment, the two of them – one reed thin and the other fat as a bloated waterskin – wore identical expressions of solemnity, their eyes wide, their chins nearly touching their chests. It was Abdul Hassan who answered. 'She'd been sitting on the ground there, near the door, when she suddenly shrieked and collapsed. We didn't realize at first what was wrong; but then Jalaluddin said it looked like she was having a seizure. She thrashed about quite wildly.'

'And?'

The merchant shrugged. 'Someone – Shahnawaz, I think – suggested we put something between her teeth to prevent her from biting her tongue. I was looking about for a spoon when Jalaluddin said it might help if we moved her out into the veranda, to get some fresh air. So that's what we did.'

Muzaffar exchanged a contemplative glance with Khan Sahib. Neither of them said anything, however, and Abdul Hassan continued. 'She came to soon enough and said she'd like to go and rest. Since there wasn't much point in our sitting around here, Shahnawaz invited us to have dinner with him. I locked up the room and we left together.'

'And when you returned, you found you'd been robbed. Who else has the key to this room?'

The man frowned. 'No one. The lock's my own. It has only one key, which I carry on my person.' He reached a hand inside the neck of the woollen shirt under his choga. A little tugging, and he drew out a heavy iron key hanging on a thin leather thong. He dangled the key in front of Muzaffar, and at a nod from the young man, pulled the thong up over his head to hand the key to Muzaffar.

Muzaffar examined the key, turning it over in long, capable fingers. 'Where is the lock?'

Abdul Hassan rose wordlessly and walked across to the wooden chest. He pushed up the lid, rummaged about inside the chest, and retrieved an iron padlock. It was a hefty, solid piece of work, with no pretensions to prettiness. Muzaffar scrutinized it carefully, then returned it along with the key.

'When did you arrive at the Begum ki Sarai, Hassan Sahib?' he asked.

Abdul Hassan blinked, momentarily caught off guard by the change in topic. 'Yesterday. Shortly before lunch.'

'And were you in the room all through the day?'

'No. While my servants arranged my personal belongings here, I went for a stroll in the garden with Jalaluddin – we wanted to stretch our legs a bit. When we returned, we had lunch in my room. The girl turned up just as we were finishing. I was hesitant at first, but Jalaluddin' – he grinned suddenly – 'Jalaluddin is fond of such things, and was insistent. When she had gone, Jalaluddin returned to his room and I closed the door and rested a while.' He looked thoughtfully at Muzaffar. 'But I checked the package and its contents when I rose in the evening. It was intact.'

Muzaffar got to his feet and went to the door. 'Excuse me,' he muttered, then stepped outside and drawing the wooden leaves of the door together, pulled it shut behind him. While the soldiers in the veranda looked on, he stood on tiptoe, then slowly and methodically let his gaze wander along the hard sheesham wood panels of the door. It was sparsely carved along the edges in a pattern of interlocking diamonds; the grooves had collected dust over time, and there were a few old scratches – even some charring at one corner – but that was all. Muzaffar bent, gathered up the edges of his choga, and sat down on his haunches. He was up again a few moments later, pushing the door open and bestowing a brief smile of apology on the three men inside.

'Well, Muzaffar?' Khan Sahib came forward.

Muzaffar merely shook his head and glanced towards Abdul Hassan. 'When the girl collapsed and your cousin suggested taking her out into the veranda, did all of you go out?'

Abdul Hassan did not need to think this time. 'Yes,' he said. 'Shahnawaz and Jalaluddin carried her out, and Ismail and I went out too. But nobody could have come in then, you know – we were standing right across the door.'

'And what about the musician?'

'He came out too, a few steps behind us, struggling with the huge shawl he was wrapped up in. It must have been quite a feat for him to play anything – just about the only part of him that was visible were his eyes.'

'Some people feel the cold more than others,' Ismail intervened with a testy sniff. 'But he offered to get a physician for the girl.'

'Ah. And did he?'

'He didn't get the chance to. He'd barely gone down the staircase when she regained consciousness. Though we told her a hakim had been sent for, she insisted on going back to her quarters. She wasn't in any condition to dance, of course, so we let her go. She said she'd stop by and tell the hakim it wasn't necessary.'

'Did the girl mention her name? Or the musician's?'

Abdul Hassan scratched his chin. 'No,' he replied after a moment's thought. 'I don't remember. Jalaluddin may recall, though.'

Muzaffar nodded and wandered over to the bed, bending down to look at the splash of gleaming red silk that spilt from under the bolster. 'I assume you pulled this out when you discovered you'd been robbed?'

Abdul Hassan joined Muzaffar beside the bed; behind him, Khan Sahib and Ismail Hyder too crowded in, the portly Persian merchant trying to peer over the shoulders of the two taller men. 'Yes,' Abdul Hassan agreed. 'I did, but when I realized it was empty, I put it back as it was.'

Muzaffar pulled out the cloth and spread it flat on the thick printed quilt that covered the bed. 'If you please, I would like you to fold this into the approximate size it was originally. I will not be able to see the depth, of course, but at least if I could get some idea of the length and the breadth –?' He moved aside to make room for Abdul Hassan. The merchant reached forward, and after arranging and rearranging the square of silk a few times, stood back. 'I think that's about how large it was. And perhaps about two hands deep. What do you think, Ismail? Is that it?'

'I think so,' the horse trader said, his voice hoarse. The cold and damp had got to him, realized Muzaffar; he would be sneezing and coughing before long. Even now, he sniffed loudly before adding, 'Or you could ask Jalaluddin and Shahnawaz. But I think that's about the size.'

'Six hands long, four hands wide, two hands deep.' Muzaffar inclined his head, eyes narrowing. 'Not a large package. And I would imagine – except possibly for the coat – nothing was bulky. The book, the aigrette, and the dagger would have been relatively small objects.'

When none of the three men made any comment, Muzaffar turned around and addressed himself to Ismail Hyder, who stepped back hurriedly. 'Would you have anything to add to Hassan Sahib's account of what happened?'

Ismail Hyder had apparently not been expecting the question; he looked bewildered and then, when Abdul Hassan patted him encouragingly on his shoulder, shook his head vigorously. 'No, nothing. I wasn't here long. I came just before the girl, and left after she fell ill.'

'Thank you. Khan Sahib, a word with you, if you please.' Muzaffar took his brother-in-law's elbow and guided him out of the room and onto the veranda.

'So? What do you think?'

'It's too early to say. But I'm sure about one thing: that lock wasn't forced.'

Muzaffar's voice was just above a whisper, and the kotwal automatically lowered his voice too. 'Which means nothing. A piece of wire in practised hands – or a forged key.'

'A key couldn't have been forged so quickly. Remember, Hassan arrived only yesterday, and that too before lunch. The wire – that is a thought, but it would take time, and I think it would draw attention.' He straightened and glanced along the veranda, his eyes quickly taking in the old merchant, still puffing placidly at his hookah. Another man had joined him and was looking towards Kotwal Sahib and Muzaffar with undisguised irritation. 'Khan Sahib,' Muzaffar said, 'I need to ask a few questions of the other occupants here. Perhaps Abdul Hassan's neighbours noticed something while he was away? Once I'm done, will you come with me to meet Shahnawaz and Jalaluddin? Thank you.' He favoured Khan Sahib with a charming grin, and was gone, striding down the veranda towards the hookah-smoker.

Muzaffar leaned his forearms on the stone rail along the edge of the veranda outside Abdul Hassan's room. The sun was rising swiftly, dispelling the last tendrils of mist from the trees. On the far end of the sarai, a pair of grey, black and white lapwings circled, calling accusingly to each other: 'Did-ye-do-it? *Did-ye-do-it?*'

Below, the main quadrangle of the sarai was nearly deserted. Along with the disappearing mist, the crowds of the morning had vanished from the courtyard, but a jostling, impatient horde of slaves, palanquin-carriers and men on horseback had gathered at the gate leading to Chandni Chowk. The gate was now open, but manned by a dozen soldiers who were systematically checking each cart, horse and palanquin that moved out of the sarai.

'I hope you're right, Muzaffar,' Khan Sahib said worriedly. 'We can't afford to have the thief walk out scot-free through that gate.'

'You'd have had a riot on your hands if you'd kept the gates closed any longer, Khan Sahib,' Muzaffar observed drily. 'You know that. None of the searches so far have yielded any results. Even your soldiers at the gate haven't found anything.' He let out his breath in a whoosh, watching it blow away, an evanescent little puff of white. It was an unusually severe winter in Dilli, and though it never got as cold as Kashmir or even Lahore, it was now cold enough to rime the morning grass with a fine crust of frost, and to make the birds fluff up their feathers. Muzaffar shivered. 'Time to talk to the other two men. Shall we go?'

Jalaluddin Hassan had the watchful grey eyes of his cousin, but was shorter, fleshier, and had a faintly effeminate air that disconcerted Muzaffar. 'I cannot imagine who could have robbed Abdul,' he confided in Muzaffar as they stood in his room. The chamber was almost a replica of Abdul's own, further down the same veranda. Jalaluddin picked at a loose thread in the sleeve of his choga. 'Of course, one cannot be surprised that there would be thieves in a place such as this; with so many people milling around, what can you expect? And Abdul should never have kept anything even remotely valuable in his own room. He should have kept the package in his warehouse here, where the rest of his merchandise is stored. All *my* goods are secure in a warehouse downstairs, with a good lock and a guard.'

Muzaffar butted in before the man could ramble on. 'You were the only one, I think, with Hassan Sahib when the dancing girl came in the afternoon to offer her services.'

Jalaluddin looked on with wary eyes and nodded.

'Did she mention her name?'

The man chewed on his moustache. 'No. Not that I remember.'

'Any distinguishing features? If not her, then of the musician who accompanied her in the evening?'

'Not really. The girl was – well, unattractive. Bony elbows and dirty feet. Her skirt was red, crumpled. The musician was all wrapped up in a huge shawl; you couldn't see anything except his eyes. He sat in the corner, where it was dark. No, I can't say what he looked like.'

The rest of Jalaluddin's recollections of the evening coincided with what Abdul Hassan had told him, and Muzaffar came away from the interview disappointed. 'The theft was obviously committed between the time the girl turned up for her performance and Abdul Hassan returned from dinner,' he said to Khan Sahib. 'And Hassan's neighbours all say they saw nobody at his door while he was away. If we agree that the lock wasn't forced or tampered with, then the possible time frame becomes even shorter. It had to be after the girl arrived and before Abdul Hassan locked the room to leave for dinner.'

'I'll send one of my men to question the dancing girls who live here,' Khan Sahib said. 'Why don't you go on to meet the other merchant, Shahnawaz? I'll join you there.'

Shahnawaz Ali was an elderly man with a wispy beard and bony shoulders on which his choga hung unfashionably ill. He was standing outside a warehouse, examining an exquisite Isfahani carpet, its ground a rich ivory woven in shades of rose and indigo. A team of porters, supervised by one of Shahnawaz's own servants, was busy loading carpets onto a nearby cart.

The merchant bowed when Muzaffar introduced

himself, and subjected the younger man to a quick, frank inspection. 'You seem to have your wits about you,' he said candidly. 'A good thing. I hope you can find Abdul's lost treasure for him. I have my doubts, but who knows; perhaps Allah will take pity.'

Muzaffar pursed his lips, not sure whether to be amused, flattered or offended by the old man's words. Shahnawaz Ali shouted over his shoulder to his servant, 'Mushtaq! Look after things here for a moment.' He turned back to Muzaffar. 'You have my full attention. You wish to ask me questions, I suppose. About what happened last night? Or who I think is responsible?'

Muzaffar's eyes narrowed. 'You have your suspicions?'

The man grinned, revealing a row of straight white teeth. 'You give this old man too much credit. No; I do not have my suspicions. But why else would you seek me out?'

'Why indeed?' Muzaffar smiled back. 'Tell me what happened last evening. When did you go to Abdul Hassan's room? What happened there?'

Shahnawaz Ali's description of events – the wait for the dancing girl, the fit, the breaking-up of the party, and the dinner in Shahnawaz's own room – tallied with what Muzaffar already knew. 'I'm surprised someone would take the trouble to steal anything from Abdul's room,' Shahnawaz Ali remarked. 'The pickings would have been richer if the thief had broken into his warehouse here. If a lock had to be broken, why not the warehouse's?'

Muzaffar did not bother to tell the old man that no locks had, in fact, been broken; instead, he simply remarked, 'But the contents of Hassan Sahib's package were more valuable *and* less bulky. They'd have been much easier to remove without drawing undue attention.'

'And more difficult to spirit out of the sarai, past all the soldiers,' said the merchant caustically. 'A bale of raw silk or a consignment of wool looks much the same, whether Abdul Hassan is the man who brought it from Isfahan, or another. And you've seen how chaotic it is here; on a busy morning, with all the warehouses open, dozens of porters and servants and merchants scurrying around, it isn't hard to create a diversion and spirit off a load meant for one cart to another –' He broke off, turning sharply to look at where his cart was being loaded.

Behind him, Muzaffar stared up absently at the sky, watching the lapwings wheel.

He was jolted out of his thoughts by Khan Sahib's arrival. The kotwal grabbed Muzaffar's elbow, and oblivious of Shahnawaz Ali's curious glance, drew the younger man aside. 'Muzaffar,' he hissed in a tense undertone, 'have you finished?'

'I think so. Why? What –?'

'A dancing girl's been found dead. I think she's the one we were looking for.'

'I thought Leela was asleep,' said the girl who had shared a room with the dead woman. She was plump, pretty enough in a coarse way, but surly. 'How was I to know she was dead?' She had made the discovery a mere quarter of an hour earlier, when the soldiers had come by, searching each room. A brisk shake of the sleeping woman's shoulder had resulted in Leelavati tumbling out of bed, cold, stiff and long dead.

'I had to go to one of the Uzbek merchants upstairs,' said the woman, folding a thin quilt. 'He wanted me to go with him into the city, to perform at a haveli. I don't usually do that, but he paid me well. I got back past midnight, and Leela looked fast asleep, huddled under her quilt. How should *I* have known?'

A series of people had passed through the dark, cramped cell that served as home to the two women. One of the local hakims had been fetched, and after a brisk examination, had given his opinion that Leelavati had been throttled. Jalaluddin, Shahnawaz, Ismail and Abdul had been brought in to identify her, and though Ismail could not be sure, the others recognized her as the woman they had seen the previous night. Muzaffar had requested Abdul Hassan and Khan Sahib – who had been present throughout the proceedings – to remain, and had politely but firmly dismissed the others. 'Are you sure she was strangled?' he asked the hakim. 'Could it have been the result of a seizure?'

'Definitely not. You can see the signs for yourself. Here' – the man threw back the quilt, exposing Leelavati's neck – 'those marks were made by a pair of strong hands. Not a fit at all.'

The other woman had turned away with a cry of distress, but even with her face towards the wall, she added a sharp retort to the hakim's diagnosis. 'Fits? Her? She never had a fit in her life. I've known her five years. Strong as a horse.'

Muzaffar lifted an eyebrow, but refrained from comment; instead, he asked the hakim, 'How many other hakims are there in the sarai?'

'Two.'

'I see. If you would wait outside for a minute or two, I have a few more questions for this woman, and then I would like you to take me to your colleagues. I need to know if she had a history of fits.'

Muzaffar turned back to the woman, who was growing restive. Having spent the past few hours in the presence of a corpse, she now seemed to have realized how macabre it all was, and had begun to gather her belongings. Even as Muzaffar had talked to the hakim, she had been scuttling about the room, gathering up bits of clothing, discarded trinkets, utensils, odds and ends that had accumulated over time. Muzaffar wondered how much of what she was collecting was actually hers by right.

'You heard the merchants identify her as the woman who was supposed to dance for them last evening. They said a musician accompanied her. Do you know who that would be?'

The woman looked up from the clothes she was piling onto a grimy sheet. 'Manohar. He usually accompanied Leela.'

But Manohar, when interrogated, shook his head vehemently. 'No, not Leelavati. She came to me in the afternoon, but she didn't need me to accompany her. Just wanted to borrow my dhol.'

Muzaffar stared. 'Wanted to borrow your dhol? What for?'

The musician looked up from the rabab he was plucking at. A hauntingly deep tone echoed round the room as he drew his fingers across the strings. 'She had to dance for a Persian merchant and his friends. One of the men was an eccentric, I think – and perhaps an amateur musician. He wanted to accompany her.'

'There's something wrong here,' Abdul Hassan said, his mouth drawn into a tense line that accentuated the gauntness of his features. 'None of us expressed any desire to accompany the woman; why should we? She brought her own musician.'

Manohar raised one shoulder and let it drop in an eloquent gesture of indifference. 'Not me.'

'Could it have been one of the other musicians?' Khan Sahib, standing beside Muzaffar, spoke up.

'I don't know. But then why borrow my dhol? He'd take his own.' The man scowled. 'Bloody woman's dead, and I don't even know where my dhol's gone.'

Muzaffar had looked in on the other two hakims on his way to Manohar's room. Both had confirmed that Leelavati was not known to be epileptic. One of the men, less busy and more inquisitive than the others, asked if the girl had been disoriented when she recovered; asked, too, for a description of her convulsions. When Abdul Hassan recounted the girl's symptoms, the hakim shook his head. 'It doesn't sound like a fit to me. Perhaps faking it.'

'I've never seen anybody suffer a seizure before,' Abdul Hassan said thoughtfully as the three of them stepped down into the garden. 'It may have been all a farce.'

'And now that the girl's been murdered, it's taken a turn for the worse,' Khan Sahib muttered.

'Don't these lapwings ever let up?' Muzaffar snapped suddenly, squinting up into the sky. Up above them, the two lapwings still flew, swooping up and then down in ceaseless circles, their cries echoing in the relative stillness of the sarai. 'They've been at it ever since I arrived.' His voice trailed off, and he came to a standstill, allowing Abdul Hassan and Khan Sahib to walk on a few paces. The Persian was the first to turn back and glance at the young man as he stood, head tilted upward, watching the birds as they circled the sarai.

But before Abdul Hassan could ask a question, Muzaffar had spun away to his left and was sprinting toward the small field that lay between the rooms and the outer wall. His path took him to a tiny pond, with a scraggy oleander bush growing beside it, at the far end of the field.

'Lapwings,' said Muzaffar, 'are avian watchdogs: alert and very skittish. I should have guessed earlier that something had disturbed this pair. They've been flying around since the moment I stepped into the sarai.' He dusted his hands and rose from his haunches beside the oleander. On the other side of the oleander, partly shielded by the bush, was the birds' nest. It was a typical lapwing nest, twigs and earth scraped into a shallow bowl that harboured three pale brown eggs, speckled with black.

Muzaffar held out the small bundle of mud-stained cloth he had unearthed from beneath the oleander. 'Only the aigrette and the dagger, I'm afraid.' He cast a regretful look towards the outer wall, where the remains of a bonfire could be seen: a pile of ashes, a few blackened strips of what looked like iron, and two charred, crumpled slabs of thick leather. Muzaffar had poked around in the ashes for more, but had found nothing of value except a hair-thin filament of gold.

Abdul Hassan took the bundle that Muzaffar handed him, and gazed at the two items it still held, both the ornament and the weapon still whole, still perfect. He looked up and smiled ruefully at Muzaffar. 'Thank you. Something is better than nothing,' he said philosophically. 'And perhaps I can unearth something from among my other goods that will appeal to the prince.'

'It was the dancing girl, wasn't it?' He added after a pause.

'*And* the musician. In fact, probably more him than her. She was just the diversion – and, of course, the one to actually bring the offer of the evening's entertainment. The fit was staged to distract all of you. Do you remember, you said the musician came out a little after the rest of you had carried the girl out into the veranda?'

'It couldn't have taken him long to empty the contents of your package into his dhol. That was why the girl borrowed the dhol in the afternoon – to give him time enough to perhaps cut away the drumhead at one end, so that the hollow interior could be used as a receptacle. He'd then just have to lightly glue the edge of the drumhead back, perhaps secure it with a strand of thread that could easily break when he wanted to open it.'

The merchant's eyes widened. 'Yes, you're right, I think. When he emerged from the room, his shawl was rucked up around his shoulders. He couldn't possibly have hidden anything under it. And the only thing he held was the dhol.' He heaved a deep sigh – Muzaffar could not tell whether it was one of relief or of exasperation – and said, 'I thank you again; had it not been for you, I may never even have got back these two things. But if you will excuse me, I must take your leave now. I must find substitutes for the book and the coat. The book's a loss; the Shahzada Dara Shukoh would have appreciated it…' His voice trailed off. He gave Muzaffar and Khan Sahib a salaam, and walked off towards the buildings of the sarai.

'But that isn't all,' Khan Sahib said, 'is it, Muzaffar? The girl was almost certainly killed to keep her mouth shut – and I'd wager the musician was the culprit. But who *was* the musician?'

'He wasn't any more a musician than I am, Khan Sahib,' Muzaffar murmured, still distracted. 'He never even got around to playing, remember? He was still tuning up when Leelavati had her fit. And he had to borrow a dhol. If he really *was* a musician, he'd have had his own dhol, don't you think?'

He looked at one of the lapwings, which had landed on the far side of the pool. 'Come, Khan Sahib, let us give these birds some respite. They've had more than enough to distress them.' As they began walking back towards the garden, he added, 'The people who stay here – especially the servants, I think – must be lighting fires in this field. There's plenty of evidence.' He indicated the scattered heaps of ash, some of them with a charred stick or two poking out.

'To keep warm, I suppose,' Khan Sahib replied. 'Allah knows, it's cold enough. Perhaps also to cook their food.'

'No doubt. And one more fire would not attract attention – even if it was to burn a book and a coat.'

Muzaffar stopped beside the lone rose that bloomed in the sarai's garden. It had been full blown, still a thing of beauty, when he had arrived in the morning. Now, with the afternoon shadows beginning to lengthen, the flower too was drooping. One petal lay beside the toe of Muzaffar's boot, and he bent to pick it up, abstractedly stroking its velvety smoothness as he fell into step with Khan Sahib. Both men were quiet as they walked back towards the gate that led into Chandni Chowk. Just short of the gatehouse, however, Muzaffar whirled suddenly and stared back at the veranda outside Abdul Hassan's room. Khan Sahib saw a look of triumph – and relief – dawn on his brother-in-law's face.

'Khan Sahib, quick. Some of your men!' Muzaffar hissed out the words, and was already racing across the courtyard, heading for the staircase, when the kotwal, having gathered up four of the soldiers at the gate, followed him.

'What made you suspect Jalaluddin, of all people?' Khan Sahib asked half an hour later, wiping a hand across a forehead that was perspiring despite the chill. Jalaluddin and his servant – both protesting their innocence, but with swiftly diminishing fervour – had been taken away by an officer of the kotwali and a small contingent of soldiers.

Muzaffar winced as he gingerly felt his wrist, which had been dealt a vicious blow by Jalaluddin in the tussle that had ensued when Muzaffar had burst into his room. Khan Sahib and his men had been a few steps behind Muzaffar, and Abdul Hassan – who had been chatting with Jalaluddin – had initially been a bewildered and indignant hindrance. In between yelling to the soldiers to get a move on, holding back Jalaluddin, and trying to convince Abdul Hassan that his cousin was in fact guilty, Muzaffar had found himself taken by surprise. Jalaluddin may look effete, but he was unusually strong and good with his fists. It had taken three soldiers to control him, and Muzaffar had emerged from the encounter with what felt like a sprained wrist.

'Something that Shahnawaz Ali said,' Muzaffar said in response to Khan Sahib's question. 'He wondered why anyone would take the risk of entering Abdul Hassan's room to steal something, especially when it would be much easier to rob a warehouse. Less conspicuous.' He reached into the pocket of his choga and pulled out a scarf.

'And then, of course, there's the fact that the book and the coat were burnt,' he continued, winding the scarf clumsily around his wrist. 'If it had been the work of a petty thief – as I initially thought the musician was – I don't think he'd have destroyed anything. Who would? If I were a thief, risking my life if I were caught, I wouldn't want to lose any of the loot. Which meant, I realized, that the objective behind the theft was not to benefit the thief, but to strike a blow at Abdul Hassan himself.'

He broke off to tie the scarf, using his teeth to help knot it. When he had finished, he grinned at Khan Sahib. 'And Abdul Hassan had three close friends, all of them merchants, who travelled with him from Isfahan and who knew well enough what Abdul Hassan carried in that red silk package of his.'

'But why Jalaluddin? Why did you suspect him, in particular?'

'Just think back, Khan Sahib. Abdul Hassan said that when the girl came to offer her services, Jalaluddin was the one who insisted on taking it up. And later, when the girl had a fit, it was Jalaluddin who suggested they take her out onto the veranda. If it hadn't been for Jalaluddin, the girl may never have been told to dance for them. If it hadn't been for Jalaluddin, the four merchants would probably have stayed inside the room until the girl came to her senses. And the musician being so completely wrapped up seemed to indicate that the other merchants were likely to know who he was. Travelling all the way from Isfahan to Dilli, they'd probably have seen Jalaluddin's servant often enough to be able to recognize him if he wasn't disguised.'

He examined the makeshift bandage on his wrist with a dissatisfied grimace. 'Also, Jalaluddin is the only one of the three who's a direct competitor of Abdul Hassan's. Shahnawaz Ali deals in carpets; Ismail Hyder is a horse trader. But Jalaluddin, like his cousin, deals in leather and wool. To have Abdul Hassan butter up the prince and perhaps bag a coveted order would do him no good.'

Khan Sahib did not say anything for a minute or so. Then he took a deep breath and squared his shoulders. 'Come, Muzaffar,' he said. 'Come home so that Zeenat can have a look at your wrist. It's been a long day.'

And putting an arm around Muzaffar's shoulders, he called to a soldier to fetch their horses.

Author's Note: *The Begum ki Sarai and the adjacent garden were destroyed after 1857, to be replaced by the Town Hall and Company Bagh.*

The Woman Who Vanished

'Uff.'

Zeenat Begum hid a private smile as her younger brother lowered himself gingerly onto the mattress lying against the opposite wall. He reached for the bolster on one corner of the mattress and tugged it behind him, leaning back gratefully.

'You are well, Muzaffar?' Zeenat Begum asked, the very picture of solicitude. Muzaffar Jang, however, caught the mischief in her voice and scowled. 'You try staying in the saddle for eight hours at a stretch,' he challenged.

'Tiring, I'm sure. But then I'm a woman, and double your age. And Khan Sahib, liberal though he may be, would certainly not allow his only wife to go gallivanting about the countryside on horseback. So, whether I like it or not, the bullock cart it is.'

Muzaffar did not deign to respond, so Zeenat tried to make amends by offering him a glass of sherbet from the pitcher next to her. Five minutes later, feeling somewhat mollified, Muzaffar grinned. 'And the bullock cart is comfortable enough, is it?'

Zeenat Begum shrugged. 'Better than sitting for hours on end inside a cramped palanquin. I cannot imagine how Shagufta can tolerate it.'

'Ah yes. Shagufta Begum. How are your protégés bearing up, Aapa?'

'Hardly my protégés, Muzaffar,' Zeenat replied. 'Just two young women who should have been travelling with decent company on the road to Ajmer.' She tapped the side of the pitcher meditatively. 'They're good girls. Shagufta could do with some cheering up, but she's charming enough. Shireen is – well, not exactly beautiful – but she has a lot of character, an interesting personality. She'll make a good wife to some lucky man some day,' she added pointedly.

Muzaffar ignored the hint. Two days before, at a sarai where they had halted for the night, Zeenat had made the acquaintance of the two sisters. The elder, Shagufta Begum, was on her way to Ajmer to offer prayers at the dargah, the much-revered tomb of the Sufi saint Khwaja Muinuddin Chishti. Her younger sister Shireen was accompanying her. Although they were part of a formidable contingent of maidservants, slaves and armed soldiers, Zeenat Begum had felt called upon to offer the added protection of her own little caravan. 'Two young women, and on their own. It's not safe,' she had said, and Muzaffar had found himself suddenly accountable for three aristocratic ladies rather than one.

'Who is Shagufta Begum's husband?' he asked. 'He must be a wealthy man; his wife and sister-in-law travel in considerable comfort.'

'A warrior,' Zeenat replied. 'Someone called Zulfiqar Ali Khan. I believe he's won a number of battles all across the Deccan.'

Muzaffar frowned. 'She's married to Khan?'

Zeenat nodded. 'Why? Do you know him?'

'I know *of* him. He has a reputation for changing loyalties with disconcerting frequency. Not the most dependable of men in a confrontation. You can never tell which side he'll end up on.'

Zeenat's eyes widened. 'Is that so? I'd never have imagined –' Her face cleared then, and she smiled, her eyes twinkling as she said, 'But whatever he may be otherwise, it's obvious he's devoted to his wife. Sends messages to her even when she's travelling.'

Muzaffar raised a polite eyebrow.

'It's true, Muzaffar,' his sister chuckled. 'In fact, I came to know of it quite by accident. I was with Shagufta last evening, and she excused herself to fetch something from Shireen's room. I was sitting there, all by myself, when one of Shagufta's maids came in. What with my being veiled and the room dimly lit, she must have mistaken me for Shagufta, and she began to say that a message had arrived from Khan Sahib. Naturally, I assumed she meant *my* Khan Sahib – your brother-in-law – so I asked her to bring me the message.'

Muzaffar grinned. 'That must have been a bit of a shock for her.'

'It was; she gave a start and disappeared from the room before Shagufta could get back.' She smiled. 'Ah, well. Whatever. Shagufta's husband's political inclinations are none of my –'

She was interrupted in midsentence by a sudden outburst from the paved courtyard outside the small cell in which they sat. One hundred and twenty-four cells, all of them identical in their square, ten-foot deep red sandstone interiors, were neatly arranged around a vast central courtyard with a well and a mosque. The courtyard, when Muzaffar entered Zeenat's cell, had been humming with activity. Servants had been drawing water, washing clothes, preparing meals – or simply chatting, discussing the journey that lay ahead and comparing notes with others travelling the same route. The courtyard had been busy, but calm and peaceful.

Definitely not the scene of what sounded to all accounts like someone being murdered.

Muzaffar got to his feet swiftly and strode out of the room, Zeenat hard on his heels. Nearly everybody in the courtyard seemed to have congregated at the far end, near the well. A shifting, babbling crowd of men and women surged around the fringes of a noisy altercation. A woman was shouting curses, and vilely intimate ones at that, in a strident voice. A man, somewhere from the safe anonymity of the surrounding crowd, was laughingly annotating the curses.

'Allah,' Zeenat Begum breathed. 'Muzaffar –'

Muzaffar was about to tell his sister that he had no intention of plunging headlong into a quarrel between a couple of strange women, but stopped when he realized that someone was already breaking up the fracas. A slim figure, swathed in a large shawl of pale green embroidered with white, was resolutely ploughing a way through the crowd. An indistinct voice, feminine and light but forceful enough to carry, drifted on the charged air of the sarai.

'It's Shireen,' Zeenat murmured. 'I'd better go to her.' And without a backward glance at her brother, Zeenat Begum followed her young friend into the melee.

Five minutes later, the courtyard was limping back to normal. The crowd was drifting back to its chores, disappointed at being cheated of a good spectacle. The two protagonists – if they could be called that, thought Muzaffar with a wry grin – were still glaring at each other from opposite sides of the courtyard. One of them, a tall and lanky female in a yellow ghagra that flapped angrily about her ankles, was surrounded by a gaggle of women, a restless mass of reds and greens and oranges, murmuring and whispering between themselves. The other woman, a voluminous orange odhni draped over her head and obscuring most of her figure, was sitting next to the well by herself.

Zeenat returned to Muzaffar, who had been watching with trepidation from the edge of the courtyard.

'The usual,' Zeenat Begum said, a little breathlessly. 'Purdah politics.'

'And that is?'

'Shagufta, when she got married, was given a few maids by her father. When she entered her husband's home, he gave her a few maids as well. So Shagufta, like many other women, finds herself being served by two cliques of women, and they can't bear the sight of each other. There's a certain amount of jealousy, of course, but also a case of generally not wanting to make any sort of adjustments.'

When Muzaffar did not say anything, she continued. 'It's a little hard on that woman, actually. Did I mention? She's the same one who took me for Shagufta yesterday.' She inclined her head slightly towards the well. 'She's the only one from Zulfiqar Ali Khan's household right now. All the other women Shagufta's brought with her are from Shagufta's parents' home. A little unfair, I think.'

Muzaffar heaved a sigh at that. 'Why? Were you hoping for a good cat fight, Aapa? No, no – I'm jesting, no more!' He draped an affectionate arm around his sister's slim shoulders. 'Come, shall we go in? You'd better get some rest. Tomorrow will be another long haul, you know.'

I must be getting used to it, thought Muzaffar as he dismounted. He was not half as sore as he had been the day before.

Behind him, the cavalcade trooped in under the high arched gateway of the sarai. This one, some fifteen miles closer to Ajmer than the one they had stayed in the previous night, was smaller, but more ornate. The gateway had octagonal bastions at either end, and an intricate pattern of glazed tiles in bright, lapis lazuli blue along the edges. Very pretty indeed.

Muzaffar watched as the bullock cart carrying Zeenat Begum trundled past, the bullocks plodding doggedly on, their dusty flanks streaked with sweat. Behind it came more carts – carrying his sister's maids, cook, and other servants; carrying Shireen and *her* maids; carrying Shagufta's maids and servants. The soldiers who were escorting the two sisters followed, strung out in a long line, some of them trailing behind the weary, sweaty kahars who bore Shagufta's palanquin on aching shoulders.

The procession trudged in through the gateway, deep into the courtyard beyond. Muzaffar stretched, then bent down to touch the dusty toes of his boots. His back creaked in protest, and almost simultaneously there came from the cool shadows of the courtyard the loud, unmistakable sound of a woman shrieking. Muzaffar straightened, gripped by a disquieting sense of déjà vu. The gathering dusk, the shrill screams of the woman, the dusty road outside, the courtyard inside: it was all so familiar. This had all happened, and less than twenty-four hours earlier. He closed his eyes momentarily, breathing a prayer that it was something very minor – a scorpion found in a sack of grain? – and then walked into the courtyard, leading his horse.

The screaming had dwindled into muffled sobs by the time Muzaffar made his way through, past the bullock carts and the soldiers – most of them now on their own two feet, moving towards the source of the commotion. Ahead of them, near the far-eastern corner of the courtyard, Muzaffar saw the white turbans of the palanquin-bearers who had carried Shagufta Begum's palanquin all these many miles from Agra. Around the four men milled a mob of women, sobbing and whispering.

A diminutive but determined figure burst through the crowd of women and made its way swiftly to Muzaffar's side.

'What has happened, Aapa? Why the clamour?'

'You'd better come and see this, Muzaffar.' His sister's voice, from beyond her veil, was anxious. 'Shagufta's disappeared, and there's a dead woman in her palanquin instead.' She paused briefly, then added, 'It's that same woman who mistook me for Shagufta the other day.'

The woman lay on the flagstones, her body contorted. Her ankles had been tied roughly together with a length of heavy rope, her arms pulled behind her back and her wrists secured with more rope. Her eyes bulged, wide open and with pupils dilated, as if terrified by her own death. Her neck was mottled, the marks a faint puce above a long, wrinkled strip of unbleached cotton that lay coiled loosely around her collarbones.

Muzaffar peered closely at the marks on the woman's neck, then briefly touched the cloth.

'That was tied across her nose and mouth,' said a soft voice behind him. 'A gag.'

Muzaffar glanced briefly over his shoulder at the slender figure that stood beside Zeenat Begum, watching patiently. He had never really wondered what this young woman, Shireen, was like; just, perhaps, a faceless female accompanying an elder sister on a pilgrimage? But no; she seemed to have a certain something. Not too many women would have ventured to comment on what purpose that strip of cloth had meant to serve. She was shapely, slim but not thin, and tall for a woman – perhaps the top of her head would come up to his shoulder if they stood beside each other. He wondered what she looked like, behind that heavy veil of hers. Was her hair black or brown? Straight and glossy, or a mass of curls and ringlets? Were her lips full or thin? And her eyes – what colour were they? How large?

Muzaffar shook his head, trying to drag his thoughts back to the crisis at hand.

'And Shagufta Begum? Has she been searched for? Among the carts? Does anybody recall seeing her?'

'Not so far.' The girl's voice was level, controlled. 'Two of the soldiers are searching, and another two are questioning everybody.' Beyond her, Muzaffar could see that the crowd had been efficiently taken in hand, thinned out into orderly ranks, each person being swiftly and briskly interrogated. 'Nothing has come of it yet.'

Muzaffar nodded absently. 'I will mount up and retrace our route,' he said, after a moment's thought. 'While the trail is still fresh – *and* there is light.'

'But what of Dulari –?' She noticed the bewilderment on Muzaffar's face, and added in explanation, 'The maid who was murdered.'

'She is beyond help. Staying here even a moment longer to investigate her death may well prove disastrous for your sister.'

The woman nodded briskly.

'I will come with you, Jang Sahib,' she said, and Muzaffar looked up sharply, wishing he could read her expression through the obscuring folds of her dupatta. 'I am her sister,' she added, as if to convince him to take her along. 'I know her well. You may yet have need of me when you look for her.'

'A bullock cart or a palanquin will be slow,' Muzaffar replied. He could not afford to lose any more time. The sun was already setting; he probably had less than an hour left before darkness fell. The light, even now, was poor enough to obscure possible clues. But to wait till dawn could be even more risky. Whoever had abducted Shagufta – if that was what had happened, and it seemed very likely – may well murder her, or *worse*, in the meantime. And clues, if any were left out there along the way, could be obliterated by the wind, by passing travellers, a scuttling lizard…

'I will ride.' Shireen's voice was firm. 'As will a maid of mine, and two of my soldiers.'

She paused, just for a moment, as if to let Muzaffar voice any further objections. Then she said, 'Besides which, I assume you have some questions you would wish to ask. We can save time if we talk along the way.'

Muzaffar inclined his head in mute acceptance. He should have guessed that this woman was not one to sit serenely by – or, on the other hand, succumb to hysterics – while storms raged all about her. She would be out there, battling the storm for all she was worth.

A very interesting woman indeed.

And she rode well, sitting easily in the saddle, her shawl ruffled by the chill breeze gusting off the desert sand, affording Muzaffar the occasional glimpse of a pale, oval face with huge brown eyes. 'I think I know where Aapa went missing,' she said, shortly after they had ridden out of the sarai. 'It must have been at about two in the afternoon. We were passing a grove of keekar trees, and Aapa sent one of her maids to summon me. When I got to Aapa's palanquin, she said she was stiff and cramped with sitting in the palanquin, and she needed to stretch her legs. The keekar grove looked secluded enough, so she wanted to stop there, just for a few minutes.'

Muzaffar chewed his lip thoughtfully. 'I don't remember seeing all of you stopping for any length of time.'

'We didn't. Aapa insisted that the rest of us carry on. She said she wanted only a few minutes of privacy. It would also give the palanquin-bearers some respite. She said they would catch up with us soon enough. I tried to argue with her, but she was adamant. One bullock cart with six of her maids; her palanquin and the men who carried it; and two soldiers. That was all.'

'Quite a crowd... twelve people? Yes, I think Shagufta Begum would probably have been safe enough.'

'So one would think. But the palanquin-bearers would withdraw from the grove after setting down the palanquin. And the soldiers would not enter the grove while Aapa was there.'

Of course. Muzaffar bit back an oath, annoyed at his own stupidity. He should have thought of that; a nobleman's wife, bound by the strict rules of purdah, would not have emerged from the palanquin in the presence of the men who served her. Shireen herself, riding beside him, would be considered by most to be guilty of extremely scandalous behaviour.

'Which means the six maids would have been the only witnesses,' he said. 'If Shagufta Begum allowed all of them to come into the grove too.'

There was a dull, sad silence for a while, then Shireen said, 'I went on. I didn't see Aapa after that.'

Muzaffar did not know what to say to that, so they rode on in silence, the darkness descending swiftly, the air growing perceptibly colder. Shireen's two soldiers rode alongside, one of them with the maid riding pillion. The woman looked distinctly uncomfortable, thought Muzaffar – as if she was scared of sliding off the horse. Which she probably was; he felt sorry for her.

'If it is not impertinent of me, may I ask how it is that you and your sister are on this journey unaccompanied?' Muzaffar asked finally. It was a question that had nagged at him for a long time. It was almost unheard of for a woman – or even two, for that matter – to be travelling without the security of a male relative to escort them. 'Surely Zulfiqar Ali Khan would have wanted to accompany Begum Sahiba on her pilgrimage to Ajmer?'

There was an awkward silence of perhaps a minute, then Shireen sighed and said, 'Yes. Khan Sahib probably *would* have wanted to accompany Aapa. If he knew she was making this trip. You see, Jang Sahib, Aapa was married to Khan Sahib two years ago at the behest of our father. Abba had fought alongside Khan Sahib in a number of battles and was all praise for his courage, his prowess in battle, and – well, whatever.

'Abba passed away a year back. His younger brother,

our uncle, inherited most of his property. Since Ammi had died when I was a child, my uncle became my guardian as well. I have been staying ever since in Agra, as part of his household. He has never approved of Khan Sahib, and when Aapa came to visit at Id, he made it quite clear that he did not want Aapa to return to Khan Sahib.'

'She is his wife –' Muzaffar blurted out. 'I beg your pardon,' he added, embarrassed.

The woman shook her head. 'No, you need not… I agree with you. Aapa has always maintained that Khan Sahib is very good to her. *She* wanted to go back to him, but our uncle has been adamant. For the past two months, Aapa has been begging and trying to coax him to let her return to Khan Sahib, but it's no use.'

'Surely Khan Sahib could come to fetch Shagufta Begum? Or send for her?'

'Khan Sahib's affection for my sister may be exemplary,' Shireen said wryly, 'but his battles and his political advancement come first, it seems.' She sighed. 'Perhaps I am being too harsh. I *do* know that my uncle gave orders that all of Khan Sahib's letters to Aapa were to be returned unopened, and that Aapa was not to correspond with him at all.'

Muzaffar frowned.

'I would think *that* harsh. Shagufta Begum and Khan Sahib are married; surely they cannot –' He realized he was again being judgmental, and broke off. 'Sorry. So Shagufta Begum has not been allowed to go to her husband, but she is allowed to travel to Ajmer?'

'Only after much pleading on her part. Aapa claimed that she was feeling stifled – that she would probably die of ennui if she stayed cooped up in our uncle's house much longer. I think he finally agreed simply to make her keep quiet.' Her voice had an amused lilt to it as she added, 'Aapa can be very persuasive when she wants to.'

'So you were chosen to accompany your sister? Along with your maids and a handful of soldiers?' Muzaffar was sceptical. For a man who had forbidden his niece to go back to her husband, Shagufta's uncle seemed incongruously lenient in this matter. At the very least, Muzaffar would have expected a trusted male relative to escort the women on their journey.

'Our brother is on his way home from Lahore. He will meet us at Ajmer, and accompany us back to Agra before he rides on further south.' Shireen glanced over her shoulder at the two men who rode six paces behind her. 'And the soldiers are – according to my uncle – handpicked. Very capable.'

'Capable enough to let someone abduct your sister from right under their noses.' Muzaffar snorted. '*And* let a dead woman be dumped inside her palanquin.'

Shireen did not say anything.

By the time they reached the keekar grove, the last traces of light were disappearing. A faint half-light, fading orange into grey, suffused the western horizon, but that was all. The little band dismounted and one of the soldiers set about lighting a couple of torches. Muzaffar took one, holding it close to the ground as he moved forward into the grove. Just as he was about to enter the copse, he looked back at the two soldiers. 'Stand guard outside the trees. We can't afford to have an attack coming out of the blue.'

Shireen nodded to the soldiers in confirmation of Muzaffar's peremptory command, and turned briefly to her maid. A quick word, too low for Muzaffar to hear, and the woman too stepped back, her eyes wide – with fear, apprehension, bewilderment, Muzaffar could not tell.

Shireen walked silently along, trailing Muzaffar as he examined the ground carefully. A mere ten minutes later, he straightened. He did not look towards where Shireen stood, however; all he did was stare fixedly at his boots as he thought.

'Jang Sahib?' Shireen's voice was soft. 'What have you found?'

His head jerked up at that, as if he had forgotten her presence. 'Would you like to see?'

When she nodded, he said, 'Come. The signs are clear enough.'

She followed him once again on a circuit of the grove, watching as he patiently pointed out the deep wheel ruts and heavy hoof-prints of the bullocks; the lighter hooves of the horses, the slipper-clad footprints of the maids, the sturdy leather sandals of the palanquin-bearers. 'The soldiers continued to sit their horses outside the grove,' Muzaffar said. 'Along with the bullock cart, which couldn't possibly have entered the keekar grove anyway.'

Shireen frowned as she gazed down intently at the footprints of the women who had alighted from the bullock cart. The track made by two pairs of feet led clear from where the cart had stood, away into the depths of the grove. 'Only two of Aapa's maids went into the grove.'

'And only one came out,' Muzaffar pointed out. 'The other tracks emerging from the grove are those of the palanquin-bearers. They left the palanquin inside the grove, then came out and waited here until they were summoned again to come in and lift the palanquin.'

Shireen was silent for a spell. 'So one of the maids who went in was Dulari? She must have been, if she did not emerge.'

'Yes,' Muzaffar answered. 'And all the while, there were other people here too, on the other edge of the grove.'

He led her around to the other side of the copse, where in the deep yellow dust were the signs of more horses, more people. 'Three horses stood here,' Muzaffar said. 'They came from over that hillock. Two horses with riders – you can see the hoof-prints are deep – and one without. But when they went back' – he indicated another track – 'the third horse had a rider as well.'

'Shagufta Aapa?'

Muzaffar nodded.

He stood still long enough to sweep a glance swiftly across the grove once again, then turned on his heel. 'Let us get back,' he said. 'I think we've seen whatever we needed to here.'

Zeenat Begum, in a fit of maternal concern, insisted that Muzaffar and Shireen join her for dinner in her cramped room at the sarai as soon as they arrived. 'Your brain will work better when you have fortified yourself,' she assured Muzaffar, and found herself thwarted by the fact that her brother toyed with his food all through the meal. Shireen was too nervous, and too curious, to concentrate on her meal, and Zeenat ended up summoning her maids to take away the dishes mostly untouched.

'Well?' she asked, turning to Muzaffar when the three of them were finally on their own.

In answer, Muzaffar turned to the young woman who sat opposite him, head and shoulders once again enveloped in the concealing folds of her shawl. 'I have a question for you,' he said quietly. 'Does Zulfiqar Ali Khan have a residence of some sort – a haveli, a palace, maybe even a camp – somewhere near Ajmer?'

Shireen hesitated, as if thinking over the question. 'Yes,' she said finally. 'I have not been there myself, but Aapa said he had captured an old fortress about a day's ride from Dilli, on the road to Jaipur.'

Muzaffar nodded. That fitted in. 'Shagufta Begum received a message from Khan Sahib two days back,' he said. 'You didn't know, did you? I'm not surprised; she obviously meant to keep that bit of communication to herself. And that's why she didn't tell you about the real reason for that unscheduled stop among the keekar trees.'

Zeenat Begum was looking all at sea. Muzaffar wondered if Shireen, with that acute intelligence of hers, had managed to figure out what had happened. He wished he could see her face, look into those communicative brown eyes, and ask her what she thought.

'Shagufta Begum is apparently very attached to Khan Sahib, and when her pleading to return to him didn't work, she began begging to be allowed this trip to Ajmer. She must have managed somehow – probably with the help of Dulari – to let Khan Sahib know that she would be travelling down this road around this time. I suppose Dulari had the trust of both Shagufta Begum and her husband; and it was through her that Khan Sahib sent a message to Shagufta Begum. That message almost made its way to you, Aapa,' he said to Zeenat, 'but it finally reached its intended recipient.'

'So Aapa is with Khan Sahib?' Shireen breathed, her voice low with hope. 'Khan Sahib instructed her to stop by that grove, and send off everybody except two maids? Khan Sahib came to fetch her?'

'It looks like it.' Muzaffar replied. 'When do you expect your brother to reach Ajmer?'

'He was expected today.'

'Excellent. I suggest you write to him, asking him to go as soon as he possibly can to Zulfiqar Ali Khan, and to see for himself if your sister is there – and well. One of your soldiers can carry the letter; the sooner he gets to Ajmer and hands it over to your brother, the better.'

Shireen nodded and rose to her feet. At the doorway,

she turned abruptly to look back. 'I suppose Dulari was in the palanquin so that her weight would make the palanquin-bearers assume Aapa was still inside. To lull their suspicions – but why was she tied up and gagged? And who killed her? *Why*?'

Muzaffar shook his head helplessly. 'I don't know.'

The veiled figure at the door nodded resignedly and was gone. Muzaffar leaned forward, drawing his knees up and resting his forearms across them as he thought over all that had happened in the past few days. It seemed selfish of Shagufta Begum to have run off without leaving any reassurances for a sister who was bound to be worried about her. But then, she was probably desperate to get back to her husband.

Zeenat Begum's soft voice cut into his thoughts. 'I think it's pointless to go to the trouble of trussing up and gagging the maid, if only to kill her. And she was a slight little thing too. Anyone who was strong enough to tie her up would have had the strength to strangle her without needing to tie her up before doing so.'

Muzaffar stared up at his sister, his eyes blank as he tried to focus on what she was saying.

The sound of rushing footsteps, the faint jangling of bangles, a rustle of silk – and Shireen was back. 'Jang Sahib,' she burst out as she arrived at the threshold. 'There has been a theft.'

Muzaffar groaned. The journey was turning out to be much more eventful than he had imagined it would be.

Shireen was, as Muzaffar had guessed she would be, swift and precise in her description of how the theft had been discovered. 'The reed pens, paper, ink – all of it is locked away in a sandook,' she said, leading Muzaffar and Zeenat to her own chamber. The sandook, a delicately carved one made of sandalwood, was an innocuous looking little chest, but with a formidable brass lock on it. Shireen drew an equally sturdy brass key from the bunch of keys hanging at her waist, and unlocked the chest. 'As you can see,' she continued, pushing back the lid to reveal a velvet-lined interior, 'it's not just the stationery that we keep here. Money and Aapa's jewellery as well.'

She glanced up. 'Two of Aapa's necklaces are missing. And a thousand rupees.'

'Nothing else? You are certain?'

'Absolutely.'

'You found it locked?' He noted her nod of assent, then reached across to examine the lock and the bolt. Both were unmarked; nobody had tampered with the chest.

Muzaffar glanced up from his swift inspection of the chest and its lock. 'Other than you, who possesses the key to this lock?'

'Aapa. She has one key; I have the other.' She hesitated, as if mulling over the implications of what she had just seen and said. 'Oh dear. If nobody's fiddled with the lock, and *my* key is safe with me, it might mean it *isn't* a theft. Aapa may have taken out the jewellery and the money. Is that what you think?'

'Unless someone stole the key from Shagufta

Begum. But I think it highly unlikely. Did she carry the key on her person?'

'Yes. At her waist, like I do.'

'Then it seems improbable that someone could have removed the key without her being aware of it. And we can, I think, safely assume that Shagufta Begum would have raised a hue and cry if she had discovered that the key was missing.'

'Tell me,' he said after a pause, 'is there more money in the chest? More jewellery?'

'Yes. A few thousand rupees, and some ornaments. Three bracelets, a necklace, half a dozen pairs of earrings – maybe a few more trinkets. Would you like me to give you a more precise list?'

Muzaffar shook his head. 'No, thank you – I don't think that's necessary. But are any of these items as valuable as the two missing necklaces?'

A few moments passed before Shireen spoke, and then her voice was low, contemplative, the words drawn out, as if she was thinking even as she spoke. 'Yes. Yes, definitely as valuable. Two of the bracelets would be even more precious… but that could mean it wasn't a theft, couldn't it? A thief – unless he were an utter idiot or blind – would not leave behind more valuable jewellery in favour of cheaper ornaments. Now that I come to think of it, why would a thief leave behind *anything*?'

'Yes.' Muzaffar sighed. 'I think you had better write that letter to your brother. And add a line, if you will, introducing me. This episode is too convoluted for me to make sense of it without first seeing for myself that your sister is where I hope she is. I will go along with the soldier you send to meet your brother, and then I will accompany your brother to Zulfiqar Ali Khan. I would like to satisfy myself that Shagufta Begum is safe and sound. *And* there are a few questions I would like to put to her.'

'What is it, Muzaffar?' Zeenat Begum's voice was hoarse with anxiety. 'What do you suspect?'

'I'm not sure, Aapa,' Muzaffar confessed. 'But while I am gone, I would request a favour from the two of you. Question the five maids who had been in the bullock cart at the keekar grove. Talk to each of them individually. Ask them if they saw or heard anything suspicious. And most importantly, find out which one of them entered the grove along with Dulari.'

'And?'

Muzaffar grinned wearily. 'How well you know me, Aapa. Yes, there is an *and*. And gather together a couple of soldiers to conduct a thorough and complete search of the belongings of all the maids. In fact, of everybody in the entourage. Leave nobody out.'

Zeenat Begum frowned. Muzaffar patted her affectionately on the shoulder, and with a courteous salaam to Shireen – who had already begun her letter to her brother – left the room.

Twenty-four hours later, Muzaffar was coming to the conclusion that Shaukat shared much in common with his younger sister. The vivid brown eyes were the same; so, too, were the keen intelligence and the readiness to plunge into an adventure. 'So that's why Aapa vanished,' he said, having mulled over what Muzaffar had recounted to him. 'I hope you're right. I think you are, actually; it seems like the only possible explanation. And it seems just like the sort of thing Aapa would do,' he added disgustedly.

He edged his horse around a slight dip in the road, then said, 'But I can't understand the murder of that maid. I don't know Khan Sahib *too* well, but I'm pretty sure he's not the type to kill a mere maidservant – and that too one of his own household. And anyway, why bother tying her up if she was going to be killed anyway?'

'Perhaps the person who tied her up was not the person who killed her?'

Shaukat drew rein. 'What do you mean?'

'My sister asked me why anybody who was strong enough to have tied up Dulari would have needed to tie her up before choking the life out of her. It made me wonder *why* Dulari was tied up in the first place. Shagufta Begum got two of her maids to enter the grove with her. One took her mistress's place in the palanquin, and was later found dead. The other came out of the grove and – what? Quietly took her place in the bullock cart?'

'She probably told the palanquin-bearers to enter the grove and pick up the palanquin. Someone would have to do that.'

'Of course. And she probably also made some excuse to the other maids to account for Dulari not emerging from the grove. Meanwhile, the palanquin-bearers had hoisted the palanquin up and set off – and because there was obviously someone in the palanquin, they never suspected anything was wrong.'

Shaukat frowned. 'I can imagine that Aapa would want someone to take her place so that her own disappearance would go unnoticed, at least for a few hours. But why tie up the woman? Aapa wouldn't do that. *Couldn't* do it,' he amended.

'She wouldn't have,' Muzaffar agreed. 'But two men had come to receive her.'

'But why?'

'Why did they come, or why did they tie her up?' Muzaffar grinned. 'I'm not sure, but I suppose it was done to protect Dulari from too much interrogation. If she'd been found sitting in the palanquin quietly, I for one would have had a lot of questions for her. Whereas if she was gagged and tied and had possibly been knocked on the head – well, she could deny knowing who had carried off your sister, and none of us would have been any the wiser.'

Shaukat sighed. 'It makes sense. But I still can't understand why she was killed. And who did it?'

'And when.' Muzaffar paused to let his words sink in, and when Shaukat looked at him quizzically, he added, 'After all, she was discovered dead as soon as we arrived at the sarai. All the way there, from the keekar grove onwards, the palanquin-bearers had been carrying the palanquin. For most of the time, they were part of the entire caravan, surrounded by others, including your sisters' soldiers. *I* glanced toward that palanquin more than once. Nobody could possibly have throttled that woman between the grove and the sarai.'

'Then?'

'At the grove. After your sister left with the two men.'

'You mean – the other maid?' Shaukat sounded horrified. 'But why?'

Muzaffar shrugged. 'A moment of utter greed combined with resentment? I think Shagufta Begum bestowed gifts on these two maids in appreciation of their service. Money, and perhaps a necklace each. At the grove, one of them – Dulari – was tied up and placed in the palanquin, while the other one was instructed to go back to the bullock cart and let the palanquin-bearers know.'

'Shagufta Begum left, and the other maid perhaps realized that she had, at her mercy, and with no witnesses around, a woman who was virtually helpless. A woman, too, who possessed a large sum of money and valuable jewellery that could be hers. As if that wasn't all, this was a woman who was not liked; in fact, was actively hated by the other maids who happened to be in this particular entourage. Dulari was the only maid who had come from Zulfiqar Ali Khan's household, and Shagufta Begum's other maids were at daggers drawn with her. I witnessed an altercation between Dulari and another woman the other day; if your younger sister had not intervened, Dulari would probably have been killed that very evening, in full view of everyone in the sarai.'

Shaukat stared. 'So you think the other maid – whoever she was – strangled Dulari and robbed her? It sounds preposterous. And what proof *is* there?'

'I'm hoping we will know soon enough,' Muzaffar replied. A few miles ahead of them, a low hillock on the flat horizon had begun to resolve itself into the straight, forbidding lines of a fortress. It shimmered like a chimera in the fraying mist of a winter noon, looking an insubstantial mirage one moment, a mighty citadel the next. 'If Zulfiqar Ali Khan brought his wife here directly from the sarai, she would have recovered enough to grant us an audience.'

'Mohini,' said Zeenat Begum. 'A very pretty name, isn't it? And a good-looking woman, too. Very delicate and lovely. I'd never have believed she could murder someone in cold blood like that if I hadn't seen the evidence with my own eyes.'

'The stolen jewellery? The money?'

'Yes. And she even took Dulari's very own bangles. Can you imagine the greed of the woman?'

Muzaffar could.

Shagufta Begum, belatedly stricken by guilt, had admitted the entire plot, including her bestowal of handsome gifts on the two women who had been a party to the entire scheme.

'Mohini and Dulari are – were – the most dependable of all my women. I knew I could rely on them to carry out my instructions to the letter, and not breathe a word of it later. They couldn't stand each other, of course, I knew that much. But then I didn't think it really mattered, you know. I hardly thought Mohini would do something so foul.' Her voice had petered into a pathetic little sob, and Muzaffar, after exchanging a telling look with Shaukat, had taken his leave of Shagufta Begum and her taciturn husband. Zulfiqar Ali Khan had looked as if he couldn't care less, thought Muzaffar as he rode away from the fortress. And that was hardly surprising. The summary strangling of a lowly maid did not merit more than a mere lift of an eyebrow for a man who had much more on his mind.

Zeenat Begum had confirmed what he had already learnt from Shagufta. The other maids, when questioned, had hesitantly admitted that Begum Sahiba had called Dulari and Mohini into the keekar grove with her. A brief while – nobody could say how long, but it must have been just a few minutes, perhaps ten – and Mohini had emerged, to tell the palanquin-bearers that Begum Sahiba was ready to move on. She herself had climbed into the bullock cart, with a sneering remark about Dulari not feeling well and wanting to rest a bit in the keekar grove. Dulari was a hardy woman, well used to walking long distances. She would catch up with them. Even if she didn't – well, none of the maids really cared. It would be good riddance.

But the necklaces – easily identified by Shireen – that emerged from Mohini's bundle of belongings, were proof enough. And frighteningly solid evidence to unlock the tongues of the most loyal of Mohini's friends. Yes, they had wondered why Dulari had actually stayed behind at the grove; she hadn't *looked* weary. And yes, considering Mohini had ostensibly seen her mistress safely ensconced in the palanquin, it did seem strange that it was not the mistress who emerged from the palanquin, but her dead maid. Yes, yes; oh yes; they had been stupid, but the gods were witness: they had not meant harm. *Never.* And they would each of them have gladly, even eagerly, laid down their lives for Begum Sahiba.

'Oh, well.' Muzaffar closed his eyes, suddenly giving in to the exhaustion of the past few days. 'That is done. I will escort you to the dargah tomorrow, Aapa, and you can say your prayers. And then, maybe in a couple of days' time, we can be heading back to Dilli.'

Zeenat Begum smiled, a deep dimple twinkling in her cheek. 'Of course,' she said. 'And we must ask Shireen if she would like to accompany us back to Dilli. What with Shagufta back in Khan Sahib's household and Shaukat wanting to travel on, Shireen will be left all alone at Agra. She may as well come to Dilli. It will do her good to spend some time with me.' She glanced pointedly at Muzaffar.

'Certainly, Aapa,' he murmured, his voice barely audible as he burrowed down against the bolster. 'Whatever you say.'

Zeenat Begum gazed fondly down at her brother, then rose to her feet and left the room. Behind her, Muzaffar turned over onto his side and dropped off to sleep.

Acknowledgments

This book owes a lot to several people.

To begin with, my sister, Swapna, who is a historian, and that too one whose enthusiasm for her subject is infectious – the many explorations we've done together through the bylanes of Delhi have contributed vastly in helping me conjure up Muzaffar's Delhi. I am equally indebted to Swapna's husband Gourab, whose passion for historical detective novels sparked off the Muzaffar Jang series in the first place. To them both, much thanks.

Gratitude is also due to Arshia Sattar and D.W. Gibson of Sangam House, who by inviting me to do the Sangam House winter residency, enabled the writing of three of the stories in this collection – writing that happened quickly, efficiently, and without the constant bother of juggling home and hearth and laptop. To D.W., especially, much thanks, for going out of his way to buy me loads of mango juice because the local beer didn't appeal to me!

Everybody at Puducherry's Adishakti Laboratory for Theatre Arts Research, where I did my residency, is also worthy of thanks, praise and affection: from Veenapani, who allowed us writers to leech off her home wifi; to Arvind, who encouraged me by reading *The Englishman's Cameo* and telling me how much he enjoyed it; to Arjun and Vinay and Nimmy, who were welcoming and full of amazing stories – and to the *ammas*, with their delicious *kaapi* and their bright smiles. I have rarely enjoyed writing as much as I did while I was with all of you. Thank you.

Thank you, Anita Roy, for first publishing a Muzaffar Jang short story 'Murk of Art', printed in *21 Under 40*, published by Zubaan Books and edited by Anita Roy. It appears in this collection as 'The Hand of an Artist'. And last – but by no means least – thank you to my editors at Hachette, Shivmeet and Nandita, for being (as always) patient and wise and amazingly supportive.